The Miura Affair

The Miura Affair

Emmanuel Kemiji, MS

THE MIURA AFFAIR
Copyright ©2020 Emmanuel Kemiji

Cover Design by Miranda Rose Creates

Foreword

As with most things worth accomplishing they are rarely the work of a single person. This novel would not exist without the inspiration of numerous friends and family members, many of whom are used fictitiously throughout this novel. To those that I did not include please know that you are not forgotten. A special thank you to Sam Barry who so patiently edited the first draught and to Leah Segawa who subsequently went over the final version and was instrumental in getting it published. To my sons Aristos and Tristan who are the best part of me, and to Isabella, Ricardo and Luna who continue to enlighten me daily. And of course to my wife Alexandra, whose patience and love in the most trying of times is forever unwavering.

The Miura Affair

"Live, love, honor, dream, fight, and let others attend to mediocrity."

— Spanish proverb by an old man counseling his young sons.

1

The old man sat with his grandson in the ancient bullring. The afternoon sun cast a shadow from his black beret that concealed the creases of a full life. As the gate in the plaza opened the crowd sighed in awe as the huge, dark beast roared out to the center of the ring. Soon thereafter the *picador* awkwardly rode into the arena on an immense horse that disguised his stodgy figure. The ground shook as the bull thundered into the horse's padding. The fence cringed as the horse slammed into it, while the *picador's* long spear pierced the animal's torso. Time and time again the bull thrust himself against the pain until the crowd could bear it no longer and the picador left the bullring, pursued by a sea of disgust.

"What heart!" the child cried out as his small hands clenched the wooden board he sat on, that fulfilled its simple function of usefulness with amazing grace. The old man smiled, realizing that the child had understood.

"Yes, it is a Miura, a bull with no equal," he replied.

The bull, drenched in crimson, looked almost beautiful. It turned towards the small opening where the matador would enter. But the matador, realizing that this animal was like no other, never did. It would have meant the greatest challenge he had ever faced— or certain death. The bull stood in the middle of the ring, not knowing what to do. Finally, one of the attendants opened the gate to let him go back into the holding pen. But the Miura had never retreated; it only knew how to go forward and fight. It stood still; a solitary figure wrapped in blood.

As the people left the bullring a tear caressed the old man's cheek. "Pity, what a pity," he muttered.

"Why?" asked the child.

"It could have been the one, the great *corrida*," he replied.

As dusk was settling upon the plaza, the child turned back one last time to gaze at the bull. It was beaten, but unbowed.

"Will the matador come back?" the child asked.

"I do not know," replied the grandfather, "the matador that fights this Miura must be very brave."

Then the child's last words lost themselves in the air, "I hope so…"

2

"*Ole!*" roared the crowd of thousands in one voice. The peasants seated beneath the scorching sun and the privileged hiding in the shade shouted it again and again, creating a mesmerizing carnival of sound.

"A real matador is back!" shouted the young boy, proudly looking up at his grandfather.

The old man looked at the boy fondly. "Yes, a true matador is here!"

The Miura attacked the thick canvas, just missing it on each occasion, but leaving behind a cloud of dust that was quickly whisked away, vanishing in the afternoon light. Again and again, at the last instant, a sudden deft flick of the wrist turned the cape into a floating palette of magenta and yellow. The matador, in a suit that reflected every ray of the blazing sun, was doing pirouettes as daintily as a Bolshoi ballerina yet as powerful as Nureyev's, as death swung by, inches away. Each time the bull leapt at the tantalizing cloth it left a spray of sweat and blood, like red rose petals littering the ground. No one had ever seen a bull fight like this. With each pass the animal seemed to gain strength, rather than tire. Finally the matador went to retrieve the long, thin, blurred steel blade, the *estoque*, that would bring the *corrida* to an end.

As the matador returned to face the Miura in the middle of the ring, the bull started to kick up the carefully raked sand with its front legs, ready to charge once more. But the matador did not unfurl the cape. Instead, it remained squeezed under the left arm, leaving the right hand to hold the sword. For the first time the bull did not move; the matador now stood less than three feet away. The matador took the *estoque*, drew a line in the sand between herself and the bull, and thrust the sword into the ground with such might that the earth seemed to swallow it. The bull's breath caressed the hilt of the sword.

"No, not today!" she cried as the crowd roared its approval with another "*Ole!*"

"What happened? Why didn't she kill it?" asked the child.

"A bullfight is not about death, it is about life: the struggle, the pain, the suffering, the honor, the joy, and this *corrida* was too beautiful to end, it was the *corrida* of a lifetime!"

As the arena emptied, the young man turned back to look at the bullring, much in the same manner as he had done as a child the day before and uttered, "I am glad she came."

The old man but smiled as a tear fell to the ground.

3

The morning sun rose with a pinkish hue, as if embarrassed to upend the peaceful dawn. The decrepit Orbea bicycle paid no such respect, noisily clanking along the narrow cobblestone-littered country road, the loose chain straining to catch the next cog, barely staving off failure with each turn of the crank. The elderly passenger slowly made his way down the palm-lined driveway, the entrance to the estate of the Count of Morente on the outskirts of the small village that bore the same name, some twenty-five miles east of Córdoba. Arriving at the end of the path, he dismounted gracefully, belying the many years that his thin legs had endured. He was the caretaker of the fighting bulls that were bred here, as modern-day noblemen had to supplement the vast expenses of their estates with other incomes. As he rested his tired bicycle against a sidewall, the noise of a horseless carriage engulfed the air. The SEAT 1500 sedan came to a standstill applauded by the clumps of dirt left in its wake.

A young, slick-haired, handsome man, whose skin had admired ample hours of sunlight, got out as if he owned the world. At that instant a tall, lithe brunette opened the large, cast iron-lined wooden door that was the entrance to the majestic villa.

"You must be Carlos. I am Alexandra," she said softly but in a confident manner that allowed no room for casualness. He instantly recognized Alexandra Maria del Carmen Vilches Benítez, Spain's most famous female bullfighter and the sole child of the 18th Count of

Morente. He tried in vain to contain the excitement within him. She was even more stunning in person he thought, her beauty barely reflected in the myriad of photographs that regularly adorned the country's most circulated periodicals. Carlos Pérez Rodriguez had been highly recommended by a family friend of the Count's in Madrid to oversee the running of the large estate. Some years before he had graduated from Salamanca, Spain's oldest and most prestigious university, having pursued the study of economics amongst other, mostly female-conquering endeavors.

Just then an elderly man walked out of the house in brown corduroys with a well-ironed, short-sleeve linen shirt that perfectly matched the color of the whitewashed walls.

"*Buenos Dias,*" he said, without looking up. He was carrying a frail wooden tray with two empty glasses, a pot of coffee as dark as India ink, and a small rectangular wooden box. Alexandra returned the greeting and then directed her stance towards the other man.

"How are you today Don Manuel?" she asked.

"Very well Alexandra, thank you— and oh, by the way, yesterday you fought well, yes, very well indeed," he replied.

"You were there!" she suddenly shrieked. All sense of formality instantly departing as she bounced towards him. "Why did you not tell me? I would have gotten you front row seats. How was I? Was I brave? Did I do the right thing by letting the Miura live, or was it cowardly for the people?" she asked within a single breath.

The two old men smiled as Don Manuel replied.

"Calm yourself child, you were splendid, and more importantly you did do the right thing. Do you not think so, Esteban?"

"Yes Manolo, she was magnificent," he answered.

Carlos was caught off guard by the exchange. Why should she care what these two old peasants thought of her bullfighting? What could they possibly know, that they could even begin to critique one of the finest matadors, man or woman, in all of Spain?

As if reading his mind, Alexandra turned towards him and her tone grew cold.

"Excuse me, let me show you to your quarters.

4

Alexandra led Carlos to a small adjacent building that housed four bedrooms and a communal living area. His room, the largest, was simple but executed in good taste. The worn furniture, still proud, showed no signs that retirement was forthcoming. A silver-plated cross hung over the headboard, the only other adornment being an old oil portrait of the Virgin of Carmen on the opposite end. Carlos started putting his clothes neatly into the large, walnut dresser under a window that lit the room. Alexandra had told him to join her for lunch and afterwards she would show him the estate's financial books. He decided to prepare a bath to cleanse himself of the grime from the long journey from Madrid. His face disappeared as the steam rose from its birthplace, and Carlos smiled smugly at his good fortune. This experience could catapult his career to heights he could not even have imagined but a fortnight ago. Spain in 1968 was not a place where there was an abundance of well-paying employers, never mind as famous as his current one.

After grooming himself more carefully than most women do, Carlos walked over to the main house where a butler directed him to a beautiful courtyard framed by exquisite Moorish archways. Brilliant blue and timid yellow tiles covered a fountain in the middle that happily spewed out its clear contents. Next to it was a table set for four, but large enough to accommodate twice that number. Just then the old man who had walked out of the house earlier with the coffee service appeared. Carlos was about to ask him for a glass of water, when a short, joyous, black-haired woman with ample bosoms and a smile to match them, marched in.

"Celia," the elderly man asked, "what are we having for lunch today?"

"Your Highness, we will begin with *gazpacho*, a stew of the red-legged partridge you shot yesterday, without the pellets," she said, adding gaily, "and your favorite to end."

"Trini's marvelous *flan*," he interjected.

For a few seconds Carlos' face turned ashen as he came to the realization that that he had almost asked the Count of Morente to fetch water for him! This look remained as the other old man he had seen upon his arrival entered the stage, laid a kiss upon the cook's cheek, and proceeded to make himself comfortable at the table.

"Come Carlos," the Count beckoned, "and do not mind my old friend Manuel's lack of graciousness. This unique quality of his seems to worsen rather than improve with age, much like cheap wine. Oh, and do not feel special, as he treats all newcomers alike," the Count laughed.

"Who was this peasant?" Carlos asked himself, that was at home here with total disregard for his lowly position?

As Alexandra announced herself just by her mere presence, the three men quickly rose from the table to greet her. Carlos noticed the gleam in the eyes of both of the other men as she warmly embraced them and then acknowledged him. As they sat down the butler served some Emilio Lustau 'Jarana' Fino Sherry. Alexandra gently caressed the small *copita* glass, lifted it up to her nose to absorb the soft perfume of hazelnuts, and ever so gently lowered it to her mouth while she closed her eyes. She took a small sip but the glass remained perched upon her full lips. Carlos was mesmerized by the scene and thus unable to stop staring at her. It was as if she was making love to the wine. Just then he snapped out of his trance as Celia softly smacked the back of his head as she made her way around the table. She poured the *gazpacho* out of an old ceramic jug, replete with hand painted red Andalusian carnations. The partridge was perfectly matched with a 1954 Marques de Murrieta 'Castillo Ygay Gran Reserva Especial' Rioja.

"So this is how the other half lives," Carlos mused to himself.

The *flan*, though commonly served in most any household, was unlike any he had ever tasted. Creamy but not too heavy, sweet but not cloying. He wished he had the audacity to ask for another serving, but that was out of the question here.

After lunch Carlos followed Alexandra to a large study. Wooden walls, seemingly hidden by so many old books that lined them, encircled a massive, ornately carved ebony desk with a chair so large that it resembled a throne. Two red velvet upholstered armchairs paid homage on the other side. A fireplace took center stage at the other end of the room, and the air was thick with the smell of Havana cigars laced with Cream Sherry.

Alexandra went over the different ledgers that outlined the estates' finances, including the various employees, their respective salaries, income from the sale of the bulls, expenditures, and so forth. She then left him to peruse them at will and offered to answer any and all questions he might have once he was finished.

The days at the estate passed quickly, as if not wanting to be noticed. As Carlos continued his analysis of the inner workings of the estate he came to realize that while the property was not poorly run, it could also be much more efficient and profitable. He also made a mental note of Celia's very substantial salary, which was three times as much as any other employee, and even more than what he was being paid! He also realized she was the wife of Manuel.

It was with the question of Celia's salary that he started his conversation with Alexandra in the study on the fourth day of his employment. He felt quite pleased with himself that he was bringing up a point that seemed to have no logical explanation, and which was probably a grave accounting error that would put him in Alexandra's confidence and good graces. Before he was able to finish his first sentence she suddenly leapt up from her chair and sat in the armchair next to his. She gripped his forearm and the emeralds that had previously adorned her eyes lost their color and turned into that of a dark cave. Carlos had never been frightened of anything before in his life, but now for the first time, he understood what fear was.

"Carlos," she said in a low, precise and terrifying tone, "you are never to mention this to anyone, do you understand? Not to Celia and least of all to Don Manuel. In fact as concerns Don Manuel you are never to direct yourself to him, unless spoken to first, and answer only what he asks of you. You will do anything he says and give him anything he wants," she continued as her grip tightened like a vise.

He started to feel the hair on the nape of his neck stiffen and began to sweat.

"But," he replied feebly, and again Alexandra interrupted him before his sorrowful plea could even let itself be heard.

"Don Manuel, as you are always to address him, has more noble blood than any aristocrat I have ever met. This topic is closed," and just as quickly pounced back on her throne and with a smile as if nothing had occurred said, "Now let us continue with your other observations."

After Carlos had finished making his commentaries, Alexandra found herself having a newfound respect for the young man sitting across from her. At first she had a certain disdain for his vanity and thought that little else of worth lived within him. She had just been hard on him, she recognized of herself, but that was necessary. In time she would explain to him that her life of privilege was not because of her title or her fame, but that it laid in the fact that she had two fathers, Don Manuel being one and her natural one the other. Still it was quite likely that no woman, other than his mother, had spoken firmly to him and that was probably not a bad thing for this striking man. She had not thought of him in that way before. Although she enjoyed the company of men, she felt that in Spain they generally got in your way instead of helping you achieve things, and hence she had dedicated little time to her suitors. She was completely committed to the pursuit of her dream— that of being a great matador— and had not let any man stand in her way. Carlos, she had assumed, was exactly the kind of man she shunned; pompous, arrogant, self-indulgent, believing that women had a designated place in life. Yet she began to feel this thick wall of doubt about him recede as she continued listening to him.

After his initial shock at her reaction, Carlos had composed himself admirably and had caused Alexandra to reassess a number of issues surrounding the running of the business. The foremost point was that either the bulls were not fetching sufficiently high prices, or that the expenses outlaid in their upbringing were too high. She made a mental note, but this was a touchy area, as the bulls were the domain of Don Manuel.

"To summarize," Carlos concluded, "either we need to sell the bulls not just as well-bred fighting bulls, but to market them as the bulls bred by the Countess of Morente, one of the modern-day icons of Spanish society, or we have to significantly curtail the costs in raising them."

13

"Very well Carlos, you are making some very convincing arguments. Give me some time to reflect on them and we will continue this discussion later," Alexandra replied.

As Carlos left to return to his quarters he thought about the exchange that had just taken place. On one hand, he was determined to find out who this Don Manuel was; on the other, he felt drawn to Alexandra's allure like he had never felt pulled by any woman before.

They began to meet customarily every day after lunch in the study. The formal atmosphere that first graced their meetings did not evaporate completely, but nevertheless dissipated considerably. Alexandra found herself strangely at ease with him, laughing and even sheepishly giggling at his humorous comparisons of life in Madrid with that of his present-day whereabouts.

"I am starting to look fondly at the female sheep in the pasture and they are starting to get nervous!" he pretended to bemoan, as the only single woman he could flirt with was Celia's sixty-two-year old kitchen assistant, Trini.

Carlos found himself looking forward with much anticipation to his afternoon meetings. He was captivated by her beauty, but now began to hear her words. He had always paid attention to beautiful women, but only to conquer them, not because of a want of listening to them. He found most women boring and vain, and the majority shared little of his interests in literature, politics, and economics, not to mention soccer. Alexandra, on the other hand, was more than a match for him when it came to academics, culture and modern-day affairs. Also, she had not only seen the magical Alfredo Di Stefano play soccer for Real Madrid on various occasions, but had actually met and enjoyed dinner with the legend! As time passed they often drifted for lengthy periods of time into other subjects not necessarily pertaining to the business at hand.

Not long after Carlos made known his initial opinions about the finances and running of the estate, Alexandra reopened the conversation about the profitability of the main source of income, the fighting bulls.

"Carlos, you will have lunch with Don Manuel, my father and me, tomorrow, and I alone," she said decisively, "will broach the subject of the bulls."

The following day Celia and Trini prepared another memorable feast. Garlic, egg and bread soup was followed by grilled hare accompanied by roasted potatoes heavy with the aroma of rosemary, and for dessert, *torijas*, made with the formers' day bread, bathed in egg yolks, then fried in olive oil and smothered with honey. A 1958 Marques de Riscal 'Reserva' Rioja provided the perfect pairing for the meal. Again everyone at the table exalted the talents of the two cooks. It was at this moment that Alexandra took her cue to begin the conversation about the bulls.

"Don Manuel," she began, "Carlos has been studying the costs and profitability of the bulls and has some suggestions that we might want to consider incorporating."

Don Manuel stiffened as his posture erected itself in his chair. "Continue my child," he encouraged, but not without the taste of sarcasm on his tongue.

"Well before we do anything differently, I feel he should spend some time with you to see how the bulls are actually reared, so as to have a better understanding of what this entails and if in fact anything could or should be changed at all," she finished.

She should have been a diplomat, not a matador, Carlos thought.

Don Manuel glared at Carlos but spoke to Alexandra, "the bulls do not like people, and I am not paid to take care of grown men."

The Count laughed as Alexandra interceded, "Please Don Manuel, do it for me, just for a couple of days!"

"Okay then, only because you know I cannot refuse you," he replied, keeping his eyes set hard on Carlos, "tomorrow, first thing in the morning, I will see you out front, and do not get in my way."

"Yes sir," replied Carlos, feeling as if he were a young teenager being scolded by an annoyed parent.

5

Carlos was waiting in front of the main house long before he was expected. He had made sure to be punctual, as he did not wish to incur the wrath of Don Manuel anymore than what was probably already forthcoming. In time Don Manuel arrived astride a huge Andalusian stallion. The animal wore a luminous black coat. He knew he was special and his flamboyant walk showed it. Carlos had heard of these legendary animals but had never seen one in the flesh. *Rejoneo* horses were trained to fight bulls with the matador solely on horseback. With no armor of any kind whatsoever to protect themselves, yet having to lure fearsome bulls towards them so that the matador could reach them with short, festively colored, but wretchedly-barbed *banderillas* or take their life with a short spear-like instrument, a *rejoneo* horse left people gasping as they tempted death, as if it was an ordinary chore time and time again.

The stallion seemed to be in a constant state of motion and responded vividly to Don Manuel's soft voice alongside his flowing mane as if he understood each word. The old man looked even more imposing atop his new podium. Beside him a young lad led a smaller white mare punctuated with gray stains.

"You do know how to ride," Don Manuel declared, more as a statement of fact than as a question, his tongue sharply engaged.

"Yes," Carlos retorted meekly, afraid to divulge the fact that he had been on horseback on only a few occasions.

17

"Well anyway I brought you Luna, the most docile horse we have here," the old man added, as the young stable hand looked downward to hide his smile from Carlos.

They trotted off and at once Carlos knew he was in over his head. He may have been given the tamest horse on the estate, but Luna was still anxious to keep up with the stallion ahead. Holding the reins, the veins on Carlos's amply muscled arms strained against the imposing strength of the equine. To his credit, or perhaps because of his foolish pride, he did not complain, at least not within earshot of Don Manuel. Instead he bounced up and down against the small black leather saddle, his feet barely able to remain in their appointed stirrups. After a couple of miles Don Manuel finally slowed down and Carlos' torture came to a standstill. About fifty yards ahead of them were three bulls clothed in menacing black skins. Even at that distance, eleven hundred plus pounds of fighting bull was intimidating. Both horses became noticeably more nervous. The stallion rocking back and forth in place but completely under the control of Don Manuel's steel grip and calm, reassuring voice.

"Noche," he said over and over again, slower each time, "remember you are a lot faster than they are. Carlos stay close behind me." Even without volume, Don Manuel's instructions could only be interpreted as scathing orders.

As they slowly shortened the distance between the trio of beasts and themselves, Carlos could hear the beating of his heart pounding against his chest, pleading for him to turn back and dash away from this scene.

"They usually do not stray too much from the main herd so it is unusual to see these three here alone."

As Don Manuel was finishing his observation the mare started shaking her head demonstrably and Carlos's natural reaction was to tighten the reigns even more so, which instinctively made Luna rear up. Carlos' eyes caught the shape of a solitary cloud as he felt himself falling backwards off the horse, seemingly in slow motion but unable to affect the outcome. The mare dashed off and now the bulls, but twenty yards away, feasted their eyes on this new prey. Don Manuel had not been looking at Carlos while he was talking and only when he caught sight out of the corner of his eye of Luna bolting back to the stables did he understand what had just occurred. As he turned the stallion around, the bulls had already started charging and he realized he did not have time to stop and have Carlos jump on Noche with him.

"Run!" he screamed.

Carlos needed no prodding, as he looked up and with instantaneous urgency, dashed towards the outlying fence some thirty yards away. He could feel the ground tremble as the bulls narrowed the gap separating the pursued and the pursuers. With ten yards left to reach the fence he knew he was not going to make it.

At that instant he caught whiff of a black wall crossing perpendicularly behind him shouting, "*Toro! Toro!*" The black stallion and its rider had just bought him the slight distraction that had slowed the bulls down enough that he was able to dive through the fence and land unceremoniously into a mud-laden carpet of grass. The bulls came abruptly to a halt, yet Carlos could still feel the warmth emanating from their nostrils. He quickly scampered further away, just in time to admire Noche leaping over the same fence.

"I take it you need a ride back. Hop on," Don Manuel ordered, this time with a thinly veiled smile.

They arrived at the stables in time to see the Count and Alexandra running towards them.

"We just saw Luna, what happened?" inquired Don Esteban.

"Well Carlitos here wanted to get a close up look at the bulls, and in fact he got his very wish!" replied Don Manuel.

"Yes I should say as much from the look of things," added the Count, which sent all three men into an uncontrollable fit of laughter.

"Well I am certainly glad you all think this very amusing, but having someone almost getting gored is anything but," said Alexandra as she hastily left the scene.

Ironic thought Carlos, such a statement coming from someone who closely comes to getting gored as a way to make a living. Both of the older men patted Carlos on the back and escorted him towards his quarters. For the first time he felt accepted and at home.

After a brief cleansing, Carlos went to the main villa. Don Esteban had invited him to join Alexandra and Don Manuel for lunch. The atmosphere at the table was more animated than usual as Don Manuel colorfully recounted Carlos' look when he fell off his horse.

"His eyes, his eyes were as big as billiard balls," he roared. "He doesn't run that fast either," he exaggerated, "thank the Lord for Noche." Carlos took the brunt of the jokes in the good-natured manner they were intended. Even Alexandra started smiling and occasionally resting her eyes on his for longer than some would deem appropriate. Celia pinched his cheeks and Trini tousled his previously perfectly combed hair and made sure he got the largest serving of the ethereal *confit* of duck that she had prepared.

After coffee had been served, Alexandra spoke up, "Carlos, let us go over the details of the upcoming bullfighting season contracts and…" but before she was able to conclude her thoughts the Count interceded.

"Sweetheart, for heaven's sake, let the poor man have a rest, he just saw his short life about to pass him by.

He will join Manolo and myself in the library for Cognac and cigars. I do believe he has earned the afternoon off."

Alexandra was about to argue but realized it would be futile. Besides, her father was right, the young man could probably use a break after all of the day's excitement.

"Very well then, enjoy yourselves," she replied. As she left the courtyard she was aware of an uncomfortable feeling looming within her. She found herself feeling slightly jealous that she would not be spending the afternoon with Carlos. She told herself not to be silly. He is only another man, just more charming that is all.

The three men accosted themselves comfortably on the large, well-worn, dark leather couch in front of the fireplace. They sipped some Delamain 'Pale & Dry' Grande Champagne Cognac from bulbous snifters while tantalizing the air with wisps of smoke from Partagas 'Lusitania' double corona cigars. Don Manuel and the Count pelted Carlos with inquiries about his days in Salamanca and Madrid. Laughter and more questions often interrupted Carlos' dialogues while the afternoon evaporated.

As the spirited session was coming to an end the Count looked at Don Manuel and said, "Manolo, do you not think that Carlos here should make it a habit of joining us for lunch?"

"I have been meaning to tell you for some time now, after more than twenty years of having lunch with you and having the same conversation it has started to get ever so slightly boring, so yes, someone new at the table would be a most welcomed addition." Before Don Manuel had finished his response the men had already broken into another laughing frenzy.

As they were leaving the library Carlos turned towards Don Manuel, "I just wanted to thank…" the words hung in the air as Don Manuel put his hand on the young man's shoulder and said, "No need my son, you are a good man, *Buenas Noches*."

Carlos was left with the solitary thought that he had just spent time with two extraordinary men about whom he knew almost nothing.

On the following day Carlos rose and as was now his customary routine, went into the kitchen of the main villa for coffee and to take in the heavenly aromas of the gastronomic masterpieces that Celia and Trini created daily. The two women loved the attention the attractive man lauded over them, and would playfully smack his wrist with a wooden spoon when he would uncover one of the pots on the large stove to discover what enticement lay within.

"If only I was older," he would chide with them, "I would take you away to a hidden paradise. My only problem is deciding which one of you to kidnap!"

"If only you were younger and more handsome we might consider your offer!" they replied jovially.

"Ah well, I am then left only to enjoy the fruits of your labor. I shall have to contend myself with this alone and brush aside other thoughts," he replied with a naughty wink, which sent both women scurrying behind a blushing facade.

But on this particular morning Trini was alone in the kitchen. When Carlos inquired as to the whereabouts of Celia, Trini told him that she had gone to Madrid with Don Manuel to visit their daughter Isabella. As he sipped his coffee in this warm and cozy setting he got up the nerve to ask the question that had been bothering him since his arrival at the estate.

"Trini, tell me about Don Manuel."

"Ah, that is a long story my dear Carlitos," she replied.

"I have nothing but time for you," he replied flirtatiously, which caused her to laugh bountifully.

6

"Long ago, before the Civil War began, things were very bad here," Trini began.

From his days at the University of Salamanca, Carlos was well versed about the events that led to the start of the war.

Spain had existed as a series of independent kingdoms until they were united by the marriage of Isabel I of Castile to Fernando II of Aragon in 1469. This monarchial system remained almost uninterrupted until 1931, with the exceptions of a provisional government from 1868 till 1871 after the Spanish Revolution deposed Queen Isabel II, and during the First Spanish Republic that existed briefly from 1873 until 1874.

The Second Spanish Republic was born in April of 1931 after General Miguel Primo de Rivera's dictatorial regime was seen as extremely oppressive by the working class and the left-leaning Republicans were voted into power. King Alfonso XIII's backing of General Rivera eventually led to his downfall and he went into permanent exile that same year. A new constitution established freedoms such as the right to free speech, to organize meetings for workers, extended suffrage for women, allowed divorce, and stripped the aristocracy and Catholic Church of most of their powers. In the elections of 1934, because of the worldwide economic depression, power reverted back to center-right and far-right parties that effectively suspended the reforms established by the recent constitution. This led to a rebellion by Socialists and Anarchists in Asturias and Cataluña that was brutally squashed by the army led by General Francisco Franco. Further elections in early 1936 saw a coalition of Socialists, Communists, and leftist Republicans avenge their losses of 1934, after which much violence ensued between right- and left-wing parties. On July 12, 1936 Lieutenant Jose Castillo of the anti-fascist Union Militar Republicana Antifascista (UMRA) was murdered by gunmen of the Fascist Falange Party. The next day the UMRA took revenge by shooting the leader of the right-wing opposition party, Jose Calvo Sotelo, who had been imploring the army to take over the country. Four days later, on July 17, General Franco began a *coup d'état* by attacking the government forces on the Spanish mainland from Morocco while General Emilio Mola mobilized another rebellious force from Navarra in the north. The war lasted till the final victory of the Nationalists forces over the Republicans in Madrid in March of 1939, and saw over half a million people lose their lives.

The Spanish Civil War was particularly damaging to the psyche of the nation. As with any ideological war, it divided the country at its very core. Thus, even in small villages you saw members of the same family fighting on opposite sides of the fronts established by the warring factions. It created a deep-rooted wound that would haunt the Spanish people for decades to come and leave the country with an ugly scar upon its history.

"Morente started to split up into two opposing bands," Trini was saying. "On one hand you had people loyal to the current Count's father, Don Cristobal, as he provided sustenance for a good portion of the village folk as well as insuring that the church and the local priest, Father Juanjo, were taken care of. On the other side you had a group of idealistic adolescent men that talked of things like needing to usher Spain into a new era, free of the power of the church and where every man was equal whether or not he was born with a title affixed to his name. Arguments became increasingly heated at the local bar, and by early 1936 the young men stopped fighting with words and instead began using their fists to make their points.

In the midst of all this an unlikely romantic confrontation started to emerge. A love story for the ages. It stars a 19-year-old girl named Maria. She had a beauty that I have never laid eyes on again; not even that of Alexandra's can compare. Her hair was the color of the darkest night, her eyes could pierce your soul, and her skin was soft, yet luminous as if the sun reflected its light upon it. She was wise beyond her years and charmed anyone that came within eyesight of her commanding presence. She was born of simple peasants, yet she carried herself in a way that showed great nobility."

As she spoke about the girl, Carlos could see Trini's eyes begin to tear while she did her best to remain composed. She continued on, "Soon two young men were desperately trying to garner her attention. One was a local village lad, a matador in training, fearless with a rough-hewn attraction that appealed to all women, young and old alike, in a way only bullfighters can, for they alone have conquered their fear of death and live every day of their life for they know another one may not be forthcoming. He became the leader of the rebellious group of youths who wanted a new vision for the country. A rebel he was, for he answered only to himself and held his principals above all else. He spoke softly, but everyone's words would come to a halt so as to not miss one of his. You know him as Don Manuel.

The other man was the son of the local aristocrat. Wealthy, handsome, dressed in clothes we could not even dream of wearing and having been schooled at Cambridge University in England. Everyone else in Morente barely had a junior high school education," she laughed.

"He was aloof, quiet, and everyone felt he thought of himself as above those in his surroundings. He seemed bored and came across as if the village people were not even interesting enough to warrant his mildest attention. But Maria most certainly captured it. Perhaps it was her allure, perhaps it was because she was the only female that treated him no differently than she treated any other young male, who knows. But around her, Don Esteban turned fragile and innocent."

Carlos was now more intrigued than ever, his thoughts racing like a rogue wave.

"When the two young men would find themselves at the bar at the same time, the tension within the room resembled a pistol duel about to take place. Don Esteban would argue about the worsening state of the country and the need for a more conservative and responsible type of government as if he were a professor lecturing students with an inherited air of superiority. Manuel was the only village male who was not intimidated by Don Esteban's title and wealth. What Manuel's arguments lacked in knowledge he more than made up with the passion and conviction in his words. All this led to a large potion of disdain for each other that became more pointed and violent with each passing week. The discussions would continue to escalate until Maria would walk into the bar, instantly diverting the attention of both men. It was as if they were afraid to say the wrong thing in front of her. She would gently flirt with them, not taking either too seriously, yet never embarrassing either one, and soon laughter would break out."

"Why do you even talk to that righteous, bullfighter want-to-be, that will never amount to anything more than a common field laborer?" Don Esteban would ask Maria afterward, as they walked around the family estate.

"Esteban my love, you only see one side of Manuel. The one who has the impertinence to argue with your beliefs. I see a brave man wanting to do better with his life. I see a good and proud man behind the mask just like I see what other people in Morente do not see in you. He is a good friend and I wish you could just see him for that. Besides, I do not wish to spend our lovely time talking about someone else and let it take moments away from us."

Just as he would get ready to retort she would brush her finger along his lips ever so slowly with a look into his eyes that would completely disarm him. Soon thereafter he would forget about everything and everyone, as Maria was apt to make one do to those who were fortunate to spend any amount of time with her."

"Why do you spend time with that self-serving ass, who no doubt bores you to death with his high and mighty attitudes?" Manuel would ask Maria when they would take a late evening stroll along the olive tree ridden orchards on the outskirts of the village.

With the moonlight illuminating her striking silhouette, Maria would smile and say, "You know that's not too different from what he said about you, and the truth be told you are both much more alike than you want to realize!"

Manuel was instantly angered by this assertion, but Maria would interrupt his violent thoughts with a soft kiss along his cheek and whisper in his ear, "We can continue talking about him or we can talk about us," as she would run away into the night. Manuel would come to his senses and chase after her, catch his prey, and get lost in her mesmerizing look. Time would float by until it was no longer appropriate to stay away from their respective homes.

On some appointed Sundays the town would gather at the small bullring to watch aspiring matadors fight young bulls in the announced *novillada*. Manuel would stand way above the rest of his competitors and constantly wow the crowd of about 250 people. Whatever he lacked in style he supplanted with bravery. Even with young bulls the crowd would acknowledge the lack of fear the young man exhibited, as he dared to get closer and closer to the charging animal more than anyone could recollect ever seeing.

He would wave his cape with disdain at the bull while yelling, "*Toro! Toro!*"

His body brushing against his foe on every pass, his facade in a defiant trance. He seemed to know what the bull was going to do before the beast did it: when he was going to charge, in what direction, and when he would suddenly raise his menacing horns. Everyone would not just say "*Ole*" on every pass, they would scream it. The women in the crowd cheered with abandon, lusting at his courage, while the men were gently jealous, but were forced to admire it nonetheless. It was obvious to everyone that they were watching someone destined for greatness. Don Esteban would watch from the solitary back row and in spite of the loathing he felt for his rival, a dose of respect inevitably surfaced. After the fight the crowd would gather at the village bar to pay homage to the brave bullfighter with much fanfare, but with the subtle absence of Don Esteban.

At first Don Esteban's parents had been less than joyous at the prospect of their noble son courting a common girl. His father in particular had not held back his thoughts on the matter.

"This is what the 18th Count of Morente aspires to, a peasant to have his heirs, we are well on our way to becoming the laughing stock of Andalusia!" he would fume. "All the money, time, schooling, for this!" as his hand would disgustingly point at an imaginary figure.

"We have introduced you to a number of lovely young ladies from very nice families," his mother would add in a softer tone, hoping to prevent another vile outburst between father and son.

"Yes mother, you have indeed, and while they are lovely and from the so-called right families, they are boring, prudish, and their noses are pointed so high up in the air they don't even know what the ground looks like!" Don Esteban would reply, adding in a more conciliatory tone, "I know that this is not easy for you and believe me I could not for one instant have imagined that after all my travels and experiences, the woman I would fall for would lie but a couple of miles from my birthplace and come from a simple household. All I ask for is for you to see her for who she is and not for who you think she is. After that we can discuss whether she should be the person to carry our name, have my children and be my companion for the rest of my days."

"Fair enough," his father finally hesitantly said, "let us find out who this Maria is," thinking in the back of his mind that in front of the whole family this girl would surely crumble and be seen for who she really was; a money-hungry, fame and power-seeking floozy.

An invitation to dinner at the estate was soon extended to Maria and on an early spring evening, alive with the perfume of birthing geraniums of every imaginary tone, Maria arrived on the arm of Don Esteban to meet his parents—but everyone knew much more than that was at stake. Her wit quickly wilted any doubts the Count and Countess of Morente might have entertained about her humble upbringing. Maria's pride, laced with a small dose of arrogance, allowed her to hold her own and withstand any sort of perfunctory intimidation at the start of the gathering.

The servants at the estate all knew her but were initially awkward about how to direct themselves toward her in this setting. She took the initiative by inquiring of each one about their son or daughter and asking them to send her regards to them. She spoke to each enough to seem genuinely interested but not that long that anyone at the table would feel that her attention to them was remiss in any way. Don Esteban watched with fascination throughout the evening as she handled any situation with aplomb and realized she belonged at this table more so than possibly anyone who was seated at it. Soon Don Esteban's mother was inviting her to come shopping to Córdoba and have lunch while Don Cristobal was affectionately chiding his son for keeping such a jewel hidden from his sight for so long, insisting that they should all have dinner with Maria's parents soon thereafter.

"Silly boy, you had no reason to be so nervous," she told him later, when he was returning her to her home, "They are lovely and genuine people just like their reputation holds."

"Yes, but until tonight, they felt no woman was good enough for their only son," he laughed. "If only they knew that I was the lucky one who doesn't deserve you."

"Yes, you are right of course!" she joked backed, and the air between their bodies suddenly fled as they embraced in a lingering kiss that neither one wanted to end.

In the months that followed Maria continued to be torn between the two men and much to her credit performed a high wire act in which neither man was offended or felt less special than the other. Inside, though, she realized things could not continue as such and knew that one day much pain would come to rest on one of the two most special people she would likely meet in her life. She constantly agonized over this burden, yet could not come to a clear decision.

"How could I love two different men at the same time? Is it not wrong? What is the matter with me?" she asked herself.

Every moment she spent with one of the men would tilt her feelings towards the person she was with, but that would end with an encounter with the other.

On top of all this the climate in all of Spain was becoming dark with talk of war dominating most of the social scenes, and tensions continued to mount between the factions; those in support of the current liberal Republican government and those of Nationalist tendencies that favored a strong-armed approach to what they saw as a decaying country spinning out of control.

"Oh my God! Look what time it is and I have yet to finish getting everything ready for lunch! Get out of here before you get me in trouble you ruffian!" Trini scolded Carlos in a not very serious tone.

He in turn walked away from the kitchen with more questions than answers.

7

The next day Carlos arose earlier than was his custom because Celia and Don Manuel would not return from Madrid for at least a few days and he wanted to take advantage of their absence. His pace was hurried as he made his way to the kitchen to continue to prod Trini to divulge more of the fascinating story she had started the day before.

"There you are," Trini commented with laughter as he entered her domicile, "I was wondering how soon you would show your face today." Without him even asking she began, "Where were we, ah yes, right before the war." She then seemed to drift off as if she had transposed herself to that time.

"As July approached, strikes, manifestations and outbreaks of violence became the norm between the leftist Republicans and the far-right Nationalists. Not a day would go by without some kind of incident, somewhere. It was awful, and everyone started talking of an inevitable war. At first people in Morente were afraid to say it, to speak the word 'war', but as the events continued to escalate, it became part of our everyday speech and it was obvious it was just a matter of months, if not weeks or even days. People started to wonder what they should do, where they should go, and to whom they should talk. You didn't know who to trust and what consequences what you said might have. The townsfolk started to avoid each other, stay in their homes, the streets of the town were deserted. It was almost as if you were living during a plague, only in 1936 rather than the Middle Ages.

Then in mid-July with the murders of Lieutenant Castillo and Jose Calvo Sotelo, the volcano that Spain had become finally erupted. It was generally held that the major cities, Córdoba being the closest one to us, leaned towards the current Republican government, while some factions of the army, particularly in Navarra and in North Africa, were in the Nationalists' corner. Some people in town who were avowed Republicans started heading towards Córdoba to feel more protected."

They were sitting facing each other on wooden chairs whose advanced age was thinly veiled. Carlos could sense the panic in Trini's voice and without even realizing it patted her gently on the knee.

"Manuel and his gang of liberal youths were gathering up any and all shotguns, as what they hunted was primarily red-legged partridges, doves and hares. They couldn't afford rifles to shoot deer and boar further away, deep in the mountains north of town. They spent most of their waking hours huddled together in Manuel's house, cleaning their firearms, scraping together every possible *centimo* to buy ammunition, and talking of the heroics they would soon be performing.

At the estate of the Count of Morente, Don Esteban was trying in vain to convince his parents to flee for safer harbor.

"Father, mother, please, you do not realize what is happening out there. A civil war is about to erupt and you would be such an easy and symbolic target for some ideological zealots who see your lifestyle as a continuation of feudal times that must be eliminated from the Spanish landscape forever."

"Son," the Count countered, "while I very much appreciate your concern for your mother and myself, I do

36

feel that you are exaggerating the circumstances. As you well know I do not support the policies of the current government, but I also do not believe that part of the army will take matters into their hands. Besides, even if they do, the rest of the army allied with the government, will squash any sort of rebellious attempt. Instead what will likely happen is that we will soon have new elections where there will be a change of government so that we can put this country back on track."

"Father, I wish I could share your optimism for an organized change but what is happening out there, in the streets of every village, town and city in this country is pointing towards a cataclysmic event such that we have likely never experienced in Spain," the son replied.

"Esteban, even if you are right," the Count asked, "where are we to go? This is the only home our family has ever known, what are the people that have worked at this estate for their entire lives going to do, where are they going to go? We have an obligation to look after them after the many years of service they have given us, and not just them, but their parents and their grandparents before them. If we abandon them now, at their time of greatest need, what does it say about the legacy of the Counts of Morente that have lived of these lands for almost five centuries?"

Don Esteban admired his fathers' stance, foolhardy as it was, and soon resigned himself to the fact that he was not going to be able to talk his parents into leaving the estate.

Within a few short days word quickly spread that General Franco was leading the army garrisoned in Spanish Morocco against the Republic from the south and General Mola was doing the same from the north. The Civil War had begun.

Later, on the day of the terrible news, Maria went to Manuel's house and asked to speak to him in private. As they took a walk on the outskirts of Morente, Maria broke the awkward silence between them.

"My love," she began, "we are in the midst of a terrifying time and I fear that horrible things are about to happen."

"Maria, although I would love to contradict you and assure you that this is not the case, I am afraid I cannot."

"Because of this Manolo, I must ask you for a tremendous sacrifice," she continued.

"Yes of course, you know that there is nothing I would not do for you," Manuel replied, curious as to what she was going to ask of him.

"You know how fond I am of Esteban and his family. I want you to promise me that you, who are in charge of the Republican youths here and are the only one they listen to, will make sure that no one moves against the Counts of Morente or raids their estate."

"I do not know if I can guarantee that. Besides…" Manuel started to say.

"Manolo let me finish please," she insisted, "as the most vocal leader of the Nationalist movement in the area, I know Esteban will not be safe here no matter what, even I realize such a thing, and that is why you have to help him get out of here to a place where he will be safe. You know this area better than anyone else, specially the mountains where you have hunted since you were a child."

"Have you gone mad!" Manuel interceded, but she held up her hand in a defiant gesture that precluded any argument.

"If you do this, I vow to you that you shall have me as your wife when this is all over."

He was still reeling from the significance of everything he had just heard when he timidly asked, "And if I do not agree to your demands?"

"Then I will pack up some things and head into the mountains with Esteban tomorrow morning," she told him assertively.

"Do not be ridiculous, you would not last a day. Neither you nor your fancy friend would even know what to pack, which way to go, never mind how to survive. How would you find food, water, or shelter?" Manuel added.

"I will take my chances, and anyway that should not concern you anymore," she replied with spite and conviction. "Look Manolo," she added in a subdued voice, "I know this is too much to ask of anyone, but if something were to happen to him or his family and I thought you could have prevented it, I could not forgive you, and my heart would be laid to rest for all eternity. Please understand, I love you more than anything, but I could not withstand the guilt I would carry upon my soul. If you agree to do this I swear that not a single being would ever find out about it. It should take less than a week to get him to a safe area. Invent a story about having being called up to a meeting with young Republican leaders in Madrid to come up with a strategic plan to quickly avert an all-out war, or something of the kind. Do this and return to me forever."

"Well then, you really give me no choice as you seem to have thought of every possible situation. I agree," she practically jumped on him and assaulted him with kisses before he could continue, "but on one condition that is not up for discussion."

"Yes, tell me!" Maria excitedly replied as he went on.

"That it is made clear to him that he has to do exactly as I say. If he does not at any point, I will not risk my life on his impertinence or foolishness and I shall leave him to his own fate, no matter what I hold that to be. Is that understood?"

"Yes it is my love," she said.

"We will depart tomorrow morning at first light and meet up at Javier Barragan's house, next to the tool shed there, about one mile from his estate." He quickly wrote a list of supplies out and handed it to her. "Tell him to bring these things and any gun he can muster, but preferably a rifle, and I will take care of the food and water."

"I shall go and tell him this at once and then I want to be alone with you this evening," Maria added in a mischievous note.

As she rode her old bicycle towards the estate of the Count of Morente she smiled. Yes, it would have been nice to be the next Countess of Morente and live a life that most people could not even begin to imagine. Esteban was a fine man, yet the love she felt for him was one of fondness and caring. She felt safe with him but her heart was finally seduced by the passion for life that only a rare person like Manolo could have. As she knocked on the door of the grandiose villa she knew had made the right decision.

"What!" Don Esteban practically screamed after Maria had finished detailing her plan in front of him and his father. "There is no way I will entrust my life to that crazed idiot."

"Esteban, my love, no one knows this land better than Manuel and while he may be stubborn, he is a man of his word and the only one whose hands I would put your life in. People are already murmuring about who are the first people the government is going to arrest as insurgents and what they should do with them," Maria calmly said.

"It seems to me son that you have little choice in the matter if the situation is this dire. I urge you to act quickly," Don Cristobal told him.

"What about you and my mother?" Don Esteban replied.

"Do not worry about us Esteban, we are old relics of little use to anyone. You have your whole life ahead of you, while your mother and I have lived long enough," said the Count.

Don Esteban had never been so proud to be his son and finally relented to the inevitable.

"My dear Maria, thank you so much for thinking of Esteban. You have grown to be like a daughter to us in the short time we have come to know you. You will always have a home here and whatever you and your family need is but a request away..."

Before he could finish Maria wrapped her arms around the Count, her tears flowing uncontrollably, "Thank you, thank you for being so kind, Your Highness."

The Count of Morente gently patted the young woman on the back while saying, "Do not worry dear, everything will be all right, and do not refer to me as Your Highness anymore, as you are making me feel older than I already am." He smiled. "Now if you do not mind Maria, I think Esteban and I need to spend some time with his mother to gently make her aware of the situation. I am afraid she is going to need much comforting and affection."

"Yes, of course, Don Cristobal," Maria replied.

As Esteban escorted Maria back to her bicycle the tears that had befallen on her cheeks moments earlier were still ample and had not dried. She kissed him deeply and rode off before he was able to make a thought come to life. She sobbed all the way back to Manuel's house, and rushed into his arms as soon as she arrived, until the night faded away.

Back at the estate, Don Cristobal and Don Esteban gently guided the Countess to the library where they told her of the impending plan, while omitting some of the details concerning the urgency of the situation. Lately her health had been deteriorating, and neither husband nor son wanted to burden her anymore than what was absolutely necessary. At first, she was naturally distraught but both men gently soothed her and before long they were talking of how soon it would be when they would all be back together again. Once she had retired for evening the Count asked his son to join him in the library for some Cognac.

"Esteban, I think we both now understand the gravity of the situation and nothing further needs to be said. I wish to give you three things for your journey," as he walked toward the large gun case in the side of the room. He removed a weapon from its allotted slot and opened a drawer at the bottom of the cabinet where he took out several boxes of ammunition.

"This is my favorite rifle, a Rigby .275 caliber, to help you protect yourself."

The oiled Circassian walnut stock gleamed against the blued barrel of the gun. John Rigby, of Irish descent but established in London, had the reputation of being the finest gun maker in the world. The rifle was the envy of every hunter. He then took out a pocket watch from his vest, unlatched the chain that anchored it in its appointed place and handed it to his son.

"Your grandfather, the 16th Count of Morente gave it to me when I turned twenty-one. I want it to be a reminder whenever you look at it, that one day it will be time to come back home."

The solid gold Patek Philippe had the family crest etched on the back and was stunning in its simplicity, its blue hands dancing around a gleaming white enamel background. Don Esteban gently put it in his pocket.

Lastly, he went up to a large portrait of one of his ancestors in full war regalia by the great court painter of King Philip V's reign, Michel Ange Houasse.

"Esteban come help me with this."

Perplexed, the son obeyed the father. He never knew that there was anything behind this painting. As they carefully lifted the ornately gilded gold frame and set it aside, a safe came into view. The Count proceeded to open the small box and took out a thin, metal cylinder about ten inches long but less than one wide. He unscrewed the metal cap at one end and carefully unfurled a document of some five pages written on parchment paper that was clearly of an advanced age.

"Esteban, tradition in our family has it that this is given to the next Count of Morente on the day of his wedding. I am giving to you now in case something were to happen here. This is the most prized possession of our family. It is the royal decree by which King Ferdinand II and Queen Isabel I granted Manuel Vilches Díaz the title of 1st Count of Morente, and deeded these lands to him in 1482. It is who we are. Who you are. It wrote your destiny the day you were born. Wherever you go, as long as you carry this, know that you are not alone."

The Count gingerly rolled the document back up in the metal cylinder, screwed the cap back on, and handed it to his son. Don Esteban's hands trembled as he accepted the baton-like instrument.

"Now help me put this painting back up on the wall and go get some rest, my son."

"We will continue some other time. Now let me finish my chores! Out! Out!" Trini bellowed at Carlos as he got up to leave.

8

Carlos hardly slept that night. The anticipation of what Trini would tell him next had kept him up counting minutes until dawn arrived. As he went into the kitchen he was greeted with an, "Oh my, we're up early again!" smile from Trini.

"The next morning," she began without being prodded, "Manuel and Don Esteban met at the shack behind Javier Barragan's house, which was out in the middle of nowhere with no neighbors in sight. At first both men barely even acknowledged each other. Manuel gave Don Esteban a bunch of provisions along with two canteens of water to put in his pack. Then Manuel took out a map and started drawing an imaginary path with his finger along the Sierra Morena Mountains north of town. Don Esteban immediately objected to the route Manuel had chosen.

"Why are we going north into the mountains when it is much quicker to go south along the plains that border the Quadalquivir River? Franco's forces are said to be heading towards Seville and south is the most direct route."

"That is exactly why we should not go there. It is the most visible and circulated route. The police will be expecting you there, as you are a big prize for the government because of your family name. They would like nothing more than to make a mockery of a prominent aristocratic family, as most are known to support the Nationalists. No one will expect us, or actually, just you,

45

since I am supposed to be in Madrid, to take the much lengthier path thru the Sierra Morena."

Don Esteban soon saw the logic in Manuel's plan and agreed.

"All right, I guess we better get started before anybody sees us."

They then set forth towards the foothills of the Sierra. While the two men were walking together their minds were locked in solitary thoughts that could not have been more distant from each other. Don Esteban wondered if he was being led into a trap. He felt largely helpless entrusting himself to a person he detested. But Maria would never put him in jeopardy, and there must be some redeeming quality about this fellow if she trusted him so. Manuel, on the other hand, was trying to figure out how he ever agreed to be thrust in this position. He knew the culprit of course: Maria, the woman who would finally be his and his alone. He started daydreaming about their wedding day, what his bride would look like, how life would be with her. He began to envision a family, a house of their own with a small plot of land, and who knows, if the bullfighting worked out, even a car, but that was some time away. Smiling, he was barely aware of the brutal summer heat of Andalusia. After about six hours Manuel signaled for them to stop beneath the shade of a large cork oak tree. They drank some water from their canteens and quietly ate the potato omelet Manuel had prepared for them. They ended the brief meal with an orange and then resumed their journey.

"We need to keep moving to be able to feel like we have put enough distance between us and those who might be looking for you."

They continued on for another four hours before finally coming to rest for the day at the mouth of a small cave. It had obviously been used before, as there were many ashes from previous campfires.

"Only a few of us hunters in town know of this place. We will not build a fire here, as that would give anyone following us a clue that someone has been here recently," Manuel said, breaking the uncomfortable silence between them.

They had some aged sheep's milk cheese with *chorizo* and bread for dinner. As they settled down for the evening and laid down on their blankets Manuel made a snide remark about Don Esteban's rifle, "Nice gun, looks like it should hang over a mantelpiece as a decoration. Does it even shoot?"

"Yes, and sometimes even straight," Don Esteban replied. Both men smiled.

"Can I take a look at yours?" asked Don Esteban.

"Sure, why not," replied Manuel as he passed his old shotgun to Don Esteban.

The gun was a 12-gauge side-by-side shotgun. It had been manufactured in Eibar, in the Basque country, from where the finest Spanish firearms traditionally come. The name of the gunsmith on the barrel could no longer be read, as age had worn away the engraving of the man who had produced it. It was a sidelock with a simple hunting scene etched on both side plates, and fine checkering on the walnut stock. Whoever had made the weapon did good, honest work, as was the custom with the Basques.

"Solid, seems like it has gotten plenty of use and not spent much time hanging over a fireplace," Don Esteban smiled as he handed the gun back to Manuel.

"Let's hope I don't have to use it, as shooting slugs with a shotgun requires one to get very close to your target, something that I can assure you I'd prefer to avoid," Manuel said as he put the gun down on the blanket.

"Amen to that," agreed Don Esteban. "Good night."

"Good night," responded Manuel, thinking that the man lying across from him had surprised him today. He had kept up with the quick pace he had imposed all day without complaining in spite of how hot it was and how much ground they had covered. "Let us see how he fares tomorrow," Manuel told himself.

The next morning they both shot up from their resting position, weapons in hand, safeties off, when they heard a rustling close by.

"Must be some small animal," Manuel finally said, "we should get going anyway."

They ate a banana and an orange, and then buried the peels so as to leave no trace of their visit. Now they were deep into the mountains and although they are not particularly steep or difficult to climb, the thorny brush beneath the cover of the oak and pine trees made it difficult to cover much ground quickly. They persevered, knowing that they had no other option. Just after noon they stopped for a bite. Canned sardines bathed in olive oil adorned a piece of bread that was harder than it should have been as it was starting to show its age.

"Not quite what you are used to?" Manuel pronounced.

"True, but after that little morning walk, I would eat anything!" Don Esteban replied in good humor.

"Let's see if we are lucky this afternoon and get a rabbit or a bird of some kind," Manuel remarked as he switched the two slugs in his shotgun barrels for pellet cartridges. They continued on for almost three hours, when all of a sudden Manuel raised his hand and signaled for them to stop. He held the old Basque gun to his right cheek and opened fire. The large brownish-grey hare never knew what hit it.

That night, as they were deep enough into the mountains, they built a small fire. Manuel quickly skinned and gutted their catch, and after inserting a thin but sturdy branch of a nearby tree through the hare, started grilling the animal, the men taking turns at slowly turning it so as to cook it evenly.

"Now we are talking!" Don Esteban announced enthusiastically as they consumed their bounty. "A pity we don't have a nice bottle of Rioja to accompany this feast," he bemoaned.

As they were coming to the end of their dinner, Manuel was solemn as he said, "How did this happen?"

"What do you mean?" Don Esteban replied inquisitively.

"A war, a war between people of the same blood, nobody will win, we are all going to lose," Manuel added sadly.

Don Esteban countered with a barrage of economic factoids.

"Well maybe it has to do with the problem that one million people, or a third of the workforce in the country is out of work, and that prices of most everything have risen 80 percent over the last five years."

"Or maybe it has to do with the fact that the church and your kind own two thirds of the land of this country, yet make up less than two percent of the population," Manuel shot back, "and why can we not sit down and talk about these issues like human beings. I never thought it would come to this. Surely we could come up with a better solution than what is happening right now." Unlike their arguments in the village bar, which had turned into shouting matches, this time both men voiced their thoughts with a calmer demeanor.

"I understand," Manuel continued, "that the situation of the country is very bad and that things can't go on in this manner."

"You cannot allow strikes on almost a daily basis, it is ruining the economy of the whole country," Don Esteban insisted.

"By the same token Esteban, you can't let a few wealthy industrialists continue to take advantage of the working class to constantly augment their already grossly overweight bank accounts. I do not disagree that free enterprise is much more efficient than government monopolies that seem to drown in their own bureaucracy, but when those businesses affect the well-being and living standards of the majority of the populace there has to be some sort of mechanism to control them. Perhaps you have to mandate that significant companies not just allow for a workers' representative to be on the board, but also that a independent government mediator sits on the same board and has the authority to resolve any disagreements between labor and management."

"By that same premise then, Manuel, you have to outlaw strikes of workers at industries that have a substantial effect on the country at large, such as railways, hospitals, police, firemen, airports, electricity, water, gas. You cannot let the interests of a few derail the country, or we will never be able to make the progress necessary to be able to benefit everyone, specially those most in need."

"Fine, Esteban, but then the Ministry of Foreign Affairs has to assist those government mediators at the major companies by finding out the average salaries of workers in those same positions at neighboring countries, so the Spanish workers can be paid fairly."

"Yes Manuel, but that pay must be adjusted for the standard of living of each country."

"Also we have to perform the same exercise with the costs to the public of those fundamental services, so that water, gas, electricity, and gasoline are all available at the lowest possible prices."

"Yet we must also make sure that there is enough of a profit incentive to lure our brightest minds into those very important industries to continue to make them competitive and efficient," added Don Esteban.

"All in all it does not seem to be such a difficult thing to accomplish," Manuel remarked.

"All it takes is a head of government with the courage and conviction to do the right thing, unfortunately money and power corrupt quickly and efficiently, so to find someone who does not just want to fill his pockets, or those of his friends, with the public's money is difficult. Such a politician is rare indeed," said Don Esteban.

"Still, such a person must exist somewhere in this country, let us just hope he is found before the country destroys itself," murmured Manuel, before turning in for the evening.

The next day saw both men awaken in a conversant mood. After burying the ashes from the previous night's fire, they started their journey in a northwesterly direction, following the curve of the Sierra Morena Mountains.

"What we need is some kind of program to put the country back to work, so that people regain their pride and self-respect," Manuel began.

"We have a recent example of such a program that has had much success in a country whose economic situation was as dire as ours, if not worse," Don Esteban said.

"Really?" inquired Manuel.

"Yes," Don Esteban replied, "the United States of America saw their economy collapse in 1929, and when their current President, Franklin Roosevelt, began his term in 1933 he started a program called 'The New Deal', whereby millions of young men were employed by the government to build roads, dams, bridges and other public works. Relief was also given to the agricultural sector, which was particularly hard hit, much like ours is here."

"If the country was in such a financial hardship, who paid for all this?" asked Manuel, thinking this was all too easy and too good to be true.

"Well I should not tell you this," smiled Don Esteban, "but it was mostly funded by heavily taxing rich individuals and businesses, while also raising the debt of the country. It was intended to be a short-term program to lift the country out of its immediate crisis and was extremely successful."

"Since you are part of the wealthy sector, how would you see such a program working here?" asked Manuel.

"It would not be easy for the rich to swallow, but I believe the country also has to have a tax structure, where every working individual pays according to their means, and there is always the incentive to make more money no matter what, or productivity will undoubtedly decrease," Don Esteban said.

Lunchtime arrived, and on this occasion, the canned sardines were served unaccompanied. Afterwards Manuel found a small stream nearby where they filled their almost empty canteens to the brim and then bathed to get rid of the grit and sweat of the last two and a half days.

"Okay Esteban, time to get some food or else were going on a diet, which neither one of us needs," Manuel added with a smirk.

They hid behind some bushes while facing the stream, and quietly waited for an animal of some kind to approach and quench its thirst. When almost two hours had gone by and Manuel was about to give up and move on, two beautiful red-legged partridges flew down to the edge of the water with barely a ruffling of their feathers to upset the afternoon silence. Manuel emptied both of his barrels and the men were rewarded with his fine aim. They gathered the birds and Manuel hung them on his belt before leaving. After trekking for a couple of hours they found a protected spot at the base of a tall mountain to stop for the night.

"I do not know how I would have ever made my way to Seville without your help," said Don Esteban in gratitude.

"Well don't get used to it, the sooner I get you to safety and we split up, the better it will be for both of us," replied Manuel, but this time with no hint of malice in his words as he had started to enjoy the chats with his traveling companion.

They awoke the following morning and Manuel started the conversation by unfolding his map and announcing that he felt they were about one day from circumventing Córdoba. After that they would be able to head towards Seville in a more direct, southwesterly direction.

"Still, we have to make sure to avoid any towns or even small villages, as it would be best to limit any contact with anyone, if at all possible," he concluded.

As they started walking Don Esteban asked Manuel a question that had always intrigued him, "What made you decide to want to become a bullfighter?"

"Actually, I remember the very day clearly. I had just turned seven when a group of us village kids were playing soccer near a fenced area about half a mile on the outskirts of Morente. One of the boys mistakenly kicked the soccer ball over the fence and went to retrieve it. Not long after he jumped over the fence, a young bull that must have been drawn to us by the loud noises we were making, appeared from behind a group of oak trees and charged the poor boy. All the other kids started screaming and running away even though we were protected by the fence, except for me. I stood next to the man-made barrier and encouraged my friend to run as fast as he could. He made it to the other side just in time as the bull crashed into the wooden structure. For some reason I did not move. It was not because I was too afraid to do so, I just did not feel any fear. He was but a foot away from me, with just some thin wooden logs between us. He snorted. It was then that I looked directly at him. It must have lasted just a few seconds, although it seemed like we were locked into each other's eyes for hours. Then, without further ado, he turned and walked slowly away. Right then and there I knew I wanted to become a matador."

"What is it like being out there in the middle of the ring with hundreds of people cheering *Ole*?" Don Esteban said, with the enthusiasm of an avid aficionado.

"Actually, it is very silent in a surreal sort of way. All I hear is the breathing of the bull. As he charges, I can feel the blood rushing through my veins, as if I put my finger in an electric socket. It is difficult to explain, but at that very moment is when I feel the most alive. I do not think, I react. I just know which side he is going to charge and when he is going to turn towards me with his horns as he is passing by. It is only when I kill him that I finally hear the crowd and begin to see the people in the stands," Manuel explained in a very matter of fact way, without the slightest hint of drama or exaggeration.

"Are you not afraid of the bull, afraid of being gored, afraid of getting killed?" asked Don Esteban.

"No Esteban," replied Manuel, saying it without a trace of swagger—not as if he were a braver man, but as a simple truth. "I am not afraid of death. I have seen enough of it to know that it is an inevitable part of life. One cannot be without the other. It is just so. Death is the ultimate Achilles heel. Philosophically speaking we all know we are going to die, but most of us never truly believe it will really happen. We do not envision the actual moment arriving, and thus go through life without really living it, as if we have the luxury of waiting for the right time to do so. In my trade the sword is my tool. I live by it. One day I will die because of it, but at least till that moment arrives, I will have lived fully. The only question that haunts my life is if I want to exist and not simply be, or do I want to be and not simply exist?"

Don Esteban realized then that the man before him was not as plain as his roots might indicate. If he closed his eyes he could imagine himself in class at Cambridge University being lectured by a professor of Philosophy about the meaning of life and death. That they need each other. That they are opposites but also the same. Yet nobody could have explained it more clearly than Manuel had just done today.

Later on that same day, at an altitude of almost 2,000 feet, they saw the outline of Córdoba southeast of them. At night they grilled two quails that had made the fatal mistake of suddenly appearing in front of Manuel's shotgun.

"We have about three more days left in the mountains before we must cross the Guadalquivir Valley to get to Seville," Manuel pointed out on the map, in what had become their planning ritual for the day each morning.

"Now that we are far enough away from Córdoba we will go down towards the valley so that we can make better time, but still remain out of sight in the foothills," Manuel continued.

As they had little food left, they agreed to skip breakfast, in case they were not lucky enough to hunt anything that day. As fortune would have it, about an hour into their walk they heard the snorting sound of a wild boar. This time Don Esteban took the safety off his rifle, as Manuel's shotgun was ill suited for this type of game. Both men slowly got on their knees and patiently waited for the fearsome looking swine to come into view. Then the animal finally appeared, about 50 yards away. It was not very large, perhaps about 100 pounds, but it was more than sufficient to feed them for the remainder of their journey. Don Esteban aimed at the animal's head and fired.

"Yes! You got him!" Manuel enthusiastically announced, but just then they heard an alarming, "Who goes there?"

Don Esteban immediately chambered another bullet in his rifle while Manuel exchanged the pellet cartridges in his barrels for slugs and pointed his shotgun in the direction of the voice.

"Just a couple of hunters," shouted back Manuel.

"Show yourselves!" replied an older sounding voice, "and keep your guns facing down."

"He does not sound like a policeman or a soldier and he knows where we are, but we don't know where he is, so we don't have much choice but to come out," Manuel whispered to Don Esteban.

"Are you sure this is a good idea?" Don Esteban whispered back.

"No, but I don't have a better one right now," Manuel replied smiling. "When we go out, stand behind me, if he fires you will know it was a bad idea. Then run like hell."

"We are coming out, do not shoot!" shouted Manuel, as both men got up and went into a clearing in front of them while pointing their guns to the ground. They stood there for about a minute or so, until a man in his sixties came out from behind a tree pointing a rusty old shotgun at them.

"Take it easy old man, we mean no harm, we are just doing a little hunting like yourself," said Manuel in a soothing voice.

"Yes, but these days one does not know whom to trust," responded the man. After looking them over he decided they were of no particular danger and lowered his weapon.

"Where are you young lads from?" he asked them.

"Morente," answered Manuel.

"You are far from your home. What are you doing all the way out here?" he inquired.

"The same as you are, looking for boar and deer. Hunting at home is not good and we need to bring some food back to our families, with the way things are lately," continued Manuel.

"I hear that," as he looked down at the prized boar they had just shot. "What are your names?" he asked them.

"I am Manolo and this is my friend Esteban."

"He does not look like he is too badly off," the old man said, examining Don Esteban and noticing his rifle and clothes.

"Well things were a lot better for him before this whole mess started!" laughed Manuel without missing a beat.

"What is your name?" Manuel asked calmly to change the subject.

"Tomas, Tomas Campollo."

"Well Tomas Campollo, I'll tell you what, why don't we split this boar in three, as you were close enough to almost claim it for yourself," Manuel suggested.

With that, the mood disarmed. Tomas expertly field dressed the animal and split it into three even parts. The men then had lunch together, as Tomas generously shared his *serrano* ham lodged in a *baguette* with them.

The two young men ate voraciously as Tomas watched.

"You have not had much to eat lately, huh?" said the elderly man, smiling. "What do you think about everything that is going on, all this talk of Communists, Liberals, Fascists, Nationalists, Conservatives, this wing, that wing, I just do not understand it," he continued.

"I am not sure anyone does," Don Esteban replied, thinking just how convoluted everything had become and how difficult it must be for the common layman to comprehend.

"Well, whatever it is they are selling, I don't want to buy it."

Both young men nodded in agreement at the simple wisdom of the old man.

"What are you going to do now?" Tomas asked them.

"We have to continue hunting, as this is not enough to bring back," Manuel said pointing towards the partitioned boar.

"Well boys, I will tell you that about five miles west of here are the lands of the Count of something or other. They are loaded with game and even though the son of a bitch does not let anyone hunt there, which would not hurt him one bit to occasionally let us do, we all sneak in every once-in-a-while and grab something. Just do not get caught, as with all those huge landowners, they will get you incarcerated for months and make you pay them a hefty fine, even though many of us are barely staving off starvation. Ironic how they call themselves noblemen, when noble is the last thing they are," remarked Tomas in disgust.

"We have the same situation in our village with the local Count," smiled Manuel.

"Bastards, inbred bastards, that is what they all are," the old man added.

"Yes!" Manuel laughed, barely able to contain himself, "I could not agree with you more."

They parted and wished each other well. Manuel was still laughing as they made their way west.

"I am glad you find it so amusing," Don Esteban remarked not finding the same humor.

"Oh, come now Esteban, it was all in good fun. Look, it is better for you to find out how people really feel about things than to think that we all live in your same paradise. Besides, your parents are not talked about in that way in Morente. While I may despise the aristocracy in this country for the disproportionate allocation of wealth that they represent, the Counts of Morente have always been generous and fair with the people of our village."

"But how will they talk about me when it is time for me to succeed my father?" said Don Esteban introspectively.

"Will they refer to me as a 'bastard' or as 'benevolent'? Do I want to have the responsibility for the livelihood of a large group of families throughout their entire lifetime? Will I do it well, as my parents have? Why did this damn 'privilege' fall upon my shoulders? Nobody ever asked me if I wanted to be the eighteenth Count of Morente, never mind whether I am remotely qualified to be it. Do I want to be anchored to a place outside of Morente for the rest of my life? Is this not but a very nice jail where I serve a life sentence?"

As he was listening to Don Esteban, Manuel began to see him in a different light. He was not the pompous, know it all rich boy he had previously assumed him to be. All of a sudden being a Count did not seem like such a wonderful thing. He began to feel strangely sympathetic to the insecurities and dilemmas within Esteban.

"Well," began Manuel, "for whatever it is worth, I think you will figure it out and do just fine."

"Coming from you, I appreciate that. Thanks," Don Esteban replied.

The grilled rack of ribs tasted especially good that evening as their hunger finally subsided.

"Manuel, I did not thank you earlier for putting yourself in harm's way by coming out into the open first, and the manner in which you handled the situation with our new friend Tomas," Don Esteban acknowledged.

"Do not worry about it— and call me Manolo. That is what my friends do."

As they were taking out the blankets from their respective packs to get ready to retire for the night, the metal cylinder hidden in Don Esteban's fell to the ground.

"What is that?" Manuel asked.

"This is my penal sentence Manolo."

"What do you mean?"

"This is the document that conferred upon my ancestor the title of Count of Morente by the Catholic Monarchs."

"You are kidding! What are you doing carrying it on your person here?"

"My father gave it to me on the night before we embarked on our little hike, in case something were to happen to him and my mother. I did not even know such a thing existed until a few days ago."

"Can I take a look at it?" asked Manuel with obvious curiosity.

"Sure, Manolo," said Don Esteban as he unscrewed the cap and took out the ancient manuscript. Manuel was awestruck.

"It is amazing Esteban. I have never seen anything remotely this old. It is like holding a piece of living history in one's hands. I am beginning to comprehend the weight that must be upon you, to have been chosen to safeguard, not just some pieces of valuable paper, but the whole institution itself."

"Yes Manolo, it is an honor and a curse at the same time."

"Do you know why your ancestor was given this title by Fernando and Isabel?"

"Ah yes, Manolo, it was one of the first things I recall ever hearing," said Don Esteban. He finally smiled as he gazed up at the lonely night to see but one shining star above them, and recounted the story of Manuel Vilches Díaz.

"It all starts back in 1482 at the beginning of the Granada War, which would end in 1492 with the defeat of King Boabdil, the Sultan of Granada, ruler of the last Muslim kingdom left in the peninsula, and result in the unification of Spain. Alhama, a small town southwest of Granada, was the site of one of the first key battles in the conflict. The Sultan was attempting to take the town back from the Christians, who had but a small force there and were waiting for reinforcements led by King Fernando II himself. Vastly outnumbered by the almost 7,000 horsemen of King Boabdil's army, they were headed by a young light cavalry Captain who had taken charge when the Castilian nobleman who had commanded them died in battle several days earlier. The 400 or so men that Manuel Vilches Díaz had at his disposal were weary, many badly injured, with almost no food or water left. Most wanted to surrender, but he refused to allow them, vowing to fight against the infidels until the death, promising that victory would soon be theirs.

Alhama was a small, fortified village that sat atop a knoll about 3,000 feet high, rising dramatically above the Alhama River some 200 hundred feet below. Up to that point the Christians had been holding off the Moors by simply using the walls of the town in a classic defense. Yet the Sultan's army was able to get close enough to Alhama to use their superior number of archers to slowly pick off the Christians, one by one. Manuel Vilches Díaz realized that it would only be a matter of days before they would succumb to their enemy. He knew he had to change their strategy, and did so in a most dramatic fashion.

He posted injured men, who would still be able to alert them of a surprise attack from below, around the periphery of the town that stood on the sheer cliffs above the river. On the western part that fronted his enemy, he saw that the hills converged above them into a small valley that was about 100 yards from the main gates of Alhama. If he could take the battle to the Sultan in the narrow gap, he might be able to defend it with only 200 hundred men. Against his cavalry, the Moorish archers in such a reduced area would be ineffective and remain too far away to harm his other men. Then, as his cavalry rode towards the Moors he would have 40 of his strongest archers run behind them until they were about 30 yards from the battle. At that point they would shower the skies with deadly arrows, aimed at the enemy bunched up near the front line. That would in turn create even more havoc for King Boabdil's men. It would leave him with about 60 cavalry in reserve to reinforce the main unit for any casualties, after accounting for a small force of men to defend the town walls. It was a daring plan, but one that might buy him the four to five days he needed before King Fernando II arrived.

The next morning as he was telling his men of his plan, one of the senior soldiers, an older Sergeant, yelled out loud, "You have gone mad! I will not have any of this crazed idea that will surely lead to our death!"

The other soldiers started to grumble in agreement with their dissenting comrade, as Manuel Vilches Díaz took out his sword and directed it towards the mutinous soldier, "You can die here right now as a coward by my sword, or you can die honorably out there for your king and queen. The choice is yours. What shall it be?"

A loud roar by the crowd made the choice, "For King Fernando and Queen Isabel!"

His plan worked as he willed them by example, fighting ferociously at the front line, reprising every attack the frustrated Moors launched against them, in spite of sustaining several serious wounds.

At long last King Fernando II arrived with his troops and the Moors fled back towards Granada. King Fernando was so taken aback by the scene he saw when he entered the town that he asked for the leader of the men to be brought to him immediately. Having heard from others about what had taken place, when he met the young captain he conferred upon him the title of Count and gave him a vast estate near his home village, Morente."

"Does not seem like much of a fellow to have to live up to," joked Manuel.

"Yeah, I know," Don Esteban replied sarcastically. Exhausted after having covered more than twenty-five miles that day, both men were soon asleep.

A cloudy and unusually overcast morning marked the beginning of their sixth day together. They were thankful for the weather as it meant the scorching sun would be gentler on them. As the day unfurled, the two men spent most of the day chatting about a number of contemporary issues. It was plain to see by now that they enjoyed each other's company and conversation. Manuel asked Don Esteban what life had been like at Cambridge University. Don Esteban remarking on the self satisfaction of the gaining of knowledge, the sense of independence of living on your own for the first time, the excitement of life in a different country, and of course, the multitude of amazing-looking women.

"Manolo, you have never seen so many attractive women in all the days you have lived! Oh my God!" he laughed out loud.

In a more sobering tone Manuel asked him, "Talking about God, how do you feel about religion and the church?"

"Like most of us in this country, I was brought up Catholic, and to tell you the truth I have not dedicated much time to questioning my faith. I believe in God and that Jesus Christ was his son sent to this world to spread wisdom and save humanity. The church ends up being an imperfect human instrument to continue his teachings. While I agree that it's crazy that the church owns almost a third of the land of this country, that the institution itself has become too politicized, there still needs to be a place for people to worship, a place for people to learn the lessons of the Bible. And you Manolo, what are your thoughts?"

"Esteban, I do not believe there is a God."

"What!" Don Esteban interrupted.

"If there was a God, then that would mean that he was perfect and all-powerful, correct?"

"Yes, I guess so," replied Don Esteban hesitantly, not knowing where this was all leading to.

"Well then how could such an immaculate being allow for wars, allow for epidemics of diseases that kill millions of human beings, how could he allow for all this pain and suffering that is a constant part of humanity, how could he allow for death, in fact how could he allow life itself?"

"There is nothing like a light morning chat to begin the day with you, is there Manolo," smiled Don Esteban. "Perhaps we make God into an image of a man because we are limited to what we can relate to. Maybe

God is more like a faith. A faith that tries to explain the reason for our existence. A faith that we need to believe in to survive the hardships of life. A faith that makes us good, moral people. A faith that makes us want to help those that are in greater need than we are."

"Yes, Esteban, I agree with you and I have such a faith, but I see the church as taking advantage of this for their own well-being. I see a few old people attending mass because today's youth can not relate to the teachings of antiquated doctrines and thus have long abandoned the pews that now lie dormant at most religious institutions."

"Manolo, I do not altogether disagree with you, but the church is caught between two difficult positions. On one hand they have to preach those doctrines that have constituted part of their teachings for almost two millennia. Perhaps some of them do have to change to conform to the world we are living in today. At the same time if they keep changing their message, then the message gets diluted. People need something strong to hang on to. I do not know that there is an easy answer to this, if in fact there is an answer at all, but I do not envy the position of the church."

"But what we cannot have is a country where almost half of its people are illiterate and where priests have become another type of aristocracy. The church is neglecting its moral obligation to take care of its flock. To top it off, the government uses a good amount of the taxes it collects to give to the Bishops to perpetuate their growing wealth, while a lot of people in this country are barely able to put a meal on their table."

"With this Manolo, I have no argument to offer you. I agree that the state has no business giving a bunch of money to a group as rich as the church already is, especially in times like these. I also think that the church has to stay out of the political culture of the country. Otherwise it should be regarded as another political party, be taxed accordingly, and lose their charitable status. Also, as a charity it should be audited by the government to make sure, that as you pointed out, it is taking care of its flock and not simply filling up its coffers or those of Rome. Still, I do not think that these constitute insurmountable roadblocks."

"I would like to agree with you, but I just do not see anyone tackling these issues."

The two men continued their trek thru the mountains, covering well over twenty miles. Only once throughout the day did they stop to rest for about half an hour. They did not have lunch, as the only thing they had left to eat was the boar, which required setting up a campfire. Time was of the essence now, as they were getting closer to populated areas and could ill afford to linger about more than was absolutely necessary. They both slept soundly after the exhausting day and a filling meal at its end.

The next morning Don Esteban awoke to find Manuel gone. Initially alarmed, he was quickly put at ease when he saw Manuel's shotgun and surmised that he had taken their canteens to get them filled. He gingerly got up, stretched his stiff muscles, and started to put his things in his pack. He was surprised at how much terrain they had covered over the last week. Never before had he done this much exercise. For the first couple of days he was quite sore, but now he felt fine and had no problem covering the 20 to 25 miles they covered daily. He was also conscious that today they would have to separate, as they were now less than 30 miles from Seville. He was not looking forward to the moment. He had become quite fond of his companion. The ill thoughts that he had about Manuel previous to their trip had long since been forgotten. In fact, he could not recall enjoying the company of any male friend at the university or anywhere as much.

"Don't move!" Don Esteban suddenly heard.

The sound sent a chill throughout his body. He quickly reached for his rifle and took the safety off. The voice that had barked out the order was definitely authoritative. Either military or police for sure thought Don Esteban. He crawled on the ground in the direction he thought the sound had come from. He came up to a thick oak tree. He stood up quietly and slowly and peeked around the side to see two army soldiers and Manuel about 40 yards away. One was holding a pistol to his head and the other was checking Manuel's pockets looking to find his identification papers. The soldier checking for documentation found the booklet he was looking for, and after leafing thru it threw it at Manuel's face.

"Communist pig!"

"Look what we have here Emilio, our first Republican. Does not look too fearsome now, does he?" he smiled maliciously.

"I think it is time to kill us our first traitor. What do you think about that, you stinking piece of shit?" he screamed in Manuel's face.

"Yes, I do believe that is the case," said his partner. "Stand back Felix so you do not get the blood from his brains splattered all over you," he added, laughing.

"Any last words you want to say, you liberal asshole?" said the other man, but Manuel just looked defiantly at him, without saying a single word.

Don Esteban carefully brought his rifle up to his cheek and pointed it towards the soldier holding the pistol. He wished he had a scope on the gun, but his father had never bought one as he felt it was not sporting to use them to hunt.

"Okay Mr. Rigby, let us find out just how good your rifles really are," Don Esteban told himself as he closed his eyes for a brief moment, took a deep breath and slowly let it escape before he pulled the trigger.

He heard a thud and saw the object of his aim go down from the single shot to the cranium. The other soldier was caught off guard just long enough for Manuel to reach down to his belt, take out his six-inch hunting knife from its sheath and lunge towards his foe before he was able to unholster his gun. He plunged the knife into the gut of the soldier, who wide-eyed could only stare at him without uttering a sound.

"Who's laughing now, you Fascist pig," Manuel sneered disgustingly at him as he took his last gasp.

Don Esteban came rushing up to the gory scene. Upon seeing the two dead men, he turned around to throw up.

"Some soldier you are going to be," said Manuel as he patted him on the back. "Now you have really gone and done it, buddy. We have to split up right away and get out of here as fast as possible: you towards Seville, and me back to Córdoba, as this place will be swarming with soldiers in no time. Also we should switch guns, as they will quickly find out that the bullet that killed this man came from an unusual caliber and your rifle sticks out like a sore thumb. I'll also grab the weapons from our dearly departed friends."

Quickly they returned to their camp to pick up their packs.

"Esteban, earlier this morning I wrote this," Manolo said as he handed him a carefully folded piece of thin paper. "Please give it to Maria if I do not make it back to Morente."

Surprisingly, it was the first time her name had come up, not that both men had not had ample thoughts about her. But they had been too personal to share.

"Do not talk like that, we will soon be arguing again at the village bar," Don Esteban replied in the least solemn tone he could muster, but without much success.

"I hope so Esteban, I really do. Thank you for saving my life earlier."

"No need to mention it Manolo. Without your help during these past days, I also, in all likelihood, would probably not be around."

As they were finally departing the two men did not shake hands, as that would have been too formal, while embracing would not have spoken enough of the gravity of the situation. Instead, they grabbed each other's forearm much in the manner Roman Centurions would have done on these same lands during their conquest of Hispania almost two thousand years earlier.

Manuel spoke first.

"Perhaps in another time we could have become friends…", but before he was able to continue Don Esteban tightened his grip on the other man's arm and quietly said, "You are wrong Manolo; because of this time, this place, this moment, we will always be friends." Manuel nodded in agreement before both men left in opposing directions.

"That is it for today!" announced Trini.

"Okay, till tomorrow," said Carlos amazed by the story he had just heard.

9

A cup of recently brewed coffee and some freshly baked *madalenas* awaited Carlos the following morning as he entered the kitchen. He could barely hold himself back, he had so many questions racing in his mind about what happened next to Don Esteban and Don Manuel, as Trini finally began, "All right, all right, you impatient youth!"

"That day Don Esteban made it to the outskirts of Seville, where he was met by a patrol of soldiers belonging to General Franco's troops. Upon identifying himself and showing them his papers he was taken to the General's headquarters, where after waiting for an hour he was summoned by the *Generalissimo* himself. He told General Francisco Franco of his ordeal in order to escape the Republican forces the past week, omitting any reference to Manuel and the two soldiers they had killed.

"Well that is quite a story, and you are exactly the kind of man this army needs to save this country from this rampant anarchism," remarked the General, aware that having the highly regarded Vilches name in his corner was a great moral triumph for his cause. Don Esteban could not help but feel uneasy in front of the man who had been nicknamed 'The Butcher of Asturias' because of the violent way he had put down the general strike in Asturias in 1934, where 2,000 miners had been killed. Whether it was the cold, steely voice or the lifeless eyes, he did not feel he could completely trust this man.

"General, I will of course be at your disposal for anything you deem necessary but request that after Andalusia is taken, I be allowed to return to Morente, to my family's estate, where my elderly parents are in need of much help."

"Yes, of course," answered the General brusquely. These aristocrats are all the same, he thought to himself, all this talk of honor, duty and nobility and at the first hint of trouble they go crawling back to their spoilt lives. Still he needed their support for his cause to be anointed as legitimate, and a dead Count would not help that.

Don Esteban was relegated to administrative work at the army headquarters in Seville, keeping track of the troops and equipment being airlifted there from Spanish Morocco by the Italian and German Air Forces. During the following two weeks the Nationalists took control of western Andalusia and started to advance on Madrid. It was at this point that Don Esteban requested and was granted permission to return to his family estate. It would prove to be a day too late.

"I will never forget that terrible day," Trini reflected, tears swelling in her eyes.

The morning had started on the most joyful of notes as we had learned that Don Esteban would be returning to the estate the following day. I was helping my mother, Rosa, with cooking duties while chatting about what a relief it was going to be for Don Cristobal and Doña Catalina to have their son back at home. She asked me to go to the well outside, to get some water to clean the vegetables we were preparing for lunch. I took a couple of buckets and headed out singing one of the many operettas my mother had taught me. I was minding my own business when I felt someone grab my waist and hoist me up in the air as I shrieked. It was one of the two guards belonging to the Spanish Foreign Legion that the Nationalist Army had posted at the entrance of the estate.

"Put me down! Put me down!" I screamed.

"I love these Andalusian girls, they are so spirited," laughed his partner. "Come on pretty girl, we spent the last three years in a hell hole called North Africa, why don't you show us a good time, we promise we will show you one!"

At that moment my mother came out of the kitchen after hearing all the commotion. With venom in her voice she said, "Put my daughter down at once."

"Oh come on honey, you look pretty good for your age, why don't you join the fun."

"Do not talk to me like that!" my mother screamed and then slapped one of the soldiers across the face. After the initial shock, he struck her back with all his might, sending her reeling to the ground, blood spewing from her mouth.

A gun went off and pellets whizzed just over our heads. It was Don Cristobal holding his favorite Victor Sarasqueta shotgun, pointed at the soldiers.

"Get off my land right now and never show your faces around here again!" he commanded the two men.

"Take it easy, sir. Put the gun down before someone gets hurt," said one of the soldiers.

"Do not dare tell me what to do in my house you piece of scum!"

At that instant the Countess Catalina came out of the house. "What in God's name is going on?"

The Count instinctively turned towards the sound of her voice, while one of the soldiers took advantage of the distraction to take out his pistol and point it at Don Cristobal.

My mother and I shouted, "No!"

As the Count turned back around and saw the weapon pointed at him, he shot off the remaining cartridge in his shotgun while the soldier discharged his gun. Don Cristobal crumbled to the ground from a chest wound. The soldier was holding his hands to his face, writhing in pain from the pellet shots. All of us women rushed towards Don Cristobal and crouched beside him, sobbing, while he attempted to reassure us, saying he would be fine and not to worry," Trini said, not being able to hold back the stream of tears any longer.

Carlos reached out to hold her hands.

"That day I learnt what it meant to be noble," she continued. "Anyhow, after a few excruciating minutes, he took his last gasp. Soon a Captain of the Nationalist Army arrived in a truck with a group of soldiers and hauled both of the legionnaires away. Later on we found that upon hearing the news, General Franco ordered both soldiers to be shot by a firing squad, but such things do not cure anything and do not bring anyone back.

Doña Catalina was inconsolable and passed away later that evening. The doctor said it was because of a heart attack, but I know this is not so as her heart died when Don Cristobal did. The following day saw the arrival of Don Esteban, who was devastated when he learned from Maria what had happened. Every single person from the village attended the eulogy given by Father Juanjo, who spoke movingly of the example the Count and Countess had given us to follow. Afterwards we all marched in the procession from the church to the small cemetery at the estate where all the Counts of Morente are buried, and where the caskets of Don Cristobal and Doña Catalina were finally laid to rest. I have never seen so many tears or bouquets of flowers as I saw on that day.

Don Esteban receded into a dark shell and Maria was the only one who could find a way inside. He would spend countless hours in the library just staring out the window. Maria became the de facto head of the house, organizing the housework and overseeing the business aspects of the estate. She treated everyone fairly and with respect, never once pretending to be high and mighty because of the power she had acquired from her close friendship with Don Esteban. Even the older women in the household grew to admire her. We became friends, but then again, everyone wanted Maria as their best friend. Slowly she nurtured the young Count back to life. Soon he was strolling throughout the house, and whenever he would see one of us he would stop to talk to us and see how we were doing. If a family member were at the front, he would ask by name if we had any news of them. Don Cristobal and Doña Catalina had always been pleasant in their dealings with us but had never shown the kind of personal interest their son was now demonstrating. I think that the time he spent with Manolo and then with Maria had changed him. The mood at the estate, in spite of all the circumstances, had never been more jovial.

"Have you heard anything from Manolo?" Don Esteban asked Maria one morning.

"Manolo?" she said back, surprised at the question. "No I have not heard from him. Rumor has it that after Córdoba fell to General Franco, he, like most of the Republican forces, fled to Madrid, but I do not know for certain. Why do you ask?"

"Well after our week together I consider him a friend, actually a very close friend."

Maria had been itching to ask him about what had occurred during their time together, but because of past circumstances had decided it was not the appropriate thing to do. Now having received carte blanche from Don Esteban she bombarded him with questions.

"Tell me what happened? How did you two get along? Did everything work out according to plan?"

Don Esteban laughed, "Actually I very much enjoyed getting to know him. I had been so caught up in my jealousy of your relationship, that it had obscured him completely. I now understand how you can be so fond of him. He is a very unique individual of great character. I sincerely look forward to seeing him again and resuming our discussions. That does not mean that I am not still somewhat envious; it is just a secondary emotion now—that is all."

Maria hugged him and said, "You have no idea how glad I am to hear you say that. Hopefully this wretched war will be over soon and the three of us can laugh about it all over a drink."

"Yes let us hope so my dear. Oh! It has been so long I almost forgot. Manolo asked me to give you this if I saw you before he did." Don Esteban gave Maria the folded paper Manuel had given him about a month earlier, then left the room so she could read the note in private. She unfolded it and saw that it was not a letter, but a poem.

My Dream

I dream of getting lost in the afternoon wind,
of walking thru meadows leading into the night,
of your footsteps gliding past the fading sunset.

I dream of holding the tenderness that lies in your hand,
of the sound of a siren that is your voice,
of your laughter that is the sweetness of your heart.

I dream of the perfume that is your body,
of the touch of ecstasy that is your kiss,
of your words that are poems for my soul.

I dream,
I dream of you,
I dream of you and me.

As she finished the poem she held it tightly against her chest and unleashed a river of tears as she looked into the distance through the window.

Days followed months and then years at the estate, where life was relatively tranquil in contrast to the turmoil elsewhere in Spain. What had at first seemed like a small rebellion that would be put down quickly had turned into a lengthy protracted struggle. The Nationalists received help from Hitler and Mussolini and became a formidable army, but they found that the Republicans, aided by foreign volunteers known as the International Brigades, were more resilient than anybody had anticipated. The war lasted until Madrid finally fell in April of 1939.

I remember having coffee alone with Maria one afternoon not long after the end of the war, when she confessed to me her most innermost secrets.

"I do not know what to do," she began.

"What do you mean? Do about what?" I asked.

"Esteban wants me to marry him."

"That is wonderful news Maria! Everyone thinks you two would make a beautiful couple."

"Trini, the only problem is I promised my heart to Manuel. I promised him that I would marry him when he came back."

No one had heard any news at all about or from Manuel in the years since he had been forced to leave Morente. It was widely assumed that he was dead. Rumors ran rampant about retributions by Franco against Republicans in the form of mass executions or deportations to German concentration camps, and it was said another 50,000 people were executed after the Civil War. So even if he had survived the numerous battles during the war, as a young leader in the Republican fold, Manuel would have been sought after by the authorities and shot immediately if found. On top of that, everyone was afraid to even broach the subject in case he was alive and we might jinx his life, Andalusians being as superstitious as they are."

"Did you tell the Count that?" I asked her.

"No, of course not. I just told him that I wanted to wait till after the war—that it did not feel right to celebrate such a beautiful moment at such an awful time. He agreed. But now I know he is anxious for us to start a family together."

"Maria, you know how highly people around here think of Manuel, even those that differ with his politics, and how much we would love to believe that he is still alive. But deep down we all have come to the realization that after all this time, chances are that he is not."

Maria was crying. "I know you are right Trini, I just haven't wanted to face it, but now I know I must. Esteban is a wonderful man and cares for me deeply. The least I can do after all he has done for me and for everyone, is commit myself to him." Then she wiped the tears from her eyes and said, "Yes! I shall marry Esteban and dedicate myself to this wonderful place and to raising a family. Yes! That is the right thing to do Trini. Thank you for listening."

From that moment on, life at the Vilches estate was overflowing with joy. All we could talk about and think of was the upcoming wedding. The women constantly chatted, laughed, and sang. Maria wanted to have it at the church in Morente, but Esteban made her understand of the multitude of obligatory invitations they would have to send out, making it impossible to have it there. The cathedral in Córdoba was the only place large enough to accommodate everyone. Maria insisted on inviting every single soul from Morente, to which she personally handed an invitation. Most of us—no, all of us, would never see so magnificent a matrimonial ceremony again for the rest of our lives. We were seated with the aristocracy of Andalusia; the Marquis' of so and so, Dukes of this and that, Counts from everywhere, Bishops, Archbishops, a Cardinal. *Generalissimo* Franco even sent a top General as his representative. People spent their last *pesetas* to buy a new dress or suit, for none had any clothes remotely appropriate for the momentous occasion. Recognizing this, Maria gave each person at the estate an envelope with more than enough money to buy ourselves a fancy dress or elegant suit and still have enough left over to give to others in our family. She called it a bonus for making her life so happy. It was so like her to never forget about where she came from and to always help others. In fact if she ever found out that someone was having any kind of financial hardship, she would discreetly give them an envelope and tell them that it was a little something extra for their hard work, but not to tell anyone. She would always do it in private, not drawing any attention to herself, and never making one feel as if they were accepting charity. Don Esteban of course, figured out all of this, even though when she asked him for money she would always say it was to buy herself something, as she knew he would never refuse her. He just smiled and gave her the money."

Trini became quite emotional and had to stop for a moment. Carlos handed her his handkerchief to wipe away her tears.

"We all wanted to volunteer to help with cutting and arranging flowers, preparing the various meals, whatever," Trini went on. The wedding day finally arrived on a Sunday in October of 1939. A large band was playing outside the cathedral as Maria arrived with her father in a pale blue and gold horse-drawn carriage. She wore a resplendent pearl-colored gown with a train that followed forever. It was the first time in my life that I saw an angel, for there is no other way to describe the light that was Maria that day.

The cathedral was packed with over 1,000 people. Photographers of all the major newspapers in Spain were eagerly snapping shots of the couple as they finally came together at the altar. The atmosphere was electric. The Count and Maria could not stop smiling at each other. The celebration lasted for days; nobody wanted it to stop!" laughed Trini.

Soon there was another event that would bring even more excitement to our lives. One morning a few months after the wedding, Maria came into the kitchen and announced, "Since you ladies are obviously having too good of a time around here and need more work to do, I just wanted to tell you that in about eight months you will have another mouth to feed. I am pregnant!"

As the news spread, screams broke out all over the estate. Everyone could not have been more ecstatic. The older women, including my mother, rushed to see Don Esteban, hugging and kissing him on the cheeks in a most uncommon display of emotion towards their employer that quite embarrassed him. But he loved it, because he knew it was a demonstration of how people felt about Maria. We all started to have friendly wagers about whether it would be a boy or a girl. A few days before the due date a doctor and a nurse from Córdoba came to stay at the estate. Finally on the first day of August of 1940, her water broke and she went into labor.

Then tragedy struck. She began to bleed internally, and just after we heard the first cries of little Alexandra, we learned that Maria had died.

My mother Rosa, as the senior woman in the household, took charge of things immediately. She gathered all of us together, away from Don Esteban, and said as she held Alexandra in her arms, "This is the gift that Maria has left us, it is now our duty to help Don Esteban raise this child and repay him for the way he has always treated us. We must put aside the pain and sorrow that we feel and show him the love and compassion that he sorely needs at this terrible time. This is what Maria, who never asked us for anything, would ask of us now, and I for one will not deny her that."

I lied earlier when I told you that I had not seen more tears than I saw when Don Cristobal and Doña Catalina passed away.

At Maria's funeral, women, young and old alike, were wailing, "God, how could you do this? How could you take away our beautiful Maria?"

The men with watery eyes, tried to console us, to no avail. I saw multitudes of people I had never seen in my life. A little boy was sobbing alone as we were about to go into the church, and as I did not recognize him, I kneeled down and asked him how he knew Maria. He was from a larger village next to Morente, Bujalance, where we often went to get groceries and things for the house. He told me that whenever he saw her, she would always have a small piece of candy for him and the other kids, and that he had never met someone so nice and kind in his short life. He had walked three miles by himself to say goodbye to her. Even Father Juanjo was at a loss for words as he gave the eulogy. He spoke of keeping one's faith even if we did not understand what had happened. He said that perhaps God chooses those of us who are so special to have them close to him. It was clear to all of us that this must be so. Don Esteban was catatonic and all the women of the house held him, surrounding him, wanting to protect him.

Slowly, over much time, the Count became consumed with Alexandra, as did everyone else. She became our glimmer of hope. In her we began to see Maria and she started to heal us. From her earliest days it was plain to see that she was feisty and independent. We lathered her with love but Don Esteban forbid us to spoil her, and whenever she did something wrong we were encouraged to reprimand her as if she were our own daughter, which is exactly what she became. My second cousin Celia and I became Alexandra's surrogate mothers. We spent countless hours playing with her and teaching her to sing and dance. Even when we neglected our duties, neither my mother nor Don Esteban would say anything to us, as they understood how important it was for us to be with Alexandra."

"What about Don Manuel?" interrupted Carlos.
"Oh, that's a story for another day," she replied.

10

"It is a day that shall remain forever embedded in my mind," Trini said, as she continued the story the following morning.

As he entered the grounds of the Vilches estate, Manuel saw a little girl that could not have been much more than five years old. She was playing with a stick, carving images on the ground. As he approached her, she looked up at him, which caused him to fall on his knees.

He just said, "Maria."

"No sir, my name is not Maria, it is Alexandra Maria del Carmen Vilches Benítez."

"Yes of course you are," Manuel replied, unable to hold back the tears within him.

"Why did you call me Maria?"

"Because you remind so much of your mother."

"You knew my mother?"

"Yes, Alexandra Maria del Carmen Vilches Benítez, your mother was a friend of mine."

"Alexandra, what are you doing? Come back here right now!" the Count shouted as he came out of the villa, alarmed by the sight of a stranger carrying a rifle slung around his shoulder, kneeling in front of his daughter.

"But Papa, this man needs my help. He is sad and is crying."

As he approached them the Count recognized his old friend.

"Manolo! My God, you are alive!" he exclaimed, falling to the ground and embracing the man he had not seen for nine years.

"Papa, you know this man?"

"Yes dear, Manolo is a good friend I thought I would never get to see again."

It was 1945. That July morning Celia and I had been preparing lunch when we went outside to see what all the ruckus was about. Both of us were astonished as we recognized Manuel.

"Manolo!" we screamed simultaneously, running out to hug him.

"Come Manolo, let us go inside. There is much to talk about," said the Count. He led Manuel to the library. As they entered the room, he looked at the Michel Ange Houasse portrait.

"I have tried to imagine for years what that painting would look like, since you told me the story about the vault behind it," Manuel commented. "I take it your family's heritage is back in safekeeping."

"Yes, thanks to your help."

"Oh, I brought your Rigby back as I hope to never have any further use for it," Manuel said, handing the rifle to Don Esteban.

"Manolo, you can keep it," replied Don Esteban.

"No Esteban, if it was yours I would appreciate the generous gift, but it belonged to your father, and the circumstances in which he gave it to you were very significant for both of you. But thank you anyway. Besides it harks back to a time that I don't care to recall."

"As you wish," replied the count, before continuing, "I have so many questions for you."

"And I for you, Esteban."

"What happened to you after we split up?" Don Esteban asked.

"After the fall of Córdoba," Manuel began, "I, like many others, made a hasty retreat to Madrid to continue the fight against the Nationalists. There I fought at the front line we established around the university. It was a bloody affair with massive losses on our side from the heavy artillery fire that we were taking, not to mention being constantly bombarded by Hitler's Luftwaffe. I saw things that changed me as a member of the human race. Friends and young boys died horrible deaths by my side, day after day. I felt useless amongst the cries of pain and looks of horror in their eyes, as death unfurled its ugly head everywhere around me. I shall never be able to escape those memories. Soon morale began to suffer, and while I did not want to admit it, I was not sure how much longer we could hold onto Madrid. Then came the arrival of the International Brigades from France, England, Canada, the United States, and many more countries. They infected us with their enthusiasm and reincarnated our belief that we were fighting a fight for the freedom of the entire world, not just that of Spain. That these men would leave the comfort of their faraway homes and risk their lives to join us in our struggle made us more determined than ever, and with their valiant aid we were held off General Franco's army. I stayed fighting along the front lines until the main Republican government decided that things in Madrid were too perilous and moved their headquarters to Valencia in November of 1936."

We learned that Manuel's courage and composure had been duly noted by a senior Republican Commander, and as a result he was assigned to the unit directly responsible for the safety of President Manuel Azaña and his wife Dolores and was transferred to Valencia.
"What was Manuel Azaña like?" inquired Don Esteban.

"Well, as time progressed and as I was constantly by his side, I did get to know the man well. He was an eloquent speaker, very uplifting. I got a sense that he was devastated that things had come to this, a war between Spaniards. He always had the well being of the common man in mind and it clearly pained him that his countrymen were suffering so. It did not matter that they were Republicans or Nationalists. He had an inner sense that he had failed them all. I think he died a tragic man. He hated the church and the aristocracy," Manuel laughed as the words came forth, "but he was taken aback by our story as I related it to him on one of the few quiet evenings we spent together."

"He thought deeply about your ideas in spite of the fact that he wanted to dispute their validity because of their origins."

"Maybe they are not all alike," he said, "referring to you aristocrats. We even talked of all getting together at the bar in Morente, after the war was over, to discuss our differences," Manuel smiled.

"As 1937 progressed things got decidedly worse for our side," Manuel went on. "Even though we were able to bravely hold onto Madrid, we lost Malaga in the south, and were witnesses to the horrific bombing of Guernica by those criminal Nazis. The loss of Santander and the Basque country meant that Franco effectively controlled the northern part of the country. By the end of that year, the Nationalists forces coming from Aragon were continually pounding Valencia. On one of the last days we were in Valencia we heard the hideous whistle of what could only be an artillery shell approaching. Instinctively I dove on top of President Azaña while the building shook from the force of the explosion. Thankfully the ceiling of the room we were in was not too high, and the small chandelier that fell on my back just caused a bad bruise. Poor Azaña was so shaken he could not even speak. A few hours later it was decided that we would move the government headquarters to Barcelona immediately.

Two days later we headed towards Barcelona along the coast in a small convoy, as we did not wish to attract the attention of the German Air Force anymore than was absolutely necessary. I was the front passenger in the lead car with President Azaña, his wife Dolores, and her brother, the well-known playwright, Cipriano Rivas Cherif, in the back. After a couple of hours of uneventful driving we were just north of Castellon, when we were ambushed by a patrol of Nationalists soldiers. The driver in our car slumped over onto me from a bullet to his forehead while the car veered out of control and was heading towards the cliffs. As the back-seat passengers shrieked, I was able to get poor Ramon off my lap and steer the Citroen back on to the road just before we would have plummeted to our certain deaths in the Mediterranean below. Still I was not able to reach the brake pedal as Ramon's foot was still on the accelerator and we careened into an orange grove on the other side of the narrow two-lane road, before finally halting when we slammed into a tree. I heard the splash of the second car in our convoy crashing into the sea just as I got out of car. I pulled the President, his wife, and his brother-in-law out of the car and used it as a shield. They were in shock but unscathed. I was bleeding from smashing my forehead into the windshield, but it was not too bad. The third car, with five soldiers inside, had managed to avoid the initial gunfire of our assailants and had stopped some fifty yards behind us. They were now under heavy attack from machine gun fire and were pinned behind their vehicle. I looked at the President, who was sweating profusely, and told him that I was going to help the other men. He grabbed my arm and terrified, shouted, "Manuel you can't leave us here!"

"Mr. President, the only way for us to get out of here is for me to aid those men." I handed him the gun from our slain driver and said, "Spain and your family need you right now. I need you to stay here and protect them until I get back."

This seemed to snap him out of his panic. He said, "Yes, yes of course, go and do what you must, we will be okay."

I could see from my vantage point that the attackers were west of us, on a small knoll. They probably thought that everyone in our car had been impaled by the crash and were focused on the other men in our group. I grabbed the Rigby rifle from inside the trunk and slowly moved behind the cover of the citrus trees to a position fifteen yards north of the car. There I could see two men approaching our vehicle. As they got closer their dark olive-colored uniforms were clearly visible. They made the mistake of staying together, assuming that we must be badly injured and stuck inside the car, as a plume of smoke rose from the engine compartment through the smashed radiator of Andre Citroen's previously, smartly styled automobile. I wiped the blood, now noticeably gushing down my face, from the cut above my right eyebrow. I could feel my heart pounding against my chest as I set down the rifle and took out my Astra M 400 pistol from its holster. Slowly, and as quietly as I could, I chambered one of the bullets from its magazine and tried to calm myself. I knew I had to wait for them to get very close as I could ill afford to miss and rely on the President to defend himself and his family. I closed my eyes, took a deep breath, said "here goes" to myself, and came around the tree firing in the direction of my foes. I hit one mortally in the chest before they realized what was happening. The second bullet hit the other soldier in the left shoulder, which made him wince in pain and bend downwards, allowing me to discharge my third bullet and take him out for good. I could hear the president's wife crying from fear as I quickly left the scene knowing the element of surprise would only be on my side for a few minutes. I ran as fast as I could, trying to outflank the remaining group. I was heaving from the exertion as I took a position to the rear of them. Lying on the ground to control my heavy breathing, I set the rifle sight on the soldier manning the machine gun. If I missed I knew he could easily turn around, spot me and splatter me with gunfire in the time it would take me to load another round and take aim again. As fortune would have it, my aim was accurate. The remaining two enemy soldiers, who were moving slowly towards our soldiers, fled. A few minutes later I shouted that it was now safe for the rest of my unit to come out from behind their bullet-ridden car. Only three of the five soldiers emerged, as several of the large caliber bullets from the machine gun had found their mark through the thin metal sheet of the automobile. Amazingly, their car could still start, but two of the tires were torn to shreds. We were able to replace them with wheels from our other, crashed vehicle, it being the same Citroen Traction Avant. I went to get the poor, shell-shocked Azaña family and the seven of us finally piled into the car. We drove in silence for the rest of the journey. President Azaña sat next to me in the front seat for the three-and-a-half-hour drive to Barcelona, which we reached late that afternoon. The five stitches that I received from a local clinic finally stopped my bleeding.

That night as we were finally parting to retire for the evening, the President held my right hand with both of his and said, "Thank you Manuel, this country thanks you for your valor."

The relief that we encountered in Barcelona after the tension that had reached Valencia would prove to be short lived. Five months later, in March of 1938, the Nationalist offensive in Aragon would cut the Republican-held territory in two. Cataluña in the northeast and the rest of southeastern Spain. At this point it was plain to see that General Franco had the upper hand, and in May, President Azaña reached out to the Nationalists to try to reach a peace accord. Franco rejected it outright. We tried to launch one last major strike to change the course of the war in July with the Battle of the Ebro, which lasted till November of that same year. After suffering heavy loses we had to admit defeat, and it became clear that it was but months away before the final surrender would take place. In the middle of January of 1939, the Nationalists took Tarragona, just 60 miles south of Barcelona. It was then that President Azaña called me in to his office and we had a private meeting.

"Manuel," he began, "we all know it is just a matter of time before the war is lost."

"Yes sir," I replied, not knowing what else to say.

"I have to stay here for the time being, until there is no more hope," the President went on, "but I will not put my wife in further danger. There is no doubt in my mind that General Franco will not be a forgiving victor, and I make no illusions to myself of what will happen to the senior Republican command and their families. That being said, I trust nobody with my life or that of my family, more than you. That is why I have called you here to this meeting in secret. I need you to do me a personal favor for which I will never be able to repay you for, except with eternal gratitude."

"Yes of course, anything Mr. President," I responded without thinking twice.

"I have been communicating with some of my old friends in French Intelligence. Fortunately, they have never forgotten my pro-French views while I was covering the First World War for several newspapers here in Spain. Anyhow, they have agreed to safeguard Dolores and her brother in a secret location near Toulouse. I need you to smuggle them over the Pyrenees and meet one of their top agents near the border with France. You are to remain with them for as long as it is necessary as their personal bodyguard. Tomorrow morning we will meet here with a Colonel in the French military intelligence agency, and he will go over the plan they have devised for you to reach France safely."

"Yes Mr. President, you can count on me."

"I know Manuel. I know I can always count on you."

The next morning at nine o'clock I walked into President Azaña's private study and met a grey-haired, mildly overweight man of about of fifty years of age, dressed in civilian clothes.

"This is my good friend Colonel Sylvain Portay of the Deuxieme Bureau," said President Azaña as he introduced us.

"It is an honor to meet you, young man. Your president speaks very highly of you and I know that Manuel Azaña is a man of sincere words," said the man. His Spanish was fluent, albeit with a thick French accent.

Carefully and slowly, he outlined his plan. We were to drive a small, inconspicuous Fiat 500, that the President had procured from a friend, wear warm clothes and hiking boots, and prepare a couple of backpacks with the minimal essentials required to trek over the Pyrenees for a day in the snow.

"You cannot drive on the main highway straight into France as unfortunately the leaders of our country have mistakenly allied themselves with Franco's benefactor, that German madman, Adolf Hitler, and are behaving like his puppets. For this, no doubt, we will eventually pay dearly. There are too many people who would like nothing better than to turn you over to the local authorities to ingratiate themselves to both General Franco and that Teutonic monster."

Colonel Sylvain Portay pointed to a map on the table. "Tomorrow morning, you will head north past Vic to Ripoll. At Ribes de Freser you will turn west until you reach Puigcerda, on the Spanish side of the Pyrenees. There you will abandon the car and head for the French side by foot. You should reach Font-Romeu, a small village about eight miles northeast, by the next afternoon. A group of three alpine refugees in this remote region should not attract much attention. One of my finest agents, a man by the name of Laurent Manrique, will meet you there at a local bistro named 'La Mer'. The code you will use to confirm his identity is, "Do you know why this place is called 'The Sea'?" He will reply, "I think it is because the owner hates these mountains."

"He will be there two days from now and rendezvous with you at six in the evening. He will wait for one hour. If you are not there he will return the next day at the same time. He will repeat this for one more day. If you have not arrived by then, he will assume you are either dead or captured, and abandon the mission. Do you have any questions Manuel?" the Colonel asked.

"Where we will go after we meet up with Laurent?" I asked.

"You will spend the first night at a small inn in town, and the next day drive in his car to a tiny village in Gascony called Roques, where Laurent is from. You will stay at the house of his aunt and uncle. Laurent's grandparents were originally from Spain, so having a few Spanish relatives there should not arouse suspicion. He will remain with you in Roques until you are settled in and comfortable."

The next morning we began our journey. I laughed when I first saw the Fiat we were going to drive. I realized why it was commonly nicknamed the *topolino*, or little mouse. President Azaña's brother-in-law wondered out loud how the three of us were going to fit in the tiny contraption. I drove with Doña Dolores, the president's wife, as the front passenger, and Cipriano squeezed sideways behind us. Barcelona was a mess. Sirens screamed everywhere while fire trucks, ambulances and army trucks raced about in a mad chaos. It took almost two hours to reach the city limits. After that it was quieter. We headed towards Vic with relative ease but limited by the Fiat's top speed, which with the three of us weighing it down, could not reach 50 miles per hour. After Vic the terrain became more mountainous and our progress slowed down considerably. Snowflakes started to fall. The engine of the Italian mouse plugged bravely along, but with only 13 horsepower it was a losing battle. It was starting to get dark and the snow started turning into ice as the temperature dropped well below freezing. Soon the tiny tires were finding little adhesion, which combined with the fact that it was the first time I had ever driven on snow resulted in us slipping and sliding all over the place. I decided to stop before we went over the precarious ledge of the steep ascent we were on.

"We will spend the night in the car," I announced to Doña Dolores and her brother, "and tomorrow, at first light, continue on to Puigcerda."

"Let us just hope it does not keep snowing," Cipriano said to the group.

Unfortunately it snowed all night long. We hardly got any sleep as it was freezing inside the car and in the morning, it took all of my strength just to open the door. The snow had reached as high as the hood of our car. We could no longer go on in the Fiat and had to hike, even though we were still over 20 miles from Puigcerda. There was no one on the small, rural road, as the weather conditions had worsened dramatically.

The going was terribly slow as Doña Dolores, although only in her mid-thirties, was most assuredly not in good shape. We were lucky if we were covering two miles an hour. We plugged along, stopping to rest more and more frequently for the sake of the president's wife. I tried not to think about missing our first rendezvous with Laurent. Late in the afternoon we found a small hostel to stay in for the night. We fixed a bath for Doña Dolores and had a good hearty meal as the poor woman was exhausted. Privately, I was having my doubts about whether she would be able to continue much longer but at least that night we were able to get some much-needed sleep and rest. The next morning we awoke to a full-fledged mountain storm. I could not see anything, the snow was falling so heavily.

What I could see was the fear in the face of Doña Dolores as we were about to head outside, so I went up to her and told her, "Everything is going to be alright, we just need to take it one step at a time and Cipriano and I are going to be right by your side." This seemed to calm her a little as we entered the blizzard outside.

To her credit, she did not complain even once, which is more than I can say for her older brother. He said how damn cold it was, what a terrible plan the whole thing had been, and how we should consider turning back.

I finally grabbed him by the shoulders and said, "There is no turning back, unless you want to get to know General Franco personally and end up in front of a firing squad, and that's if you are lucky! I was put in charge of getting you and your sister out of this hellhole of a country. You are welcome to stay here, turn back, or do whatever you want, but shut up and get out of my way so that I can at least take her to safety, as our president requested. He stayed so you could get out. He might not be able to get out now, but he sacrificed his best chance for you…"

"Enough!" Doña Dolores interrupted. "He is right Cipriano, my husband went to a lot of trouble so that we at least have a chance to escape. Most people will not get that opportunity. Let us at least try or die doing so."

"I am sorry, forgive me, you are both right. I am ashamed of my selfishness in light of what is happening to so many of our people," Cipriano finally said.

We continued forth without any more words being spoken until we finally reached Puigcerda that afternoon, having missed our second rendezvous with Laurent. There we found an inn to spend the night and the next day we set forth to Font-Romeu.

The snow was still coming down incessantly and now that we were in the open country, the going was even tougher. If I never see another snowflake in my life it will not be too soon! About halfway to Font-Romeu we had another mishap. Doña Dolores tripped on a fallen branch hidden by the snow and sprained her ankle. She tried to soldier on, but it was soon apparent that her ankle was badly swollen and she would not be able to continue walking. Cipriano and I took turns carrying her over our shoulder. Doña Dolores was so embarrassed, but her brother and I made light of the moment, which seemed to divert everyone's attention from our arduous task. As much as Cipriano and I yearned for a break, we all understood that we could ill afford to stop and lose precious time as it was the last day that Laurent would be waiting for us. We finally arrived after ten hours, exhausted and starving, in Font-Romeu at six thirty in the evening. Shortly thereafter we walked into the unassuming, but pleasant bistro named 'La Mer', where I saw a tall, lanky, slightly balding, dark-haired man sitting at the bar.

I walked up to him and asked him, "Do you know why this place is called 'The Sea'?"

"I think it is because the owner hates these mountains!" he responded laughing. "Hello Manuel," he went on, "I almost gave up on you, especially with this storm."

"I almost gave up on us," I replied smiling. After a warm onion soup and a delicious grilled chicken with roasted potatoes and red peppers we all went to bed at an unassuming inn next to the bistro.

"The sun finally decided to show itself the next morning and after fortifying our bellies with *croissants* and coffee we climbed into Laurent's spartan but spacious Peugeot 201 four door saloon. We were all in high spirits, as the painful memories of last few days faded. The swelling of Doña Dolores' ankle had gone down and she was not overly uncomfortable. By lunchtime we had arrived in Roques, about four hours drive northwest of Font-Romeu. Laurent had called ahead and there we were warmly greeted by Laurent's mother, Nicole, his uncle Jacques, and his aunt Gladys, who had prepared a veritable Gascogne feast for us. We started with *garbure*, which is what they call a cabbage soup, but it's more like a stew. Then came an amazing grilled duck breast, cooked over the wood of old vines and accompanied by green beans that had just been plucked from the garden. We finished with *canneles bordelais*, cupcakes flavored with rum and vanilla. It was here that I also got my first introduction into the wondrous world of fine wine, as we were served a red wine from the small village of Saint-Emilion in the nearby Bordeaux region. Up until that point I had not realized wine could smell and taste that way. I used to think the wine from the local co-operative in Morente was pretty good. Now I would not dare put such a awful liquid in my mouth!"

"Talking about all this food and wine has made me hungry. I think it is time for lunch. Manolo let us go to the kitchen and see what Rosa is concocting for us," interrupted Don Esteban.

"As they entered the kitchen, they could feel the heat of the grill cooking the baby milk-fed lamb chops. Leaves of lettuce dressed in oil and vinegar obediently accosted themselves in a large wooden bowl. Next to them was a ceramic jar immersed in a bucket of ice that held *salmorejo*, the thicker, more concentrated version of *gazpacho* native to Córdoba. A whole wheel of sheep's milk cheese from the nearby Los Pedroches Valley sat alone at the edge of the counter.

"Rosa, as usual you are tempting me such so that I will have no choice but to grow fat," the Count laughed.

"Don Esteban, look at poor old Manolo, he must be starving. I am only thinking of our guest. Besides a little extra weight does not hurt anyone when it is incurred by gastronomic pleasures."

"Wisely spoken, Doña Rosa," added Manuel.

My mother went up to Manuel and gave him a big hug and then held him by the shoulders.

"You have been missed around here Manolo. I know how your parents have suffered. Your mother Araceli, whom you know I have been friends with almost since the day I arrived on this earth, has shed many tears on my shoulder. While your father Eugenio seems composed on the outside, I see his pain inside. I know that your arrival will breath life back into them."

"Yes Doña Rosa, it is also good for me to be back."

"Now go sit down so that I can fatten that scrawny body of yours!" she said, dismissing us laughing.

On our way out of the kitchen Don Esteban approached Celia and asked, "Would you go to the cellar.

Manolo seems to have acquired for a taste for fine wine; let us show him what Spain has to offer, so as to make him forget French wines forever. Take out a bottle of a Vega Sicilia. See if we still have any of that 1920 left. Decant it and please bring it to us."

At lunch Manuel ate voraciously, having had little in the way of nutrition for the last month.

"This wine is amazing, it smells of a hundred things. A forest, an orchard and fields of flowers. It is full, yet light on its feet, powerful but elegant. It reminds me of a top Bordeaux, yet it is finer, more aromatic. Tell me about it, Esteban!" implored Manuel.

Don Esteban responded, laughing, "Vega Sicilia is the finest wine made in Spain. It comes from the area of Ribera del Duero near Valladolid. You are right to note that it reminds you of a French Bordeaux, as it is a blend of several different Bordeaux varieties with Tempranillo grapes, locally known as Tinto Fino, and interestingly enough, a tiny bit of a local white grape called Albillo, which I think adds a unique perfume to the wine. I dare say you are going to be an expensive and difficult guest to satisfy from now on!"

"It was obvious to us that the two men had missed one another and that they enjoyed each other's company immensely. Hours passed at the table and then in the library. We had not seen the Count so animated since the days when Maria was still alive. Meanwhile Manuel continued on with his story.

"We quickly settled into the tiny village of Roques. There were but 100 people that lived there. Most of them were quite friendly, with the exception of perhaps the owner of the local bar, Blanc et Rouge, who seemed weary of anybody he had not known for at least twenty years! The village itself was quaint, being founded in the

Middle Ages and not having suffered from the effects of modern architecture. It even had a small but stately Chateau that enjoyed a commanding view of the countryside. The locals were predominantly involved to the tending of Ugni Blanc vines from the vineyards that lay upon the rolling landscape that surrounded the village. The grapes were mainly sold off to a nearby cooperative where they were distilled for the production of the wonderful brandy they call Armagnac. The small amount of still white wine made from the Ugni Blanc grapes was acidic, bland and about as unpleasant as Isaac, the owner of Blanc et Rouge. Laurent though, had a nice cellar replete with Bordeaux and some of the better red wines from the region, which he generously shared with us without hesitation. Nicole, it turns out, was the schoolteacher for the village. There was but one classroom and about fifteen children of all ages attended the same class. She had a commanding presence that prevented any thoughts of foolishness from her alumni. On the weekends we would go over to the Blanc et Rouge, where Jacques would play the accordion and Nicole would show her softer side, jovially giving any and all ballroom dancing lessons, laughing whenever somebody mistakenly stepped on her feet and joining Gladys in bellowing out delightful French ballads to a small but very appreciative audience. Gladys, who was Nicole's elder sister by some years, and Jacques were wonderful hosts and made us feel as if we were in our own homes in no time. Gladys was a marvelous cook, like so many French women, but Jacques was no slouch in the kitchen either, and on the grill he had no equal. Laurent loaned me his very capable Verney-Carron 16-gauge boxlock shotgun to go out and hunt duck and geese, which were everywhere. It was no wonder the Gascons ate so much goose and duck liver, or *foie gras*.

Jacques who must have been in his early fifties walked with a slight limp in his left leg. I soon found out from Laurent that he had been a First Lieutenant in the French Foreign Legion.

"Do not ever underestimate that old bird," Laurent once told me, "he can still take out a whole platoon on his own. They do not make soldiers like that anymore, *mon ami.*"

As I got to know Jacques better I asked him about his days as a Legionnaire. The hours would pass by as we sat on a long wooden table out in his small garden, admiring the beautiful scenery replete with vines and sunflowers whilst sipping old vintage Armagnac.

"I was born in Algeria where my father was a Major in the Foreign Legion," Jacques said, "having been assigned there after graduating from the military academy at Saint-Cyr."

"The famous Saint-Cyr?" I interrupted in awe. I had heard about the legendary institution from several French members of the International Brigades when we were fighting together in Madrid.

"Yes, the same one. One of my forefathers was a General in Napoleon Bonaparte's army and fought alongside him in what might have been his greatest victory, the Battle of Austerlitz in 1805. Since then all the men in my family have traditionally attended the academy at Saint-Cyr, which was founded by the Emperor Napoleon I himself, and have been officers in the French army. My father missed France terribly and after he retired from the Legion we moved to Toulouse, where his family was from. I quickly learned that the sacrifice my father had made by serving his country in Algeria was not appreciated by his fellow countrymen, who instead viewed all of all North Africa as a huge sand pit and the presence of the French army there as a waste of time and money. To add insult to injury, my sister and I were often discriminated as if we were children of a lower class for not having been born in France! After I graduated from Saint-Cyr, I asked to be assigned to the Foreign Legion in Algeria. I was quickly granted my request, as the postings in North Africa were the least popular. For me though, it meant going back to my true home. At the academy I had heard that the Legionnaires were an impressive fighting force, but more of the talk about them concerned their unruly and almost criminal makeup. When my father had been in the Foreign Legion we lived outside of the army barracks, so my recollection of the Legion was limited to parades and other ceremonial events that my entire family attended, watching soldiers march by in immaculate uniforms and perfect unison. I could not imagine the horrible rumors about the Legion being correct and dismissed the rumblings as exaggerated and almost envious. When I arrived at my post in Sidi Bel-Abbes as a newly designated Cadet from Saint-Cyr I was in for the surprise of my life. I reported to my company Commander, a portly, short, thick-mustached and bald Captain by the name of Jean-Pierre Dubray. As I stood at attention, he looked over my file in his bare office. After a few minutes he told me to be at ease and finally raised his eyes from the brown folder within which lay my whole life's achievements. Needless to say, the file was not very thick!" said Jacques laughing.

"Why the hell did you ask to come back to this inferno?" Captain Dupray asked.

I mumbled something about wanting to come back to the place I was born, to fulfill my duty and follow in the footsteps of my father, at which point I was interrupted.

"Yes, your father. I knew your father. I was a stupid Cadet much like you are now, and he taught me to be a soldier, because believe me, Saint-Cyr does not teach you how to be a soldier out here. Tough but fair, your father. A good soldier. I doubt that you will be half as good as he was."

"I shall do my best sir," I replied trying not to lose all of my composure at this brusque reception.

"Unfortunately, your best will likely not do," replied Captain Dubray thru his grayish-tinged mustache. "Let me show you to the officer's barracks and introduce you to Second Lieutenant Jean-Louis Dumonet, who will be your direct supervisor.

Jean-Louis was a jovial chap from the town of Amboise on the banks of the Loire River. We soon became good friends and I quickly learned the ropes around the fort.

"These men," Jean-Louis told me, "obey only one thing and one thing only, and that is authority. But you must first earn their respect. Saint-Cyr means nothing here. Our motto is not 'Honor and Country' like it is in the French Army, it is 'Honor and Fidelity'. Above all, we are loyal to each other. You must never ask a soldier here to do something you would not be willing to do yourself, and you must set the example for others to follow. If we go on a march of 20 miles in the desert, you must march with them and not on a horse like some superior and pompous officer. They are a rough bunch. Most of them are trying to escape from somewhere, trying to find a fresh start in life. Some are criminals, some are mercenaries, some just don't know how to be anything but a soldier, but if I ever have to go into battle there is no one else I would rather have behind me than these guys."

Meeting the soldiers in our company was intimidating. I could tell from their eyes that they hid many secrets, but one that they did not hide was a dislike for any newly arrived Cadet!

It was a unique bunch made up of Germans, British, Italians, Spaniards, Swiss, Russians, with less than a quarter of the men actually being French. A few of them wore some kind of scar from a skirmish as a badge of honor. Their skin showed the punishment that the incessant sun cast upon them and was brittle, like cracked leather, dyed with the color of mahogany. Their uniforms were barely presentable and the air was filled with the smell of sweat and dust. Soon after my arrival, Jean-Louis suggested that I go on a march with his section so as to get a feel for the pace and heat.

The next day we set forth in a small patrol of twelve men led by Jean-Louis along an oasis south of the fort. At first the slower 88-step-per-minute pace of the Legion seemed awkward to follow and much too slow compared to the traditional 120-step-per-minute pace that I was used to at the academy. After a few hours in a sun that already smothered us with ninety-degree heat by ten in the morning, I was grateful for the slower pace. It had been over a month since I had been training at Saint-Cyr, that coupled with a heat that no one at my academy could have possibly imagined, made for an exhaustive endeavor. Yet I dared not to complain or ask for any sort of reprieve in the form of a small break, as that would have showed the men weakness, and if there is something these men would disdain it is that. After three hours, Jean-Louis called for the patrol to come to a halt and rest for 30 minutes in a valley amongst the palm trees that stingily handed out shade. The rest of the soldiers started chatting and smoking strong Gitanes cigarettes in between quenching their thirst with water from the thin aluminum canteens they each carried. They barely seemed to break a sweat, while I was drenched in it.

"How are you holding up?" Jean-Louis asked me.

"Let us just say I have had better days." I responded as enthusiastically as I could muster.

"Well do not worry, we will head back soon, before it starts to get hot," Jean-Louis went on.

"You mean this is not hot?" I said, as my face turned pale. I did not think it could possibly get any warmer than the suffocating oven we were currently in.

"Ah *mon ami*, this is nothing, believe me," he replied, laughing.

"Anyhow, what are we doing here in the middle of nowhere?" I asked.

"We have heard rumors that some Tuaregs are in the region and that could spell trouble," Jean-Louis informed me.

"Tuaregs this far north?" I responded, surprised.

"Yes, apparently the attacks on them in Mali and Niger has forced them to migrate north."

I had heard of the proud people that roamed the most desolate parts of the Sahara since I was a child. These Berber tribesmen established a series of travel and trading routes thru the vast dessert sands thousands of years ago and guarded them ferociously with their broadswords. They are known as the 'Blue Men of the Sahara' because of the indigo blue-dyed veils they wear that cause their faces to appear blue. Interestingly enough, the women do not wear veils, have a great deal of freedom, and participate in family and tribal decisions far more so than their Arabic counterparts. Unfortunately, they also have a dark side, as they delve into the slave trade by raiding villages of neighboring countries and using black African males to tend to their lands or herd their animals. But then again, is not the colonization of many countries by western powers a thinly disguised form of enslavement?

"Anyhow, doubtful that they will come this close to the fort, so think of this as an early morning recreational walk," Jean-Louis went on, smiling, and then all of a sudden the smirk vanished from his face, replaced by a look of great concern as he yelled out, "Enemy above!"

Everyone turned around to see what he was looking at. It was an awesome sight— more than 60 Tuareg warriors on their camels were poised atop a hill overlooking the valley. As everyone reached for their Berthier rifles, a spine-chilling scream from one of the warriors made several hundred other Tuareg warriors appear from out of nowhere, completely surrounding us.

"*Mon Dieu*, this is going to get ugly. Get ready!" ordered Jean-Louis, as everyone automatically chambered an 8mm Lebel bullet into their rifle, fell to their knees, and formed a circle.

I do not know why, but instinctively I told Jean-Louis, "Let me talk to them."

"What!" he bellowed back.

"Jean-Louis I can speak Arabic fluently, maybe I can talk us out of this mess. Besides, what have we got to lose? We are about to get massacred."

"Alright, go ahead, although I do not like it," he said hesitantly.

Slowly I got up, held my Berthier rifle over my head with both hands, and bent down and put it on the ground. I then put my hands in the air and walked slowly towards the warrior who had screamed moments before, as I thought that he might be the leader. When I was 20 feet from the warrior, I put my arms down. Although I could not speak the Berber language of the Tuaregs, I knew many spoke Arabic.

"*As-salaam 'alaykum*, forgive me for I do not speak your language," I started.

"Peace be upon you," replied the warrior in perfect Arabic.

"My name is Cadet Jacques Lemaitre."

"I am Moussa Ag Amastan, chief of the Kel Ahaggar Tuaregs."

"You are far from your home Moussa Ag Amastan."

"And you Jacques Lemaitre— are you not far from your home in France?"

I smiled, "I am and I am not. I am French but I was born but a few miles away."

"You should go back to your faraway land. This dessert has been in the hands of my people from the time of countless moons ago," replied the chieftain in a sharper tone.

"I do not disagree with you, great leader of the Kel Ahaggar Tuaregs, but swords and guns are not the instruments to see the path where the light shines. I know we have wronged your people. I know we have stolen your land. I know we have not treated you fairly. I know your great warriors could kill all these men," I said, pointing towards the other legionnaires, "but many others will quickly come to seek revenge and we will all lose. Are you not weary Moussa Ag Amastan? Do you not miss your home? Do you not miss your family? Are you not tired of all the blood upon your hands?"

"You speak wisely for one so young. You are right. The time without peace has lasted too long. Perhaps it is the moment to talk like you and me today," the Tuareg spoke solemnly.

"It is you who are wise to see this, great chief of the Kel Ahaggar people. There are many in my country who feel that the battles with your people should come to an end," I replied.

Then as the Tuareg chief started to turn his camel around, lift his arm into the air to signal to his warriors to follow him and head south, he looked at me and said, *"Lla-llqaa"* and I responded in kind, "Until we meet again."

When I walked back to our patrol, I was greeted by a multitude of appreciative handshakes and pats on the back. It was the last time they ever questioned whether I belonged as part of their family. I reenacted the whole conversation with what was now a very animated group.

At the end Jean-Louis pulled me aside and said, "You know that as soon as we get back and Captain Dubray finds out about this, he will send an entire company to go after the Tuaregs."

"What?" I replied.

"Jacques, he will not care that you had this peaceful little dialogue with them. He hates them and would love nothing better than to annihilate a large group of rebel soldiers."

"Jean-Louis, you know that is not the honorable thing to do after they just spared our lives," I insisted.

"You are right, of course, but what can we do?"

"Well," I replied after pondering the situation for a few moments, "we can take our time in getting back to the fort and try to arrive slightly before dusk, so that Captain Dubray has to wait till morning to go after our new friends. By then they will be long gone."

"Excellent idea! Yes Jacques, that will work, but let us keep this conversation between the two of us so that neither of us gets into any trouble."

"Alright then, lets relax and enjoy this wonderful weather and thank God that we are still alive!" I replied, laughing.

"You say Moussa Ag Amastan was his name?" asked Captain Dubray back at the fort.

"You are fortunate to be alive, as he has evaded us for years and caused more casualties to the Legion than practically all the other Tuareg tribes put together. I cannot believe that he let you live. It is unfortunate that we have to wait till morning to go after that scum!"

continued Captain Dubray after I told him a brief version of the days' encounter.

"Yes sir," I replied, as stoically as I could.

"In what direction did he go after he left you?" Dubray asked.

"Sir, he went due west," answered Jean-Louis, knowing full well that that was wrong.

"Pity, the wind throughout the night will wipe any trace of their tracks," bemoaned Dubray to himself. "Still, tomorrow we will see if we get lucky. Get some rest, both of you. You will need your energy, as you will accompany me to try to catch and kill the madman. Dismissed!" he commanded.

As Jean-Louis and I were leaving his office he added, "Oh, and you Lemaitre, you might end up becoming a halfway decent soldier after all."

We never found even a trace of the Kel Ahaggar Tuaregs, and although the march in their pursuit was exhaustive, I did not mind at all, and was chuckling inside all day long.

A couple of years later, in 1910, I heard that Chief Moussa Ag Amastan of the Kel Ahaggar Tuaregs was in Paris, being treated like royalty by the French government, after agreeing to sign a peace treaty that would end the fighting between the Tuareg tribes of Algeria and the French Foreign Legion. I happened to be in Paris at that time visiting an uncle and decided to go to the Champs-Elysees to see the parade in his honor. Bands were playing lively marching music and eager crowds bordered the entire avenue from the Place de la Concorde to the Arc de Triomphe and beyond, anxious to see what this foreign and feared warrior looked like. After watching wave after wave of neatly dressed battalions march by, I saw a royal carriage with the Tuareg chieftain aboard. I smiled at the scene as the carriage approached while recalling the much more austere circumstances of my first encounter with Moussa Ag Amastan. At that moment a thunderous yell caused the carriage to come to a standstill. I realized that the Tuareg had spotted me in my legionnaire uniform and had recognized me. Chief Moussa Ag Amastan got down from the carriage and started walking towards me, which caused all manner of commotion amongst the politicians and soldiers accompanying him.

As he approached, he gestured with his right hand toward me in the traditional Arabic greeting as he said, "*As-salaam 'alaykum* my young friend."

"Peace be upon you also, great leader of the Kel Ahaggar Tuaregs," I responded.

"You are far from your home, are you not?" he continued smiling.

"As you are from yours," I replied.

"I am not sure that all will be well between our peoples, but at least the blood has stopped flowing," the Tuareg added.

"It is a good beginning," I mustered, not knowing what else to say.

At that point he put his hand on my shoulder in a fatherly way and said, "I want to thank you. Till we meet again may Allah continue to cast his wisdom upon you." And with that he walked away.

My memories of the rest of my time stationed at Sidi Bel-Abbes were full of the camaraderie that one only finds in army barracks in a desolate place. The daily grind became a reassuring friend and as I got to know my fellow soldiers, I realized that life carves a different path for each of us and one should refrain from judging individuals too often or too much. It is at end of that road when we are all alone and have to look at a mirror that we will know whether our short time on this earth has been worthwhile for us and for the others whose lives we have touched.

Our monotonous routines got disarrayed with the arrival of the Great War. We spent all of our free time glued to the sound of static emanating from the large radio in the common area of the barracks. News from the front lines was the subject *'du jour'* everyday. The constant advances of the Germans on French soil drew the ire of everyone and we longed to join our brethren in the fight against them, for although many of the soldiers were not French, there was a feeling of unanimity that the freedom of the entire continent was at risk.

Finally, in the spring of 1915 I was given my orders to go to the front and first fought under General Philippe Petain at the Battle of Artois. Initially we were successful in halting the German advance and even started to gain ground back from them, but as the weeks and then months went on, the fighting became akin to a chess stalemate with neither side making any significant inroads. In July of the following year my unit, made up of mostly Legionnaires was transferred to hell, because the Battle of the Somme near the border with Belgium can only be described in that way. In five months one million men lost their lives. *Mon Dieu*, in the first day of fighting alone the British lost 60,000 men— 20 percent of their entire army! They made the grave error of underestimating how well prepared the Germans were, as they had been able to plan for the allied offensive since October of 1914. The British, worried about the safety of their artillery guns, made the mistake of keeping them almost 300 yards away, which rendered them totally ineffective against the opposing fortifications and put their infantry at the mercy of the firmly entrenched German machine gunners. The result was a massacre. While the British vainly tried to attack north of the river Somme, we attacked from the southern sector. Having had more experience in this type of warfare, we took greater risk with our artillery and positioned our guns 55 yards from the enemy. It proved to be the right decision, and we slowly started making progress in our quest to drive the Germans back.

Hell is a place where the stench of sulphur permeates every breath. The cries of pain and suffering from the burns of mustard gas and the wounds from shrapnel were dwarfed by the constant thunder of incoming artillery fire. The ground shook uncontrollably, the sky was constantly grey, and the trenches became cemeteries. It is something terrible when there is so much death and torment that humans become numb to it.

"Why?" is the question that haunts your mind and is the main protagonist of your nightmares. In November, as the battle was coming to an end, my unit was put in charge of securing a perimeter around the area where thousands of German prisoners were being held. It is easy to hate someone when you do not see them. You imagine them to be a sort of demonic monster. But when they become your prisoners you see the humanity in their frightened eyes. You see that most are only boys that should be playing soccer in some faraway village. Boys whose innocent childhood is forever lost.

On one of those dreary winter days when we had long forgotten the sight of the sun, we came under fire from a sniper. Olivier Reginensi, a tough, grouchy, but gentle-at-heart Corsican that I had befriended in Algeria was standing next to me enjoying a cigarette, when a bullet he had no idea was coming killed him instantly. My first instinct was to pull him towards a ditch nearby and just as I was falling in, I heard the sound of a tree branch breaking and crashing down, except that it was no tree, it was the femur of my right leg. The young doctor at the overcrowded infirmary who set the bone had not slept in several days and only had a few minutes to attend to me before moving on to others in more dire need. So I do not blame him for this limp that has been my constant companion ever since. I do not even hold a grudge against the German who shot me, for it was there, in the infirmary that I met *mon amour*.

Gladys was a nurse whose smile and soothing voice took us away from our pain and suffering. I was in love from the moment my eyes first saw her, attending one patient after another.

"I am going to marry you," were the first words out of my mouth upon meeting her.

"Delusional, definitely delusional!" she said to the doctor who she was accompanying on his rounds. But she smiled at me.

"I can not blame him," said the attending doctor.

As the days progressed the banter between us became less silly and more serious, less light and more forthright.

"I cannot believe I am falling in love with a Legionnaire—of all people!" she said, laughing gaily.

"We are all God's creatures!" I answered.

"Well some might disagree with that assessment of the Legion, Jacques Lemaitre!"

"Well someone has to fall in love with even us!"

Then the conversation took a different turn.

"Jacques, I want to get out of here, I want to see only you, I want to hear only the sound of your voice," she would say.

"Soon *ma cherie*, soon it will only be you and me," I said, trying to reassure her.

We talked about everything— where we came from, what we believed in, what are dreams were.

I even remember asking her on day, "How in the world did your parents choose that beautiful but most un-French name of yours?"

"Well," she said, "it is a story that my mother told me that I have never repeated to anyone else."

"It all started when my mother was a beautiful and young adolescent living in a small village high up in the Pyrenees near the border with Spain. It was a popular destination for mountain climbers and in the summer was overrun by all sorts of aspiring alpinists. One sweltering July she met Pedr Griffiths from Cardiff, Wales and fell in love. Her name was Gurutze but Pedr decided to anoint her with the closest Welch equivalent 'Gladys'. The summer came and went, leaving her with tears and memories of a love found and lost. A few years later she met another climber from a small village in Gascony. Love was found anew and this time she followed it to a village called Roques, my father Pierre's hometown. When I was born she convinced my father to let her name me Gladys, telling him she fondly remembered the name from a medieval fairy tale she had read as a child, in which a handsome prince had rescued a peasant girl named Gladys from some ferocious wolves and fallen in love with her. She told my father he was her prince. Who could possibly argue with that!" Gladys laughed out loud.

It was only after my father died three years ago that she told me the true meaning of my name, telling me she had never quite gotten over that first love.

"Why did you not tell me this before?" I asked her.

"Out of the respect and the love I had for your father, who was a good man. I never wanted you to think that I could love another man and not be completely true to your father. Plus I do not even know if what I feel for Pedr Griffiths is love, or the love of a memory that one can never have back."

In November of 1918 the war finally came to an end. All those lives lost, all the pain, and for what?

Sometimes I think politicians just use us as pawns in a game that feeds their demented egos. Because of my permanent injury I could not return to the Legion and since I had no other home, I moved to Roques with Gladys. Soon afterwards, we got married and I came to realize how little one needs to be content. With the small pension I received for my services to France, plus the salary that Gladys makes as a senior nurse at a nearby hospital, we have more than enough. I discovered that one is truly rich when one has more than one needs and can share their life with someone they love more than they love themselves. Now I tend to my roses and vegetables and read novels when it becomes too warm or too cold. It is a simple life but one but I would not exchange for another."

"Do you have any children?" I remember asking him soon after we met.

"No, my dear Manolo, it was not meant to be, but not for lack of trying," he answered, laughing. "Laurent became my son as his father left him and Nicole right after he was born. If Gladys and I would have had a son, he would have been treated no differently from Laurent. I am very proud of the man he has become and his role in the Deuxieme Bureau, as evidenced by Colonel Portay's decision to use him to extract the three of you out of Spain."

"Okay, enough! I am exhausted from talking so much!" said Trini, "We should finish the story tomorrow, as I hear Manolo and Celia are coming back the day after."

11

Carlos left the kitchen shaking his head, thinking that just when the story could not get any better it became even more amazing. He made his way to the stables, where he was sure to see Alexandra taking care of the many Andalusians. They would start by discussing the main topics of business for the day, and that would lead to light conversations pertaining to current news events and local gossip in Morente. As he walked into the stables, he saw Alexandra brushing the long, flowing mane that adorned Noche. It was one of the few times he ever saw the stallion stand perfectly still. Usually Alexandra would be humming one of the many operettas that she had memorized since her days as a child, but today for some reason she was quiet. As he said his customary but lively *"Buenos Dias!"* he noticed she had been crying.

"Alexandra what's wrong?" he asked.

"Oh nothing, it is just one of those mornings," she replied.

"Alexandra, look at me," he said softly.

She turned to face him, and now could see that she was quite upset.

"Let's take a little walk," he suggested.

"Okay," she replied meekly.

They meandered thru a meadow next to the stables without exchanging words. Carlos had never seen her like this and as anxious as he was to find out what bothered her, he knew that he needed to give her some time for her to feel comfortable enough to confide in him. After walking for about half a mile in silence, Alexandra suddenly blurted out, "They will not let me fight!"

"Who will not let you fight?" asked Carlos, perplexed.

"The managers of the main bullrings. They all say that they are already full for the upcoming season, when I know that most, if not all, of the main *corridas* are yet to be formalized. When I asked the manager of the bullring in Pamplona, who was fighting during the whole week of the San Fermin festival, he got caught in his own lie, and just said that people want to see male matadors," replied Alexandra.

"Well," Carlos said, "that is not altogether surprising."

"What? What do you mean? Just what exactly do you mean by that!" retorted Alexandra.

"Please Alexandra, just listen to me for a moment," Carlos told her patiently. "I know that it is very difficult for women to break into the matador world. Look, even *Generalissimo* Franco prohibited women from being matadors after the Civil War ended, and it has only been in the last decade that he has relaxed that rule. Most serious aficionados still scoff at the idea of a woman as a matador. They see them more as a circus act intended to gain a wider audience. You know full well that in Spain things are dominated by men. A bullfighter is the epitome of courage and manhood. To have a woman in that role shows that man is no longer superior, questioning the very essence of our society. Yet in your case what has happened transcends even that. Your prowess as a bullfighter has reached the level of the most-skilled matadors. You are no longer just a sideshow. You now command center stage and you often outshine the other matadors that fight alongside you. It is not the bullring managers nor the aficionados that do not want you to fight, it is your fellow matadors whose egos can not tolerate being second best to a woman!"

"I thought I had advanced past that, but I guess not," said a dejected Alexandra.

For the following few minutes nothing was said, as the profound impact of Carlos' words slowly settled upon Alexandra.

"I never wanted to be a bullfighter to prove that women were just as strong or skilled or brave as men. I wanted to be a matador because I love how it makes me feel in the ring. The fear mixed with the excitement, the sadness with the joy, the failure with the accomplishment."

"Well," interrupted Carlos, "you do have an alternative."

"Pray tell," replied a curious Alexandra.

"*Rejoneo.*"

"What are you talking about?"

"Before you immediately discard the idea, stop and think about it for a second," said Carlos. "*Rejoneo* is as much about being a great horseman, or excuse me, horsewoman, as it is about being a matador. In *rejoneo* that machismo tone of a matador is much subdued. I know that many bullfighters regard *rejoneadores* as second rate matadors, but you have already proved yourself on the ground. This would be a great new challenge for the fearless Countess Alexandra de Morente. You are an expert equestrian. We also have Noche and a few other *rejoneo* horses at the estate already. We have plenty of young calves to practice on in the small bullring here, or when we do the *tientas*, to test them to see if they are brave enough to become fighting bulls. On top of all this Don Manuel could easily be your teacher, as I understand he also did some *rejoneo* in the past. From a business and promotional point of view there are also far fewer *rejoneadores*, who are thus always in high demand.

Besides, my dear countess, you are not getting any younger and soon you will not be quick enough to get out of the way of charging bulls!" ended Carlos, smiling.

"Well, that is something to think about. I love riding and I love bullfighting, so this could be a way of continuing to do both. Not a bad idea altogether from a city boy, although I definitely disagree with the getting older bit," replied Alexandra as she playfully gave him a shove. "All I need to do now is convince my father and Don Manuel," she added.

"I do not think that will be much of a problem for your considerable charm, my dearest countess," said Carlos smiling, "and besides, it is a lot safer than fighting on the ground."

The walk back was a direct contrast to the solemn way it had begun earlier in the morning. Alexandra was practically skipping along from her newly gained enthusiasm. The more she thought about the idea, the more she liked it. Carlos was amazed by how quickly she had come to terms with the realization that her matador days were numbered. She had wasted little time sulking and feeling sorry for herself. Instead, she immediately recognized that *rejoneo* would be a parallel venue and was embracing it swiftly.

"I want to wait till Don Manuel returns the day after tomorrow, to tell him and my father together, as I know Don Manuel's feelings would be hurt otherwise. Besides I am asking him for a lot of help, not just in teaching me the fine points of *rejoneo*, but also in allowing me to use his calves for practice," Alexandra said.

"Are not the calves and bulls yours, and is this not your estate?" asked Carlos.

"My dear Carlos, while that might be technically correct, neither my father nor Don Manuel would agree with you. Trust me! Don Manuel is closer to my father than a blood brother would be if he had one. He, and he alone, has made the bull-breeding program as successful and respected as it is today, and no one has to remind my father about that. While there are things that we can improve to make it even more profitable, there is no denying that the income from the raising of the fighting bulls has been a godsend in these past two decades to help offset the considerable costs of running this estate in these most difficult of times. Carlos, my father does not view Don Manuel as another laborer at his dominion. He thinks of Don Manuel as a partner in his enterprise, which is the continuation of this estate and the well being of the many people who depend on it for their livelihood, just as sixteen generations of his family have done before him. He would never agree to a change in the program without the approval of Don Manuel, and Don Manuel in turn would never consent to anything that was not in the best interest of the estate of his closest friend. Thus, while I might be the legal heir to this entire place, without the blessing of both my father and Don Manuel I cannot do a single thing here!" laughed Alexandra.

"Promise me that you will not tell anyone of our *rejoneo* plans before I get a chance to."

"Of course, I will not tell a single soul," replied Carlos, smiling. "I know you told me before not to ask this, but Alexandra, if Don Manuel is as important to the estate and to your father as you say he is, and I understand this to be true without question, why then does he receive such a small salary for his significant contribution, while Celia gets paid three times as much?"

"Before I answer your question you have to promise that you will never repeat what I tell you," Alexandra said, her tone suddenly serious.

"You have my word," replied Carlos.

"Naturally you are right to be so curious about the discrepancy in their pay. On paper it does not make any kind of sense. However, as you are learning, many things with regards to Don Manuel that at first do not appear to be logical, turn out to be quite so. Don Manuel has been getting paid the same amount of money for years. In fact, he rarely even sees his check as most of the time it is Celia who picks it up when she gets her own. He will not accept any sort of raise, so my father years ago decided that he simply would circumvent Don Manuel's stubborn refusal to get justly compensated and made a secret pact with Celia, making her swear that she would never tell Don Manuel what she gets paid, which is in fact what Don Manuel should be getting. Since Celia is in charge of their household finances and makes the deposits at the local bank, Don Manuel has no idea of any of this."

"I will tell you another little secret. You may have noticed in the books that several times a year there is a substantial payment to the Complutense University of Madrid."

"Yes," Carlos replied, "as a matter of fact I was meaning to ask you about it."

"Well," continued Alexandra, "I will save you the trouble. No one knows about that transaction either, except for three people; my father, Don Ricardo Curias, the Chancellor of the Complutense University of Madrid, and me. When Isabella, Don Manuel and Celia's daughter, was growing up, it was apparent to all who came in contact with her that she was quite bright. Her grades in high school were exemplary and it was obvious she was destined for much more than Morente could possibly offer her. One day while they were enjoying their usual morning coffee ritual, I overheard Don Manuel talking to my father about what he thought of the possibility of Isabella going to a university to further her education."

"Splendid idea Manolo!" my father replied and continued, "Isabella is way too bright to settle for anything else and who knows, she might eventually be able to teach a couple of old men a thing or too!" he concluded laughing.

"The only thing is Esteban, as you know, I never even finished high school, and thus have no idea as to how one goes about getting into a university, never mind which one."

"Not to worry Manolo, I have a couple of friends who will be more than happy to guide us in this matter. I will make a few phone calls and in no time, we will figure all this out," my father assured Don Manuel.

"I can not thank you enough," replied Don Manuel.

"Don't be silly, and besides, I am not doing this for you, I am doing this for my beautiful goddaughter," said my father smiling.

A short time later my father asked me to see him in his private study.

"Alexandra, I want you to do something for me," he started.

"Yes, of course father," I answered.

"I want you to find out exactly how much it costs to go to the Complutense University of Madrid. I want to know everything: tuition, books, room and board, every possible cost."

"Yes father," I replied.

"And Alexandra, no one is to find out about this, is that understood?" he added sternly.

"Yes father," I replied once again.

It was not for some time that I came to find out what my father was really up to. He convinced Don Manuel that the Complutense University of Madrid was the best choice for Isabella.

"Esteban," he told him, "the top intellectuals of our country have attended this illustrious institution. Men like the poet Federico Garcia Lorca, the filmmaker Luis Buñuel, the philosopher Julian Marias, and even your old friend President Azaña. Such luminary professors as Jose Ortega y Gasset and Santiago Ramon y Cajal have taught there. It is a place where Isabella's mind will be free to explore and discover."

Meanwhile he had talked to Don Ricardo Curias, who is an old friend of the family. He convinced the Chancellor to give Isabella a full scholarship, promising that he in turn would make a substantial endowment to the university. My father knew of course that there was no way Don Manuel and Celia could possibly afford to send Isabella to university. He also knew that Don Manuel would never ask him for the money and would instead probably find an extra job on his days off to pay for it. Father even made Don Ricardo agree never to tell anyone about their pact, especially Isabella and her parents, for he knew Don Manuel was too proud to accept any kind of charity."

"My God! That is an incredibly generous and kind gesture," exclaimed Carlos.

"Actually Carlos, my father would disagree with you, and instead tell you that it was simply his obligation to his dearest friend. Don Manuel and my father are men cut out of the same stone. There is nothing they would not do for each other, even give their life for one another, and they would do so blindly, without asking a single question and with no hesitation," replied Alexandra.

"Yes, yes of course, I am beginning to see that clearly now," responded Carlos.

12

"Today you are fortunate my dear," Trini said as Carlos entered the kitchen the following morning, "for I do not have much work to do and I can finish our story so that you leave me in peace forever!"

"Manuel," began Trini, "continued to recall the days in Roques to Don Esteban."

"The days passed by quietly, in sharp contrast to the last three years. We heard on the radio that Barcelona fell to the Nationalists on January 26th, and just over two weeks after our arrival in Roques, on February 5th, we got word that President Azaña had safely crossed the border into France while Girona was succumbing to Franco's men. Two days later Laurent arrived with his weary passenger at Roques. When we saw the President, for a moment we were all in a most festive spirit in spite of the gloomy circumstances that had forced us to meet in this most unlikely of places, far from our homes and country. Colonel Sylvain Portay had instructed Laurent that the President was to stay at Roques for the time being until things calmed down. The Colonel felt that Roques was the ideal hideaway, as President Azaña would attract the least amount of attention there. No one- even those at the Deuxieme Bureau- knew of the Colonel's plan. In the following months, bad news continued to spew forth from Spain. On March 3rd, Manuel Azaña officially resigned as President of the Spanish Republic, after England and France recognized Franco as the new leader of the country. On April 1st, General Francisco Franco proclaimed victory and the civil war was over, or so we thought.

President Azaña became consumed with writing his memoirs and spent innumerable hours sitting on the terrace of Nicole's house with his pad and pen, scribbling away. Life was simple. I would typically accompany Dolores on her morning walks and then go hunting on my own for a few hours on the outskirts of Roques. I would get lost in thoughts about Morente and bullfighting and then have to shove them aside because they made me too melancholic. I would return to Nicole's house at lunchtime, where my mood would be instantaneously lifted by the wonderful gastronomy and the spirited conversation. The impending talk was of a new war that was waiting to happen. Adolf Hitler had seemed to come out of nowhere, or actually from the American stock market crash in October of 1929, which had a disastrous effect on Germany as several large banks collapsed, throwing millions of its citizens out of work and causing economic mayhem. Hitler capitalized on the unpopular austerity measures imposed by the government. His oratory prowess and nationalistic themes had an almost hypnotic effect on audiences and in 1930 his National Socialist German Workers Party, commonly referred to as the Nazi Party, came in second in the national elections. By 1933 he had become Chancellor of Germany, and the next year anointed himself as *Fuehrer und Reichskanzler*, leader and Chancellor of the Reich, which effectively made him a dictator.

We began to see that Hitler had used Spain as a testing ground to train men and test equipment and tactics for his ambitious plans. He also saw in General Franco a new Fascist ally that would help him in the coming conflict with France and Great Britain. Without Germany's support it is doubtful that Franco's

Nationalists forces would have succeeded in winning the war.

The afternoons were reserved for a short nap followed by a sip of Armagnac with my newly found friend, Jacques. And so, the hours, days, and months passed until that fateful day of September 1, 1939, when the Germans invaded Poland. Two days later, France and Great Britain declared war on Germany, marking the beginning of World War II. The daily conversations became more anxious as Germany, now allied with the Soviet Union, seemed to have no bounds on its ambitions. In April of 1940 the Germans invaded Denmark and Norway and on May 10th our worst fears grew to fruition as Belgium, the Netherlands, Luxembourg, and finally France came under siege from their bullying neighbor to the north. Before June was over, France had surrendered and Vichy France was formed which amounted to little more than a puppet government led by Marshall Philippe Petain but effectively under German control. It was at this time that we began to get really nervous about the safety of President Azaña. Now France was at the mercy of the Gestapo, who at Hitler's bequest made it a top priority to round up as many prominent Republican exiles as they could and turn them over to General Franco's government, where many were summarily shot. It was Hitler's way of ingratiating himself even more with Franco to try to convince him to join Germany and Italy in the war.

In spite of all of the turmoil going on around us we had a false sense of safety due to the isolated nature of the little village that had temporarily become our home. The war seemed a thousand miles away, but all that changed one morning in the waning days of October of 1940.

Dolores had decided to remain at her husband's side, as he had come down with an awful bout of the flu, so I grabbed my shotgun, slung it over my shoulder, and started my day walking alone through a meadow resplendent with sunflowers. I was about a mile away from the village when I saw three men smoking cigarettes next to a black sedan a couple of hundred yards away by the side of the road underneath a large oak tree. I started walking towards them in the hope of encountering some much-needed conversation. When I was fifty yards away I thought one of them finally spotted me, but the three men slowly got into the sedan and drove off, in the opposite direction. I don't know why, but I kept walking towards the area where the men had been smoking. When I got there a plume of smoke was still drifting upwards from one of the cigarettes that had been tossed by the side of the road. I was about to head back to the village when an empty and crumbled paper box caught my eye.

I picked up the small container and read its contents under my breath, *"Cigarillos Populares - Labor de Guerra - 14 cigarillos."*

For a few seconds I just froze. I could not even move as my mind tried to understand the words I had just read. Who was smoking Spanish cigarettes from the Civil War? Why were they smoking them here, in the middle of nowhere, so far from Spain? At that instant I started to sprint towards Roques, shotgun in hand with the safety off. All sorts of alarm bells started going off in my head.

I practically shattered the side door leading into the living room as I burst into Nicole's house. Nicole, Gladys, Jacques, Cipriano, Dolores and President Azaña where all sitting placidly on couches and sipping Floc de Gascogne, a popular local aperitif. I tried to catch my breath as my mind registered that everyone was safe. Everyone was staring at me as if I were a lunatic.

"Manolo, what the hell is the matter with you?" the President asked.

Struggling to catch my breath, I finally answered, "I just thought something was wrong, that's all. I'm sorry, sir."

"It's okay my boy, but take it easy before you have a heart attack, for God's sake," and everyone started to laugh as the shock from my most unceremonious entry subsided.

I walked out to the terrace and sat on a bench, still trying to catch my breath. After a minute or so, Jacques came out with a glass of cold Floc.

"I think you can use a drink, my young friend,"

"Thank you, I sure can!" I replied.

"What happened out there, Manolo?" he asked.

I related the incidents of my morning walk to him.

After a brief but measured pause he added, "All right, it could be reason for alarm, but I can not imagine how anyone could have found out that President Azaña is here and that those men you saw were secret Spanish police, sent to kidnap or assassinate him. Still it does not smell right. Let me call Laurent and let him know what happened and get his thoughts. Meanwhile let us keep this little story to ourselves so as not to cause undue panic amongst our residents. President Azaña is still not looking very well and any additional tension will definitely not aid his health. Why don't both of us stay on guard duty tonight— you here in the living room, while I keep an eye on the front door from the kitchen window of my house."

"Sounds like a plan," I finally said.

Later on that same afternoon, while Jacques and I were having our customary Armagnac in his garden, he relayed his telephone conversation with Laurent.

"Laurent agrees with me and thinks it is highly unlikely that anyone would know that President Azaña is here in Roques, as only he and Colonel Portay in the Deuxieme Bureau know of his whereabouts. Still, he agreed with me to err on the side of caution and keep alert just in case. He will talk to Colonel Portay tomorrow and see if he thinks there should be a change to the current plan."

"Okay, that sounds good," I replied.

That night, after a couple of cups of strong coffee, I sat on a comfortable armchair in a dark corner of the living room. The moon had decided to abstain itself and the sky was pitch black. It was also cooler than usual, accented by the wind endlessly whispering eerie chants. After about four hours I began to doubt danger was forthcoming and started to feel the weight of my weary eyelids. I was about to succumb to the temptation of sleep when the sound of a twig breaking brought me back to consciousness. I reached for my Astra M400 pistol on the small table next to me and chambered a 9mm bullet. My hand clenched the cold grey metal within its confines. Nothing changed for what seemed an eternity.

"There I go again, thinking of non-existent dangers," I said to myself and just as I was about to put my Astra back on the table, I saw a dark silhouette appear outside on the terrace. My heart started pounding so hard I thought the man outside could hear it. I had just crouched on one knee in the corner of the living room when another man appeared. It hit me then that the third assailant would come in the front door. With no way of alerting Jacques, I prayed that he had not fallen asleep on his watch. I waited while the first man slowly turned the handle of the door. It wouldn't open, so he pulled a couple of small tools from his pocket and expertly picked the lock. They waited for about thirty seconds to make sure no one had been alerted by their intrusion, then gently stepped into the room and shut the door. In that instant I pulled the trigger of my pistol, shooting the first assassin squarely in the upper chest. My next bullet failed to hit its intended target, as the second assassin used his comrade's body as a shield. He fired blindly, not knowing exactly where I was. My second bullet struck him in the right arm, just above the elbow, causing him to drop his gun. He screamed in pain, opened the door, and rushed out of the house. I fired two more shots, shattering the glass panes that had previously acted as windows, but missed. I jumped over his fallen accomplice and ran after him. As the wounded man was taking his first step down the stairs of the terrace, I shot him in the back and saw him tumble down the concrete steps towards the street below. I waited for a moment to be sure he was not getting up, then rushed back into the front of the house where the stairs led up to the bedrooms.

Just as I reached the base of the staircase, I saw that the front door was open. I had just darted halfway up the stairs when the word "Stop!" came thundering from behind me. I knew I had made a deadly mistake in assuming the third killer was already upstairs. I slowly lifted my arms over my head in surrender and was turning around when the sound of another bullet shattered the air, followed by a loud, hollow sound. At first, I thought I had been shot and half expected to see blood gushing from somewhere on my body, but as I finished looking behind me I saw the corpse of a man slumped on the floor at the base of the narrow stairs, blood spewing from his head.

Jacques, I later found out, had fallen asleep earlier, and it was not until I fired the first shots at the first two assailants that he suddenly awoke to see a man in a dark suit with a fedora trying to open the front door of Nicole's house. He quickly grabbed the old German pistol next to his side, but as he chambered the first bullet into the barrel it jammed.

"Merde!" he muttered to himself, frantically trying to insert the 9-millimeter projectile. Finally it clicked into place, just as he saw the man taking aim and about to shoot me.

Right afterwards Jacques entered the house holding a Luger.

"It's about time you decided to show up, old man!" I said, accompanied by much nervous laughter.

"Well it seemed that you had everything under control," Jacques replied, smiling.

"Where the hell did you get that antique?" I said, pointing at his gun.

"I borrowed it from a German prisoner at the Battle of the Somme and forgot to give it back," he said sarcastically.

"Well, I am sure glad it still works!" I replied.

At this point I shouted towards the bedrooms upstairs, "Everything is okay. You can all come out now. Do not worry."

Slowly each of the bedroom doors opened and their contents came forth, trembling.

First came Nicole, who upon seeing the dead man at the foot of the stairs, screamed, *"Mon Dieu!"*

Next, Cipriano appeared and asked, "What happened? Who is that person?" pointing towards the dead man.

As Jacques was about to answer, Dolores and a very frail looking President Azaña came out of their room with the President, asking, "Yes, who is that man, and what about the other gunshots fired?"

"Monsieur President, I can find no identification of any kind on this man," began Jacques, as he went thru the man's pockets.

"I will check the other two men I shot, but I have the feeling that neither will have papers. These men were professional. They would not make that kind of mistake, but give me a moment to make sure," I volunteered.

"Jacques, help me take this man out to the terrace," I said.

"Sure, no problem Manolo," he replied.

132

As we were about to pick up the dead man, the President started coughing uncontrollably. Alarmed, we all looked towards him until Dolores led him back to their bedroom.

As Jacques and I carried the man out of the house, Jacques quietly said, "He does not sound good. We have to get him out of here and to a doctor."

I interrupted him by saying, "I agree with you, and anyway after this little intrusion by our three friends, our days, if not our hours here, are numbered."

"After we check the other two men, let us go over to the Blanc et Rouge and call Laurent to see what the next plan of action should be," Jacques suggested.

"Good idea," I concurred.

As I suspected, the other two men had nothing on them that would give away their identity. From their southern European looks it was easy to ascertain that they were definitely not German, and thus not Gestapo. Their clothes confirmed what I had started to suspect. They were of Iberian manufacture, and because of their crew cuts and well-built physique, I surmised that these men had to be Spanish secret police. Jacques agreed with me as we made our way down the dimly lit, narrow main street from Nicole's house to the Blanc et Rouge bar about 200 yards away.

It was almost five in the morning and although the bar would have shut down hours earlier, the front door was always left unlocked in case anybody needed to make an urgent call, as it was the only telephone in the entire village. Next to the phone, that sat stoically on top of the zinc-clad bar top, was some paper and a pen, on which people were expected to write down the number they had called and their name for later payment. As we approached the bar I noticed the light was on. Strange, I thought— maybe the shots awoke Isaac or Anne, his wife, although the building was a fair distance from Nicole's house. Isaac was on the phone and as soon as he saw us enter he hung up without saying a word. Odd. Who was he calling, and why had he ended the conversation without bidding the other person farewell? I saw him stuffing a small piece of paper in his pocket. I quickly rounded the bar as I pulled my Astra out of its well-worn brown leather holster.

"What are you doing?" he yelled at me, "I was just calling the police because I heard some gunshots."

"Since when don't you know the number of the police by memory?" I snarled back at him.

"Give me the piece of paper you just put in your pocket," I continued in a threatening tone.

"What paper?" he replied, trying to hide his obvious guilt.

I chambered the Astra and looked right into his spineless, bespectacled eyes. "I am going to count to three before I shoot you in the head Isaac, unless you give me what is in your pocket. One, two ..."

"Okay! Okay! Here it is," Isaac said, as he pulled the crumbled note from his right pocket.

"Jacques, dial this number and give me the phone," I commanded. Jacques did as he was told and handed me the phone.

"If you make one move towards the gun I know you keep in the drawer underneath the cash register I will blow your head off," I told Isaac, who was overcome by fear.

"*Jawohl?*" a German voice said in a curt military tone. I slowly put the receiver back on its cradle.

I handed Jacques my Astra and pulled the large hunting knife from its sheath on my belt and lunged at the owner of the bar. Issac was no match for me. He was of average size and had a large gut fueled mostly by the local beer. I shoved him back against the bar and grabbed his hair and yanked his head down violently against the bar, resulting in a loud thud which made Isaac wince in pain. He resembled a large black beetle on his back, his arms and legs flailing helplessly in the air.

"You fat piece of scum!" I yelled at Isaac, my knife securely lodged against his throat.

"Whom have you talked to? What have you told them?" The knife drew blood as it broke the skin.

"I didn't know they meant to kill you! I swear!" Isaac muttered, tears gelling in his eyes. "I recognized President Azaña from a picture in a newspaper article around the time of the defeat of the Republican forces at the hands of General Franco. We are close to starving here, so when I found out that the Germans were offering large rewards for information leading to the whereabouts of prominent Spanish Republicans hiding in France, I called their headquarters in Toulouse. I swear I meant no harm." The smell of urine filled the air, as a stain appeared on Isaac's pants.

"What the hell did you think your Nazi friends would do, invite us out to dinner for some wine?" I shouted in his face. At that moment Anne came into the bar from the rear entrance. Seeing me holding a knife at her husband's throat, she rushed to his side.

"Manuel, why are you doing this?" she asked.

"Because your son of a bitch husband almost got me, my friends, and the rest of Nicole's family killed tonight by selling us out to the Germans."

"Is that true, Isaac?" Anne asked her husband.

"Yes, it is. I told the Germans, but I had no idea they would try to kill them! I though they would just be deported back to Spain. It is the truth!" Isaac cried.

"Manuel, I know my husband has many faults, but he is all I have. I beg you not to do this!" This plea, and the look of supplication in her hazelnut-tinged eyes, caused me to have mercy.

"Against my better judgment I will not cut your throat off Isaac, but you will gather what you can fit in your car and be out of Roques in one hour. If I ever hear that you have come back to this village again, not even your wife, whom you obviously do not deserve, will stop me from returning here and taking your sorry life. Is that understood?"

"Yes! Yes! Yes!" was all the shameless man could offer in return.

"Get out of my sight before I change my mind," I said. He scurried off, his hands wrapped around his throat.

"Jacques, please ring Laurent's number for me," I asked, handing him the phone. Jacques dialed the numbers of his nephew from memory and passed the receiver to me.

Laurent had obviously been asleep when he answered the call and uttered a groggy, *"Oui?"*

"Laurent, it's Manuel. There has been an assassination attempt on President Azaña's life."

I could sense Laurent bolting upright in his bed.

"What?" Laurent screamed.

I related the events of the past few hours to him.

"Thank God you are all alive," he said, once I finished.

After a brief pause, he added, "President Azaña's health worries me. Is this bad cough you say he has, something new? Has he seemed tired lately? Does he sweat easily or complain of headaches?"

"He has had the cough for a few days now and it is definitely getting worse. Actually, now that you mention it, he is easily exhausted. And yes, he is constantly wiping perspiration from his forehead," I answered.

"Manuel, this may just be mental exhaustion, but it could also be more serious than it appears. It could be the onset of pneumonia. We need to get him somewhere safe and find a doctor right away. I'll call Colonel Portay and get back to you right away," Laurent said.

"This is getting more exciting by the minute," Jacques said after I hung up.

"Are you going to be alright?" I asked, worried about any repercussions for Jacques, Gladys, and Nicole in the aftermath of the incident.

"Do not worry yourself, my friend. The Germans will not concern themselves with three silly old people, responded Jacques, smirking, "I am just glad I am not on your bad side! I now fully understand why President Azaña keeps you close by."

Barely fifteen minutes had elapsed when the phone rang. Jacques answered it and passed the receiver to me.

"Manuel, I will be in Roques in less than an hour to pick you all up. When I get there, I will go over Colonel Portay's plan," Laurent said.

"Okay, I will make sure everyone is ready to go," I replied.

"Good."

I ripped the cord out of telephone to make sure no one else would be alerted before Laurent arrived, and Jacques and I headed back to Nicole's house. Cipriano, Gladys, and Nicole were all in the kitchen having some coffee and were eagerly awaiting our return. I related my brief conversation with Laurent but omitted the incident with Isaac. I told Gladys and Nicole to go up and help Dolores and President Azaña get ready.

Within forty-five minutes we heard the screeching of tires in front of Nicole's house. I cautiously peered out one of the front windows and was relieved to see Laurent with his trusty Peugeot. By this time the whole household had assembled in the living room. I had moved all three bodies to the garage next door, and Nicole had swept the shards of broken window glass from the floor. Laurent quickly went over the elaborate plan that Colonel Portay had devised.

"Colonel Portay has always had a backup plan in case something went wrong while you were in Roques. Apparently since the end of your Civil War, Mexico's very progressive president, Lazaro Cardenas, has been offering political asylum to Republican refugees and many have taken him up on his generous offer. Germany, fearing the possibility of another country getting into the war against them, is turning a blind eye towards these refugees and doing little to hinder their evacuation from France. Colonel Portay contacted the Mexican ambassador here in France, Luis Rodriguez, some time ago about the possibility of moving you out of the country if things started to get dangerous. President Cardenas personally called Colonel Portay and let him know that his country would be at your disposal. A plan was drawn up to go into effect at the first sign of any threat."

"We are to drive to Montauban, north of Toulouse and about forty miles from here. Mexico has established a temporary consulate there, inside the Hotel du Midi. Once we are inside the hotel, the proper formal procedures can begin for you to be extradited to Mexico. We have two choices of how to get to Montauban. The first is by taking back roads that are much less prone to be used, but if we were to encounter any Germans, we would surely get stopped, questioned, and handed over to the Gestapo. The second option is to take the principal road towards Toulouse and then on to Montauban. This route would take us right under the Nazi noses, and because it is a lot more daring and something they would likely not expect, we might just get away with it. It is up to you, President Azaña," concluded Laurent.

"What do you think we should do, Manolo?" the president asked me.

"Well it is definitely riskier to travel on major thoroughfares and although it is against my instinct, it might just contain enough of an element of surprise that it could work. If we do get stopped it would be easier to make a run for it in a well-heeled area than on an isolated country road," I answered.

"Okay, let us see if we can outfox our German friends," said President Azaña.

"One last thing," continued Laurent, "once we reach the outskirts of Montauban, we will transfer from my Peugeot into an ambulance that will be driven by a colleague of mine from the Deuxieme Bureau. The Germans, knowing that the Hotel du Midi is a safe haven for Republicans, now have a number of patrols around the hotel but will likely not interfere with an unexpected emergency. Now let's go— there is no time to waste."

As everyone was helping load the suitcases into the Peugeot, Laurent asked to talk to me in private. "Manuel, you know that if we get pulled over we will have no choice but to fight, so have your gun loaded and ready. There is no stopping once we get into that car."

"I know," I replied solemnly.

The final goodbyes to Nicole, Gladys and Jacques were not easy. More than hosts, they had become a new family. Nicole and Gladys were in tears while wishing us a safe journey. Dolores would not stop hugging them. President Azaña was effusively thanking everyone for their service to Spain. At long last I went over to bid Jacques *adieu*. He had become a second father to me and I knew I was going to miss our afternoon Armagnac sessions. On top of this, he had saved my life a few hours earlier.

"Jacques, I do not know where or how to begin to thank you for everything you have done for my president and especially for me," I began, but before I could continue, he interrupted.

"There is no need to thank me. I thought Laurent was the only son I had, but I have found a second one— a Spanish one from a small village in Andalusia," he said, putting his hands on my shoulders.

"There will always be a bottle of old Armagnac waiting for you at this house."

I was so taken by his words that I could not think of anything else to say except, "*Merci, merci beaucoup* Jacques."

I decided that Dolores should sit in the front passenger seat alongside Laurent, thinking this would raise fewer eyebrows. There was little or no conversation on the journey north, as everyone understood the severity of the situation. Surprisingly there were few German patrols out and the ones that were present paid little attention to an inconspicuous Peugeot saloon. Traffic was relatively light and we made it to Montauban in about an hour. Once there, we made our way to a quiet neighborhood where we met the affable Christian Rassinoux, who was to be our ambulance driver. We all hopped in the large, grossly utilitarian, converted Renault van, and with sirens blaring started driving towards the center of town. Only Christian was in the front, and both Laurent and I, seated on a bench near the back door, had our guns out and loaded, just in case.

After less than ten minutes of driving on the bumpy, narrow, cobblestone-lined streets of Montauban, Christian let us know that we were within sight of the hotel. But a moment later he said, "Oh God, get down, everyone!"

The olive green-draped van slowed down to a standstill. We crouched as low as we could so as not to be seen through the windshield. Dolores prayed quietly and

Cipriano held his head in his arms, while President Azaña simply looked down at the floor.

"What's going on?" a voice barked.

"We got a call that the Mexican consul may have suffered a heart attack," replied Christian.

"I have not heard any such thing," replied the Waffen SS Captain. It was the Nazi party's military arm, and not the regular German army, that was guarding the Hotel du Midi.

"Well, maybe I could just sit here while you make a few calls, and then maybe you can explain to you superiors why you impeded me from reaching the hotel to try to save the consul," Christian said, sarcastically. "Take your time, he probably has at least one or two more minutes to live."

The German thought for a moment, and deciding he did not need any additional headaches in his life, said, "Okay— go!"

We all breathed a heavy sigh of relief. Shortly thereafter the ambulance backed up to the main entrance of the hotel so that the Germans outside would not see us getting out of the back of the van.

A few minutes later Laurent and I bid Christian goodbye. With sirens blaring he made it past the German patrols outside, which did not realize they had just let General Franco's most sought after enemy slip through their hands. The Mexican consul Jose Pedraza, and his lovely wife Mercedes welcomed us in the lobby, as Colonel Portay had let him know to expect us.

"Please, President Azaña, take my suite, which has its own study, as yours for as long as you need it," offered the consul.

"Thank you, Mr. Pedraza, that is most gracious of you," replied a weary Manuel Azaña. We all settled into our respective rooms while a private doctor examined President Azaña.

I shared my room with Laurent, who in the last twenty-four hours had seen his life transformed.

"Laurent what will you do now?" I asked.

"Once the Germans get wind of what has happened in Roques and start asking questions, they will start looking for me. Fortunately, only Colonel Portay and I knew of this plan. If I leave this hotel the Germans will arrest, torture, and then shoot me. Even if I got past the patrols outside, I would put the lives of my mother, aunt, and uncle at risk, as the Gestapo would surely use them as bait to get to me. Therefore, I have only one choice. Colonel Portay has secured my extradition to Mexico, where I am to assist you in protecting your president."

"That is quite a sacrifice you are making for my country," I said, overwhelmed.

"Manuel, what is left of mine? We are mere pawns of a fascist ogre. I will come back to France when the last Nazi is gone from my country, as there is little I can do here now," Laurent said. But in spite of his defiant tone, he seemed dejected.

After about half an hour Jose Pedraza knocked on the door of our room and told us to follow him to a private office where Dolores, Cipriano, and a well dressed, middle-aged man in horn-rimmed spectacles were waiting.

"I am Doctor Pierre Meslier. Forgive me but I will come straight to the point. The situation with President Azaña is quite serious. I cannot be completely sure, since it would require chest X-rays to confirm my prognosis, which is obviously something not at our disposal here, but he seems to have an advanced case of pneumonia compounded by the fact that he is not very fit. For now, the best treatment is having him take cold baths to get his fever down and getting as much rest as possible. Do not even dream of moving him anywhere. It will be some time before he gets better and is able to travel."

"About how long do you think doctor?" asked Dolores, who was more concerned than ever after hearing her husband's prognosis.

"It is difficult to say, *Madame President*. It could be as little as one week to as much as a month. I shall personally stay at the hotel and check on his progress daily. More than this I cannot do."

"Thank you very much, Doctor Meslier," answered Dolores, trying her best to maintain her composure.

After the doctor left the room, we all tried to lift her spirits by telling her that with some much-needed rest the president would be back to his normal, witty self, continuing to write his memoirs and entertain us with intellect-filled conversations. After accompanying Dolores back to her suite, where the president was already sound asleep, Laurent and I decided to take eight-hour shifts at guard duty outside the room.

The hotel was filled with prominent Republican refugees and in spite of our dire situation it was good to hear the voices of Spaniards, even if they were those of defeated ones. Everyone was very concerned about Manuel Azaña's health, the main topic of each passing day, as November came upon us.

On the morning of the third day of our stay at the Hotel du Midi, as I was getting up to relieve Laurent at guard duty, I heard a loud exchange coming from the front door of the hotel. As I peered out of my window, I saw a Waffen SS Major with a squad of ten SS soldiers behind him, barking out orders at the Mexican consul. I quickly finished getting dressed and rushed downstairs, gun in tow, to see what was going on. As I reached the lobby, I could hear the irritation in the SS Major's voice.

"Get out of my way before I not only arrest the traitor Azaña, whom I know is inside, but also you."

"My dear Major," the consul calmly replied, his hands crossed behind his back, "the president of my country has personally invited Mr. Manuel Azaña to stay here. As I am sure you can understand, I cannot undermine the leader of my country, just as you would not disobey a direct order from your Fuehrer. I need not remind you that this building is a consulate of the sovereign nation of Mexico and as such you have no jurisdiction here."

The German's face was turning so red from anger that it looked like he was going to burst a vein in his forehead.

"I do not care what you think this building is— if you do not move aside right now I will..."

"You will what, Major?" interrupted the consul. "You will shoot me? I am sure you could and would, but unless it is your wish to declare war on Mexico, which I am certain is above your pay grade, I believe this little meeting is over."

The major knew his attempt at intimidating the consul had failed, and looking at the group of about 20 men standing behind him and sensing that they would not be easily subdued either, recognized that his ploy was doomed.

"This is not over!" the SS officer shouted back.

The consul simply replied, "Oh, but it is. Good day, Major."

With that, the German and his squad abruptly left.

As Jose Pedraza turned around and faced us, he smiled, "Okay gentleman, I believe that is enough excitement for today. I know it is early in the morning, but I am going to the bar because I can sure use a little tequila! For those of you who will join me, I'm buying!"

We all laughed and headed to the bar and had tequila shots for breakfast as everyone congratulated Jose on his show of courage.

Shortly thereafter I went to relieve Laurent at guard duty and after about half an hour Dolores came out of the suite to tell me that the president wanted to speak to me alone. He looked very pale as I approached the large, wooden, four-poster, ornately draped bed. His eyes were shut and I was hesitant to say anything in case he had fallen asleep. Suddenly he coughed and opened his eyes.

"Oh Manolo, my loyal and trusted Manolo," he began with constant interruptions caused by his incessant coughing, "who will protect me if I do not end up in heaven?"

"Do not speak like that, sir. Soon you will gain back your health, you just need to rest," I answered feebly.

"Manolo, you and I know that my final days are arriving and in spite of the huge debt that I owe you, I must ask you for one final favor," the president said, having to pause momentarily to regain the strength to go on. "I need you to promise me that you will make sure that my wonderful Dolores gets out of France."

"My president, you need not worry, I will not leave her side until I know she is safe," I replied.

"Thank you, thank you my friend," the president said as he shut his eyes again and fell asleep. I stood there for a few minutes, my thoughts swirling. I felt like a piece of history was fading right in front of me and I was afraid to let it go. I finally left the room and went to speak to Jose Pedraza in private.

"Mr. Pedraza."

"Please call me Jose," he said at once.

"Jose," I continued, "I am afraid President Azaña does not have much time left. We need to quickly make arrangements to get Doña Dolores out of France."

"Not to worry Manuel," answered the consul, "I will call the ambassador in Paris right away to take care of this."

"Thank you, Jose," I replied before heading back to take up my post outside the president's room.

Later that afternoon I told Laurent of my conversation with both President Azaña and the consul.

"What are you going to do now?" asked Laurent.

"Well, once Doña Dolores is on the way to Mexico, I doubt that our Nazi friends will be interested in her, and anyhow, with you at her side I know she will be well protected. My fight here has not ended. I cannot forget how the many men of the International Brigades came to the aid of my country when we most needed help. I feel a debt to those men that I must repay," I answered.

Laurent was pensive for a moment before saying, "Let me call Colonel Portay. I know that General Charles de Gaulle is a close friend of his and that the General is organizing a resistance movement against the Germans from London. Let me see how he thinks you could help."

"Okay," I replied.

The next afternoon the Mexican ambassador, Luis Rodriguez, arrived at our hotel. Soon afterwards, Laurent, Jose, the ambassador, and I met to discuss Doña Dolores' situation. The ambassador told us that as soon as President Azaña passed away he would personally escort Laurent and the president's wife to Paris, and from there, to Le Havre where they would catch a ocean liner to Mexico. After our meeting, Laurent told me that Colonel Portay had made arrangements for me to leave the hotel during the funeral, which would create enough of a diversion for me to evade the German patrols outside the hotel. I was to meet our old ambulance driver, Christian, two blocks away at a bar on the northwest corner of Rue Notre Dame and Allee Mortarieu. From there we would take his car and drive towards the town of Espelette, and then on to Ascain in the Basque region where we would meet Jean Moulin, who was one of the principal organizers of the French Resistance.

That evening of November 3rd, at 11:15pm, the President of the Second Spanish Republic died, although his death was not officially registered till the following day. I will never forget that day of the 5th of November. Even though the president was not a religious man, Doña Dolores, who was a fervent Catholic, insisted that his funeral take place in the Cathedral of Montauban across the street from the hotel. As we were leaving the hotel and carrying his casket with the Republican flag covering it, the French prefect in charge of the region stopped us, saying that Marshall Philippe Petain would not allow such an act of defiance against his country's German and Spanish allies. With a German patrol looking on, a shouting match broke out between our group and the French police that had the feel of a riot about to break out. At that moment the Mexican ambassador stepped in front of the casket and held his hand up.

"Jose!" he yelled. "Go upstairs and remove the Mexican flag that hangs out over the balcony."

Jose Pedraza dashed back into the hotel and up the stairs, returning quickly with the flag. With the utmost reverence, the ambassador removed the Republican flag from the casket, folded it neatly, and handed to Doña Dolores.

He then took the Mexican flag and carefully placed it on the casket, turned towards the French official and said, "The flag of Mexico will proudly cover him. For us it will be a privilege, for the Republicans a ray of hope, and for you a painful lesson!"

We all erupted cheering, "Long live Manuel Azaña! Long live the Republic!" as we marched towards the imposing wooden doors of the Ionic façade that marked the entrance of the cathedral, with the statues of the four evangelists looking down upon us.

I was one of the pallbearers, and once the eight of us set his casket down at the foot of the altar, I casually walked towards a corridor that circumvented the altar and slipped out a side door into an alley. Vast crowds had gathered around the cathedral, and this allowed me to make my way to the rendezvous point without drawing any unwanted attention. Christian was drinking a *café au lait* at the small, quaint drinking establishment. I joined him in a coffee and we left a few minutes later. We got into his pale burgundy-colored Simca Huit and headed south towards Toulouse, then west towards the vast Pyrenees Mountains. We did not speak much during the six-hour journey. Laurent had warned me not to mention my meeting with the French Resistance leader and Christian was too professional to ask, so I was left alone with my memories of President Azaña. It was then that it hit me that the Republic was lost forever and that the Spain I knew would never be the same again.

Nightfall was fast approaching when we reached the picturesque village of Ascain, nestled in a valley at the foot of the imposing La Rhune Mountain with the River Neville running through it. Christian dropped me off at the intersection of the Rue Ernest Fourneau and Chemin de la Fontaine, where we quickly bid each other *adieu*. I made my way to number 16 Rue Burdin Bidea. As I walked up to the traditional red-roofed, timber-lined white house, I could not help but feel I was starting a new life.

I knocked on the large door twice, paused for a moment, and then knocked three more times as Laurent had instructed. The door was partially opened and a man with an imposing nose and wearing a black woolen beret asked me my name.

"Manuel," I said, as he stepped aside. In his right hand was a distinctive Welrod pistol.

"Follow me," he said after bolting the front shut. He led me through the dimly lit foyer into the back of the house, where a man was sitting on a bench next to a large and rustic wooden kitchen table. He was wearing a smart Fedora, an unbuttoned trench coat, and had a scarf around his neck.

"Welcome, I am Jean Moulin and this is Gerald Hirigoyen, the commander of the resistance is this region. General de Gaulle has been told that you might be of assistance to us."

"I hope so," I replied.

"Well Gerald, let us open a bottle of *Irouleguy* and get to know our Spanish guest," continued Jean in a friendlier tone.

The wine was rough, but I was thirsty, plus the ham from Bayonne and a local sheep's milk cheese, *Ossau-Iraty*, hid most of its coarseness. The wine also served to break the ice, and soon I was peppered with questions about my days in the Civil War. In return I learned of Jean Moulin's mission to go to England and meet with General Charles de Gaulle and devise a plan to try to unify the various resistance groups. Gerald told me that most of his time was spent rescuing Royal Air Force pilots shot down by the German Luftwaffe, or gathering intelligence on troop movements of the Germans and their Vichy allies and passing it on to the British.

"Every once in a while, we get bored, so we sabotage a railway line or blow up a munitions factory!" said Gerald laughing.

"Well it seems like our friends in the Gestapo like you as much as they like us, so we should all get along just fine!" concluded Jean smiling. "I will be leaving in the morning to Saint-Jean-de-Luz, where I will meet up with some other resistance leaders and make my way to London to enjoy some tea with General de Gaulle, leaving you guys to have all the fun."

With that, the evening ended and I was finally able to get some sleep. A few years later I was saddened to learn that Jean Moulin died while being tortured by the Gestapo. It is a testament to his courage and devotion to his country that he never divulged a single word to his Nazi captives.

The Basques are a curious bunch. Initially they are very leery and untrusting of strangers. It is difficult for them to open up and completely confide in someone they do not know well, but once they recognize you as a friend, there is no one more loyal. Like most Basques, Gerald was a very private person and divulged little about his persona. He seemed to have no family and we spent hardly any time in Ascain, instead seeking refuge in an isolated cabin high up in the mountains with the three other members of our resistance group.

Bixente, Mikel, and Julen were all in their early twenties. The war had cost each of them a personal tragedy and they were ardent in their hatred of both the Germans and the French who stood by their side. We spent most of our days out of sight and usually only ventured away from the cabin as the day succumbed to darkness. We had a flock of about 100 sheep that we tended with the able help of a couple of very large Pyrenean Mountain dogs. The dogs kept any wolves at bay during the cold and dreary nights. In the cabin we usually played cards or dominoes, or had to listen to Gerald's awful voice chanting old Basque ballads after vast amounts of Patxaran, a liqueur typical of this land, made by soaking sloe berries, a few coffee beans, and a vanilla pod in Anisette. In spite of this, my initial months of pastoral life were a welcome change from the anxiety and stress of the previous five years. It allowed me to regain a sense of normalcy, if one could call life normal in the midst of a World War.

It took some time for Gerald's gruff demeanor to subside, but I began to really understand the man when one morning while tending to our sheep with Julen, who had been the first of the group to warm up to me, I asked him, "Gerald never mentions anyone in his past. What happened to his family?"

Julen turned around to make sure no one was within earshot. "He is an only child and both of his parents died tragically just after the Nazis invaded France. They had been celebrating their thirtieth anniversary at a restaurant and were walking back to their house when a truck, whose driver must have been drunk, veered off the road near their home, ran them down, and took off without stopping. They died instantly. A neighbor, who heard the loud noise, stepped outside his house to see what was going on. A German military truck was racing away from the scene, swerving all over the road.

This was when Gerald decided to get involved with the Resistance. Before that he was mostly here, tending to the animals. When he did come down into town to check on his parents and have a drink with friends, I often heard him say that this war did not involve him, that he was Basque, not French. That it was their war, not his. All that changed after the death of his father and mother. He became the most fervent and brazen guerilla amongst us, and quickly assumed the leadership of our loosely organized resistance movement. That in turn led to another terrible event in his life.

Before his parents' death, he had just gotten engaged to the woman of his dreams, actually of all our dreams: a beautiful young blonde with eyes the color of

151

the clearest sky named Karmele. She was charming and brought a smile to anyone who crossed her path. The Gerald you know now is not the man that I knew just a year ago. She took that hard edge away from him. She made him laugh and forget about the mad world we were living in.

Across the street from Karmele's house lived a man by the name of Joseph Bataille. Originally from Alsace, he had moved to Ascain when the war had started because his wife was from there. He never did integrate well into the Basque culture. He felt like an outsider, and quickly came to resent his new neighbors. It was not uncommon for Alsatians to have German roots, and in Joseph's case his grandmother was from Munich and he actually spoke German fluently. His was not a dislike towards those across the border to his north. In fact, he secretly admired the strength and superior attitude that Adolph Hitler has instilled into the Teutonic people. The French army had been a pitiful opponent to the Wehrmacht forces and as the months passed and he saw how quickly the German army was overpowering the rest of Europe, he knew they would be the new masters of Europe in no time. He thought he could use his German roots to ingratiate himself with the Germans. He might even be rewarded with a much more prosperous status than the lowly automotive production line worker he had been at the Bugatti factory in his hometown of Molsheim.

One misty evening while sipping some Schnapps and staring out the window of his living room he noticed a group of four men approaching Karmele's house. It was the way they moved that caught his attention. They were constantly checking to see if anyone was behind them, as if they were afraid of being spotted.

He called his wife Antxone over and offhandedly asked her if she knew who they were.

"Oh yes," Antxone replied, "those are the brave local boys that make life difficult for those terrible Nazis."

It was at that very moment that he saw his opportunity.

Using the pretense that he was going to go shopping for some groceries, the next day he went to the town's Vichy police headquarters and related the events of the previous night to the local chief.

"Thank you, your deeds will not go unnoticed my friend. We have been looking for these traitors for some time with little success, as everyone in this town is afraid of those cowards," the police chief told Joseph. Ascain being a town of less than 1,500 people, his visit to the police headquarters did not go unnoticed by an older man who was enjoying a glass of wine while reading a newspaper at a bistro across the street.

Later on that same afternoon, a truck carrying six armed Gestapo agents pulled up to Karmele's house and dragged her away kicking and screaming.

It was Gerald's uncle, Iker, who told him of the suspicious visit of Joseph Bataille to the police station that he had witnessed on the same day that Karmele was taken away. Two days later our worst fears were confirmed when we found out that she had been tortured to death without revealing any information.

That night I noticed Gerald putting on his overcoat and I remember asking him where he was going, as we were all very nervous about his state of mind. He seemed like a caged, rabid animal.

"I am just going out to get some fresh air," he replied.

"Do you want some company?" I asked him.

"No thanks, I need some time alone."

"Okay," I said.

The sound of the door of the cabin opening some five hours later woke me up as Gerald returned from his so called 'walk'.

I asked him if everything was all right and he responded, "No, but it is better now," and with that we all went back to sleep.

The next afternoon we heard from a shepherd friend of ours that they had found the body of Joseph Bataille in the main square of town. His head was in a pool of blood with his entire tongue cut out.

"He got what he deserved," said the shepherd. "Gerald would never speak about the incident."

"Jesus!" I said astonished, "No wonder he has an ax to grind! I assume no one else has divulged information about our whereabouts!" I added.

"No *mon ami*. I think everyone got the message," replied Julen smiling.

When we returned to the cabin, Gerald had a pair of headphones and was listening to a small British MCR-1 radio that was hidden in a kitchen cupboard with a false back. The crackling sound of the radio was interspersed with an English voice spouting out coordinates and military times. These radio transmissions were kept short to avoid detection by the German radio direction finders.

After Gerald turned off the radio and stowed it back into its hiding place, he turned towards us and said, "Okay boys, it looks like we are going to be busy tonight. The British Royal Air Force is going to launch a bombing raid against the Manufacture d'Armes de Bayonne at 22:00 hours. A squadron of twenty Bristol Blenheim bombers will be escorted by Spitfire fighter planes. This is the largest pistol producing facility in the southwest and is about eighteen miles away. We are to provide search and rescue duties in case someone gets shot down over land. Julen, Manuel, and I will drive together, Bixente and Mikel will follow us on the motorcycle about 300 yards behind. We will leave at 20:00 to have plenty of time to scout the area and decide where to watch the fireworks from. Any questions?" When no one responded, Gerald continued, "In that case go clean your weapons and get ready."

After that the only sounds heard inside the cabin were that of rifles and pistols being taken apart, oiled, cleaned and then put back together again.

A few minutes before eight o'clock we all gathered our things and headed to the barn. Inside, a pale blue Renault 6CV with its awkward looking nose stared at us as Julen, Gerald, and I got in. Bixente and Mikel hopped on the black Motobecane 250cc motorcycle parked behind the automobile. Not much was said on the thirty-minute drive through the small country back roads.

We stopped about half a mile away on a hill overlooking a series of plain looking, large industrial buildings surrounded by multiple barbed-wire fences. There were lookout towers positioned at each corner of the complex. We parked under some trees so as not to be seen from the road. Gerald took out his binoculars and checked the surrounding area, before we separated into various groups. Mikel stayed close to the vehicles, Julen and I headed to another hilltop some 300 yards away, while Gerald and Bixente headed in the opposite direction and stationed themselves about 500 yards away from us. From our vantage point and with the pair of extra binoculars Gerald had given me, I could see two groups of 6 guns each at opposite ends of the pistol factory. Each of the large 88mm Flak guns were manned by four soldiers, who were mostly standing around chatting and smoking cigarettes. The towers had large searchlights that roamed the skies and surrounding fields.

Two minutes before ten o'clock all hell broke lose as alarm sirens pierced the night air and searchlights lit up the black sky. We could hear officers shouting orders as the gun batteries started to deploy. The noise from the anti-aircraft guns was deafening, but nothing compared to the sounds of 500-pound bombs as they descended from the skies and sent the ground shaking as they exploded. The lead squadron of the Bristol Blenheim bombers was not successful in hitting their intended target as their bombs fell short of the factory, but it helped the bombers behind gauge when to drop their payloads and soon a series of explosions rocked the complex, destroying several buildings. As the rear squadron was finishing their run one of the German's 88mm guns had a direct hit on a bomber. Part of its wing was missing and the left engine was on fire as the plane spiraled downward, heading towards a field of wheat directly below where Julen and I were.

"Come on, let's go!" I urged Julen who was staring mesmerized as the large plane plummeted to earth.

The aircraft crashed landed moments later. The left side collapsed, as the wheel on that side had been destroyed. The rear of the plane was barely attached and fire was starting to spread from the engine towards the main body of the aircraft. I could feel tremendous heat from the blaze as I got closer.

I heard Julen shout behind me, "Stop, it's too late!" as I finally reached the bomber. The crewmember in the back bay was dead and then I turned to look into the cockpit. The co-pilot in the bottom part of the nose section was covered in blood and was also obviously dead, while the pilot did not look much better. I was about to turn and leave before the smoke inside overcame me or the whole thing blew up, when the pilot moaned. I unstrapped the poor bastard from his seat and dragged him out of the plane before throwing him on my back and running for my life. I was but thirty yards away when a huge explosion threw both of us to the ground and the plane went up in flames. Julen helped carry the airman to the road that bordered the field, where we saw the fast approaching lights of a car followed by a motorcycle.

The Renault came to a screeching halt as Gerald and Bixente jumped out and helped us get the injured pilot into the vehicle. Within seconds we were racing away from the scene, as the Germans would soon be coming to collect any prisoners. Back at the cabin we laid the wounded flyer on the kitchen table. Gerald fetched a first aid kit from one of the bedrooms. We cleaned him up, administered ointment for some minor burns, stitched a nasty cut above his right eyebrow, and removed several pieces of glass shards imbedded in his shoulders and arms. The poor man had lost a fair amount of blood and was barely conscious. Gerald radioed our British friends to let them know we had rescued one of their own, but that he probably needed a few days rest before we could think of extracting him out of France and back to England. Afterwards we sat down in the living room and started to enjoy our customary nightly Patxaran ritual.

Julen was the first one to break the silence. "I'm sorry Matador," which had become my nickname, "I should have helped you get the pilot out of the plane. I thought it was going to blow up before we had a chance to see if anyone inside was alive."

"Not to worry Julen. If I had stopped to think about it, I probably would not have committed such a foolish act either," I smiled at him.

"Nice work Matador," said Gerald in a rare compliment, raising his glass in a toast.

"Here, here!" chimed in all the rest.

Our guest slept for over fourteen hours till the next afternoon, and was quite weak when he got up. Gerald prepared a hearty white bean and vegetable soup, which he devoured in no time as we smiled, looking on.

"Boy, you lads can sure cook. I have not had anything this tasty since I left home!"

"What happened to my mates?" he asked after he had finished several bowls worth.

"Unfortunately, they did not make it," answered Gerald somberly.

"The last thing I remember is trying to land old Bess, urging her to hang on and not break up, and then I passed out."

"Well you can thank the Matador here," said Julen, pointing towards me and relaying the events leading up to his rescue.

"Jesus mate, I don't know how to thank you!" he exclaimed.

"Just doing my part in the war, much like you are," I replied in the broken English I had picked up during my warring days in Madrid from my comrades in the International Brigades.

"What is your name?" I asked him.

"Flight Lieutenant Aristos Stelios Kemitzis," he responded.

"That is a mouthful," I smiled, "and it does not sound very British."

"Actually I am a Greek-Cypriot. I come from Karavas, a small, sleepy fishing village on the north side of Cyprus. My father is a Colonel in the island forces and although the army was a natural path for me to follow, as a child my dreams were always filled with planes soaring into an endless sky and thus I joined the air force instead, much to my fathers' chagrin. Cyprus has been part of the British Empire since 1878, so when the war with Germany broke out, as there was a shortage of pilots in the Royal Air Force, I volunteered to get transferred to England. I was sent to RAF station Biggin Hill in Kent six

158

months ago and at once started flying bombing missions over France. This, even though I had become a pilot just one month earlier having logged a paltry total of 80 hours flying time! Two days after I arrived at Biggin Hill I got five hours of instruction in one of the Bristol Blenheim bombers that we were going to be flying and the next day I was off on my first mission!"

"What is life like as an RAF pilot?" asked Mikel.

"Well," Aristos started answering, "because during the day we would be easy prey for the German Messerschmitt Bf 109 fighters, we mostly fly night missions. In the late afternoon or early evening, we get briefed on our upcoming mission by our Wing Commander, John Dhillon, who gives us details of patrol areas and what enemy activity we can expect, the bomb load we'll carry, and take off times. The Meteorological Officer, Robert Hackman, tells us what the weather should be like and what airbase to divert to if conditions get ugly. The Intelligence Officer, Roger Lethander, goes over enemy troop and transport movements and the bomb line."

"What is a bomb line?" interrupted Bixente.

"A bomb line is the line between enemy and allied troops and of course no bombs or attacks are allowed on the allied side of the bomb line," answered Aristos. "Routes to the bombing areas are suggested to avoid major flak areas. After the briefing I get together with my navigator and bomb aimer, Flying Officer Tristan Hawke, and plan our entire route and study a topographical map, noting any high ground or major obstructions, and any known anti-aircraft positions."

At that moment the Royal Air Force Pilot stopped and began sobbing, the thought of his fallen crew having just hit him. Nobody spoke, but Mikel and Bixente, who were seated at either side of him, gently patted him on the back.

"Sorry guys, it just that Tristan and I had become close friends, having survived more than a few close encounters and our gunner, Steven Andrews, was just an eighteen-year-old, pimple-faced kid," Aristos muttered.

"Please Aristos, there is nothing to apologize for. We have all lost someone in this horrible conflict. It touches everyone," I said, as the rest of the group nodded in agreement.

"Tell us how it feels to be in a bombing run," Mikel asked, trying to divert Aristos' attention.

"We take off singly and climb to an altitude of 12,000 feet, which is where we can hit our maximum speed of 265 miles per hour, and then fall into winged formations. Once we get close to the enemy lines we drop down to about 4,000 feet, where we will patrol for more or less an hour and search out any movements on the ground while keeping an eye on our fuel as our range is only around 1,400 miles. If we spot something suspicious, we go lower and investigate to see if it is a train, army lorries, tanks or barges and then attack with 250- or 500-pound bombs or use the 7.7mm Browning guns at low levels, sometimes just above trees, which could be quite scary. In the last six months my squadron alone has lost almost a quarter of its pilots. Anytime Tristan would yell "Up!", I did not even think twice and would immediately pull up on the stick to gain height as quickly as possible. It's ironic that we got shot down on one of our high-altitude bombing runs, which are supposedly less dangerous," ended Aristos.

"Okay, let's have a little lunch Carlos. I need a break!" said Trini.

13

"Not all were tales of fighting though. There were also stories of romance," Trini resumed, after she and Carlos had finished lunch in the kitchen.

"I remember the first time Gerald came to visit us, right after the war ended. He came with his wife. They were an odd couple. He was pleasant enough, but had a rough, almost crude edge to him. His wife, on the other hand, was tall, thin, and elegant, with silky black hair. She loved cooking and came into the kitchen immediately after they arrived. The Countess Christiane Wenckheim could not be nicer and soon she put on an apron and started helping us prepare dinner. At first we were taken aback but she made us feel so comfortable that, as typical Andalusian women are prone to do, Celia and I started asking her all kinds of personal questions that she readily volunteered the answers to.

"How did you meet *Monsieur Hirigoyen*?" Celia asked her.

"Oh my dear, that is a story!" she answered, laughing.

She talked about growing up in Vienna. Her family owned prominent breweries there and in Budapest. In fact, she was the fifth generation of the family to run the brewery business since it was established in 1837. When Germany annexed Austria in March of 1938, business at the brewery there continued without much interruption. Most of the workers were of German background, so there were no issues with the Nazi's anti-Semitic policies. When Hungary joined the Axis, on the other hand, it was a whole different matter. Almost fifty of the 300 people that worked for them in Budapest were Jews. During the initial stages of the war minorities in Hungary suffered some repression, but as a prominent businessman her father was able to keep the authorities from persecuting their workers.

However, things changed dramatically with the defeat of the Germans by the Soviets in January 1944. At that point the regent and prime minister of Hungary, seeing that the German defeat was eminent, secretly tried to negotiate a peace accord with the United States and Great Britain. When Hitler found out about this, he ordered the invasion of Hungary. The Nazis began to deport Jews in masse to concentration camps.

Shortly after the Nazi regime had attained power, a group of SS soldiers led by an officer arrived at the brewery and asked to see her father.

The SS Captain came to the point quickly, "*Herr Wenckheim*, I want a list of every Jewish person working at this brewery by tomorrow morning."

"And *Hauptsturmfuehrer*, what if I do not provide that list to you?" my father asked him.

"*Herr Wenckheim* I do not think you and your family want to find out the answer to that. I believe you have a beautiful young daughter, do you not?"

"How dare you threaten my family!" my father shouted.

"How dare you disobey an order from an officer of the Third Reich! I will see you tomorrow morning to pick up that list. Do not disappoint me!" said the SS Captain as he stormed out of the office.

"Anna!" my father called to his secretary. She came into his office with tears in her eyes as she had overheard the confrontation moments before. She had been my father's secretary for twenty-five years and she was Jewish.

"Anna, it is going to be okay, but I need you to be calm right now as we do not have much time. Get me the company check book and the list of every Jewish person that works here right now and arrange for them to go to the main conference room within the hour."

My father took all the cash from his office safe and counted it. Anna returned within fifteen minutes with the check register and a list of forty-nine names, including her own. My father divided the cash into 49 equal portions and then wrote a check to each person for the equivalent of four months salary, as any more would arouse suspicion at the bank.

"Anna," he asked, "get me the addresses of the four main branches of our bank." My father's plan was that the workers would cash the checks at different locations so as not to attract attention to what he was doing.

Just over an hour later he walked into the brewery's largest meeting room, where a panicked group was wondering what fate would befall them. He held his hand up to silence the murmuring.

"Ladies and gentlemen," he began, "my family started this great brewery one hundred and seven years ago. But it is great not because my family owns it; it is great because of your work and the work of generations of your families before you. I wish I could do more to help you in this difficult time, for you deserve much more than what I can give you at this moment. Please take the cash and check I am going to give each one of you and go into hiding as soon as possible, as we do not have much time left. I pray that these terrible days will soon be behind us so that we can all resume our life here. Know that when this all ends, you will always have a job and a home at this brewery."

Each of the forty-nine workers lined up to pick up their check and some cash. My father thanked each one and wished them well. Most of them hugged him with tears in their eyes like the ones my father had in his, profusely expressing their gratitude for his generosity. After the war twenty-two of those people came back to work for us. To this day when I go to visit that brewery, those same workers come up to me in tears and hug me," said the Countess, tearing up.

Next my father called on me at our house in Vienna.

"Christiane," he told me, "listen to what I am going to tell you and do not argue with me as there is not a minute to waste. You are to go to our bedroom and open up the large armoire. There is a safe in the back."

After giving me the combination, he continued.

"Take all the money in it, get your identification papers, and pack a small bag for a weekend trip. Grab some casual clothes, a good pair of walking shoes, and make your way to the Suedbahnhof station. When you get there buy a round trip passage to Milan. If anyone asks you where you are going, say that you are going to visit your elderly aunt who lives by herself in Milan for a few days, as her health is failing. When you get to Milan go to your aunt's apartment on the Corso Buenos Aires. I will call her and tell her you are on the way. Someone from British Intelligence will call you tomorrow. Do whatever they tell you unless you hear from me to do otherwise. Is this all understood?"

"Yes father, but you are scaring me. What is happening? Are you safe in Budapest? Is everything alright?"

"My dear, I am being careful, that is all. We are having some small problems with the Germans here at the brewery that should be resolved soon, so do not worry any further. Your mother and I will be fine," he said, trying to reassure me.

I gathered some things and followed my father's directions without incident and within four hours I was on a train headed towards Italy. Late that evening I arrived at Milan and went to my aunt's apartment. She welcomed me and assured me that all would be well. I would soon find out how wrong she was. The following afternoon, the phone rang at my aunt's apartment.

"Countess Christiane Wenckheim?" inquired a man with a British accent.

"Yes, this is she," I answered.

"This is Lawrence Stone from British Military Intelligence, Section 6. I need to meet with you immediately. If you do not mind, I think the best place is the apartment where you are currently staying on the Corso Buenos Aires in about one hour."

"Okay," I consented.

Exactly fifty-seven minutes later there was a knock on the door.

I opened the door and a well-dressed man in his late thirties politely asked, "Countess Wenckheim?"

"Yes," I replied.

"I am agent Stone."

"Please come in Mr. Stone," I beckoned.

"Thank you," he answered as he entered my aunt's apartment. He followed me into the ornate living room and I invited him to take a seat on one of the large rococo armchairs. I sat on the couch with my aunt.

"I am afraid I am the bearer of bad news. Your father was arrested this morning at your brewery in Budapest. Initial reports seem to indicate that he told a Gestapo Captain that he had fired all the Jews working for him yesterday and he had no idea of any of their whereabouts. When the Gestapo command learned of this, they did not find it at all amusing and decided to make an example of someone well known in the community to deter others from not cooperating with them. They took him, and a few hours later your mother, to their main headquarters. We have since learned that they are being deported to the Auschwitz concentration camp in Poland."

"No!" I screamed.

"Oh dear God!" exclaimed my aunt, clutching her face in her hands.

"I am truly sorry, but now we need to get you to a safe location as the Gestapo has no doubt started looking for you and it will not be long till they piece two and two together. We need to be on our way."

"Where are you taking me?" I asked him.

"Miss, I prefer not to give out any details in front of your aunt in case she is questioned," replied the MI6 man.

"It is alright my dear, I understand. You had better do as the young man says and go," said my aunt.

"I grabbed the bag that held some of my clothes and followed the MI6 agent down the Corso Buenos Aires for three blocks, and then we turned into a small side street.

"There we got into his grey Fiat 1100 that appeared to have a big smile on the hood," said the Countess, laughing. "We drove for about twenty minutes and ended up in a quiet, upper-middle class neighborhood on the outskirts of Milan. We parked the car and went into a large, non-descript white house. Inside we were met by several British agents and ushered into a room where a camera on a large tripod stood with what appeared to be a dark room off to the side. I was introduced to station chief Byron Kingston, who explained to me that they would take several pictures of me to prepare both French and British identification papers in case I was stopped along my way. Agent Stone was to drive me the following morning to the port of Imperia, west of Genoa. There I would hop on a fishing boat to Banyuls-sur-Mer, just north of the Spanish border. A French Resistance agent would pick me up on my arrival and we would cross southern France and make our way to Saint-Jean-de-Luz. There I would catch another small boat that would rendezvous with a vessel from the Royal Navy, before heading towards the town of Brighton on the coast of Sussex. Lord Richard and Lady Leah Cook would be there, waiting to drive me to their estate, twenty-four miles north, just outside of the village of Horsham."

Lord Richard Cook had been a classmate of my father's at Eton College and afterwards at Oxford University. They had been friends for almost twenty-five years, and I remember as a child going to their beautiful estate with a large lily-covered, swan-filled lake amongst the immaculately manicured lawns and the majestic 500-year-old castle that housed them. Lord Richard Cook also happened to be a cousin of Winston Spencer Churchill.

"Just a walk in the park, as they say," said the station chief.

"I imagine Mr. Kingston, that whomever came up with that phrase has probably not taken this particular walk," I said.

"Yes you are quite right, I imagine not," he responded somewhat embarrassed before continuing, "Diana here will help you find clothes that will be more appropriate for your journey."

"Come my dear," said a very pleasant, matronly woman.

After Diana found some rugged working clothes that more or less fit me, she led me to one of the guest bedrooms on the second floor of the house, where I made myself comfortable before heading downstairs for dinner.

The next morning agent Lawrence Stone and I left Milan and drove south towards Genoa, before heading west towards the fishing village of Imperia. The journey of over 150 miles took almost four hours in the slow-moving Fiat. Lawrence Stone was a jovial chap though, and made the journey go by pleasantly.

"Two days ago, station chief Kingston picked up the phone in his office and the operator told him it was a call from 10 Downing Street. I have never seen Kingston jump up from his desk so quickly. Anyone close by could hear the gruff voice of Prime Minister Churchill on the line. All poor Kingston could manage to say was "Yes Sir!" and he must have repeated it at least twenty times," said the agent, laughing.

We spent the rest of the journey in the car talking about how the Allies were on the verge of taking Rome and the hope was that the rest of Italy would fall shortly thereafter.

"We spend most of our time keeping an eye on troop movements in and around the major bases and reporting them back to London, so chaperoning you is a nice break," he said.

"I just wish the circumstances could be different," I replied.

"Yes of course my dear girl, but we must keep our chin up even in the worst of times," he added.

Imperia was a quaint village. We parked the Fiat near the harbor and headed towards the area of the port where the small fishing boats were anchored. Soon enough we found *Maruxa*, a twenty six-foot turquoise and yellow-trimmed wooden boat and were greeted by Vincent and Xavier. I said goodbye to agent Stone and hopped on board. The boat had a small cabin underneath that housed a cot, a small kitchen and a toilet. As soon as we were in open water, Xavier showed me a compartment, more like a coffin actually, in the front of the engine bay where I was to hide if anybody stopped us. I soon found out that both father and son were descendents of a liberal-thinking Catalan family and had volunteered to fight on the Republican side of the Spanish Civil War. When that conflict ended, and France was besieged by Germany, they joined the Resistance.

The going was slow on *Maruxa*, so named for Vincent's Spanish mother, as it was difficult for her to cruise any faster than 12 knots an hour. But Vincent and Xavier were lively hosts, probably because they had not had a female companion for some time! Vincent in particular was a wonderful cook and made a terrific *Bouillabaisse*, the fish stew typical of the Marseille region. After dinner we drank Banyuls, the delicious sweet red wine made with Grenache grapes from the town that Vincent and Xavier were born and raised. Vincent, who had a lovely tenor's voice, broke out signing old French ballads while Xavier accompanied him on harmonica. I could not remember the last time I smiled as much. I felt like I was a million miles away from the war. Like true gentlemen they insisted that I sleep on the cot while they took turns at the helm and getting some rest up above.

The next morning, I awoke to a day so calm on the Mediterranean Sea that it looked like we were floating on glass. Vincent went down into the galley and started making some scrambled eggs and sautéing a few andouillette sausages. Mesmerized by the tranquility surrounding me I could not stop staring at the water.

At first the faraway speck looked like a grey bird flying just above the sea. As I kept looking it soon became obvious it was too large to be anything but a boat, and a fast one at that.

I turned to Xavier who had his back to the scene and said, "I think there is something moving towards us."

Xavier took out a pair of binoculars and looked towards the approaching vessel.

"*Merde*! It is a German S-boat!" he said.

Vincent came up from the galley and grabbed the binoculars.

"Okay, everyone keep calm. Xavier, keep cruising at the same speed. That boat is four times faster than ours and has a bunch of powerful guns to boot, so do not do anything to make them think that we are trying to evade them. I am going to go back down and keep cooking as if nothing is happening. Christiane, get into the hiding spot below."

I climbed down into the engine bay and crawled to the back part, where out of sight was a wooden box that I got into and then shut the lid above me. The diesel engine fumes made it difficult to breathe. I tried to close my eyes and be calm as a feeling of claustrophobia overcame me.

The *Kriegsmarine* patrol boat soon announced its presence over a loudspeaker, commanding us to come to a standstill as it approached. Three huge twenty-cylinder Daimler Benz diesel engines spewed out smoke as the imposing 100-foot attack boat came alongside us, with various 20mm canons aimed directly at us. A rope was thrown towards Xavier and Vincent and they tied it up to *Maruxa*. An officer and three soldiers climbed on board our boat, as eight others aimed their weapons at Xavier and Vincent.

"I am *Oberleutnant Hans Reisden*, commander of S-7. What are you doing in these waters?"

"*Bon jour* commander, I am Vincent Casas, and this is my son Xavier. We are just two simple fisherman, trying to make a living."

"Show me your papers," commanded the German officer. They took out their identification papers and handed them over to the German.

"Banyuls-sur-Mer, where is that?" asked the officer.

"It is a small fishing village just southwest of Perpignan," answered Vincent.

"Are you not a little too far from where you live?" asked the officer.

"Normally we do not stray this far, but we have not had much luck on this trip, so we decided to venture further. Yesterday and this morning we had a good catch, and are now heading back."

"Show me your catch," ordered the German. Xavier opened up the fish box at the back of the boat that was brimming with Red Mullet, Turbot, and Sea Bream.

"You do not mind if we check your boat?" asked the German, which was not intended as a question at all.

"Of course not!" answered Vincent jovially.

I could hear the thud of the boots on the deck above me as I prayed silently.

A soldier went down into the galley and came back out after a couple of minutes saying, "Nothing here."

Then I heard the floorboard that concealed the engine creak open. I held my breath, as I was even afraid that it might be heard.

"Nothing here either, *Herr Oberleutnant*," said one of the seamen. A loud thud accompanied the closing of the engine bay.

"You will not mind if we take some of your fish, *ja*?" asked the boat commander.

"No, of course not," answered Vincent as the Germans practically emptied the whole compartment of fish.

"Good day," said the German as he climbed back on the S-boat.

"Bastards," said Vincent under his breath as the S-boat quickly disappeared from view.

"Okay *ma cherie*, you can come out now. They are gone," I finally heard Xavier say a few minutes later.

I crawled out coughing and covered in grime.

"Wow, that was close," I said.

"Yes my dear, we were all very fortunate," acknowledged Xavier.

"Okay, time for breakfast," announced Vincent cheerily, as if nothing had happened.

It had almost been twenty-four hours since we had left Imperia when we first caught a glimpse of Banyuls-sur-Mer. A short man with a well-worn brown leather jacket was awaiting our arrival on the main pier of the harbor. He introduced himself as Gerald and brusquely asked me if I was ready to go. I gave Vincent and Xavier each a big hug and jumped off the deck of *Maruxa* and followed my new companion to a street nearby.

"A motorcycle? We are going to cross all of southern France on a motorcycle?" I exclaimed as I looked at the Motobecane.

"Unfortunately, my car is indisposed at this moment as it is having engine trouble. So, you can get on this motorbike with me or you can walk on your own. Whatever you wish, Countess," Gerald answered sarcastically.

"This man was the first rude person I had encountered on my exodus from Vienna and the thought of riding a motorcycle with him for over 400 miles was not in the least bit appealing!" said the Countess, laughing.

"From Banyuls-sur-Mer we made our way north to Rivesaltes, and then headed east. To say the ride was uncomfortable is the understatement of the year! By the time we reached Foix, south of Toulouse, it was getting dark and Gerald decided that we should spend the night at an inn.

"That evening as we were having dinner at a bistro near our inn, I asked him, "If we are only about four hours away from Saint-Jean-de-Luz, why did we stop here? We could have made it there by midnight."

"My dear Countess," he started to answer in what was now becoming a typical cynical tone, "even though we are driving on back roads to avoid our Nazi friends, if we were to be spotted at nightfall we would raise alarms as to what we were doing, while during the day we would likely not arouse much suspicion."

"Ah, that makes sense," I replied.

"Yes, it does," answered Gerald acerbically.

The next morning after a breakfast of *croissants* and *café au lait* we continued on our journey. As he headed west we passed Bagneres-de-Bigorre, then Pau, and had just ridden by the town of Espelette when disaster struck. Our Motobecane started spewing black smoke and backfiring and then just stopped altogether. Gerald tried to kick start it for the next ten minutes to no avail.

"*Merde! Merde! Merde!*" he yelled.

I just stood quietly by the motorbike trying not to panic or think about what we were going to do now.

"It looks like it has overheated. Perhaps if we just let the bike cool down for a while it will start up again," he said optimistically.

An hour later he tried to start up the old Motobecane, but it was fruitless.

Sweating profusely, he finally gave up and said, "Okay we are about twelve miles from where I live in Ascain. Once we reach there, we can find another means of transportation so that I can be done with this stupid mission," he said angrily.

I finally had enough and said, "Stupid mission?"

"Yes Countess, I prefer not to babysit royals as I have better things to do with my time, like kill Germans!" he replied mockingly.

I answered back with a barrage of insults. "The only good part of riding a motorcycle with you is that I did not have to talk to you. I am sick and tired of your unpleasant nature, your constant complaining, and your hideous, overgrown Basque snout!"

Gerald just stood there and looked at me for a few seconds before bursting into laughter.

"Alright, alright, I am sorry. I have behaved like an ass, but how do you breathe out of that tiny thing?" he said, pointing at my nose smiling.

We both started laughing hysterically.

Finally he said, "Okay, let's get on our way to Ascain before it gets dark."

As we began our long walk he asked me, "Who are you anyhow, that you can have British Intelligence mobilize all of us into instant action?"

I related the story of what had transpired in the last days and my father's friendship with Lord Richard Cook.

"I am very sorry to hear about your parents Christiane. Your father seems like a very honorable person, of whom there are few left," said Gerald as he addressed me by my Christian name for the first time, putting his arm gently around my shoulders when he saw me tearing.

We spent the next few hours on foot chatting about our families, our pasts and what the future had in store for us. As time passed, I very much warmed up to this man who hid his soul from view. I had never talked so openly, so frankly, with a man. The sun was going down as we made our way up a steep hill.

"Just a couple of more miles and we will be there," Gerald was saying reassuringly when just an instant later we heard, "*Halt!*"

We turned around and saw a German army motorcycle and large truck about 50 yards down the hill on the road that traversed it. None of the soldiers had gotten out of the truck yet when Gerald pulled out his peculiar Welrod pistol and aimed it at the motorcycle driver and his passenger in the sidecar next to him. The gun barely made a sound as one of the riders yelled for help from his comrades, as he hunched over from the bullet that had hit him.

"Run!" screamed Gerald at me, as he followed directly behind. Bullets whizzed by as I ran as fast as I could.

We were about to reach a protective mound I heard Gerald say, "Damn it!"

I turned around I saw him on the ground clutching his waist with his left hand. Blood oozed from the side of his abdomen.

As I went to help him, he shouted at me, "No! Go on!"

I screamed back, "No!" as I helped him up and dragged him to the mound.

"Okay, listen to me," he said, heaving from the effort of even talking, as he took another gun out of his jacket and handed it to me. "Take this pistol and let me show you how to use it."

"You mean like this," as I took the safety off the Star Model 14 and chambered a 7.65 mm Browning caliber bullet.

"A woman after my own heart," said Gerald smiling.

"My father has taken me hunting since I was a little girl. Not all of us spent our youth playing with dolls," I replied.

"I will cover you from here while you make a run for it. Go north until you reach Ascain. Soon you will see the lights from the town that will serve as your guide. Make your way to my uncle's house on Rue…"

"That will not be necessary," I said interrupting him.

"What are you talking about Christiane?" he asked me puzzled.

"I am not leaving here without you," I answered.

"Christiane, my dear, please do not be silly, and let me die in vain. Give me the pleasure of seeing you escape to safety. Give a dying man his last wish," he said, almost begging.

"Gerald, I just left my father and started running. I am not doing that again. Besides, I am finally starting to enjoy your company." With that, I reached over and gave him a passionate kiss!

"Okay!" we heard and both spun around to look behind us where the voice had come from, weapons in hand.

Four men came out of the dark.

"Sorry to interrupt your *petite* love fest my Basque friend, but don't you think it is time we get out of here?" asked Manuel, grinning.

"You always have the worst timing," replied Gerald. "Christiane, this is Manuel, my Andalusian brother from another mother. He is also known as the Matador. Bixente, Mikel and Julen form the rest of our merry gang of outlaws."

The three Resistance fighters just nodded in acknowledgement. Manuel took off Gerald's jacket to take a closer look at his wound.

"You are losing a lot of blood my friend, but at least the bullet went completely thru and looks like it missed any major organs," he said, taking off his shirt and tying it tightly around Gerald's waist, who winced in pain.

"You would make a lousy doctor," Gerald growled.

"And you a worse patient," Manuel replied, smiling.

At this point Manuel, who even though was the youngest in the group, took command.

"Mikel and Bixente, circle down around the hill and come in from behind the truck and the motorcycle. Since our Nazi friends believe they are chasing two people and know one is injured, they will probably only leave a couple of soldiers guarding the vehicles, one of them being the radioman. Take them out when the rest of the group is at least 60 yards up the hill. Knife the tires in the truck, grab the radio and take off in the motorcycle. Break the rear light so that they cannot use it as a target as you drive away. Dump the motorbike in a ditch before you get to Ascain and cut the brake cables so that if somebody does find it they will not be able to use it. Then make your way to the cabin. Christiane, on my signal you will run up the hill. Find the best hiding place you can and get down on the ground. I will carry Gerald on my shoulder and will be right behind you. Julen, you will cover us as we go up the hill. As soon as the three of us reach a spot with decent protection, we will take our position and start firing at the Germans. Julen, this will be your sign to rush towards us while we cover you. We will continue to make our way up the hill until Mikel and Bixente create a diversion down below. At that point they should be confused enough and will probably head back to their truck, giving us enough time to lose them. Any questions?"

No one said a word.

"All right then, Mikel and Bixente get going."

The two men took off and were quickly out of sight.

"Okay old man, let's see how heavy you are," Manuel told Gerald as he lifted him over his shoulder. Gerald was in excruciating pain but did not utter a word.

"You ready to get some exercise, Countess?" asked Manuel, smiling.

"I have never been more ready Matador," I answered as bravely as I could.

"Good, because I need you to run like the air in a hurricane. Julen, on my word, start firing. First take out the headlights of that motorcycle and truck that are pointing at us. Countess, as soon as the lights are out, start running. Okay Julen, go!" ordered Manuel.

I could feel an adrenaline rush overcome my body as I dashed up the hill, the sound of gunfire all around me. I just kept looking forward for somewhere where we could momentarily take refuge. After about thirty-five yards I found a place and dived to the ground. A few seconds later Manuel and Gerald slumped to the ground next to me. Manuel was sweating profusely and breathing heavily. He rested for a few seconds to catch his breath.

"Jesus you are heavy! I am going to put you on a diet if we ever get out of this one!" he told Gerald.

"Very funny Matador, but I think you need to work on bulking up, so you get stronger. You seem quite weak. I cannot believe that you can hardly keep up with a girl!" Gerald grinned through his increasing pain.

I was amazed at how calm both men were in the face of the danger we were in. Manuel started firing his rifle at the approaching Germans and I could see Julen dashing towards us.

After Julen reached us, I asked Manuel, "How did you know we were here?"

"Gerald had called his uncle Iker last night from Foix, and he let us know that you were spending the night there. We figured if all went as planned that you would have arrived at our cabin sometime this morning. So when you did not show up and with our car broken down, we decided to go on a walk in the direction of Espelette, where you should have been coming from. You are very lucky because we were about to turn back when we heard the gunshots that led us to both of you."

"Okay my Basque brother, are you ready to get going again?" Manuel asked Gerald.

"I am as ready as I am ever going to be, my friend," replied Gerald.

"Alright, let's get this over with," said Manuel as he hoisted Gerald over his shoulder and followed me again as I sprinted back up the hill.

A small outcropping gave us another place to rest as Manuel was wheezing from the effort of carrying Gerald. Manuel started firing his Rigby again, while Julen sprinted once again to our temporary hideout. Just as Julen was about to reach us he went down from a gunshot to his right shoulder. Manuel jumped out and dragged him to safety.

"*Mierda!* Now we are really in trouble, we have lost our cover man," exclaimed Manuel, as it was apparent that Julen could no longer shoot a gun. "Matador, I can stay back and keep the Germans at bay while you guys go on," I suggested.

"I don't like it, but it looks like we have no other choice right now. Okay Christiane, take Julen's rifle and take over his duties. Julen you will leave first like Christiane did before, and I will follow with Gerald," commanded Manuel.

Just then we heard gunshots coming from far below.

"That must be Bixente and Mikel firing at the Germans. Alright let's all get out of here now, as they will not be able to hold the Germans for long!" said Manuel.

We all rushed up the hill and soon were on the other side, as the German soldiers were preoccupied with their vanishing transportation.

The diversion created by the earlier gunfire on the hill, plus the fact that it was getting dark, had allowed Bixente and Mikel to go unnoticed as they took a wide arc down the hill and behind the German vehicles. The two German soldiers never had a chance, as simultaneously they felt a hand over their mouths and a knife plunge into their lower spines, paralyzing them instantly before they both keeled over dead. Mikel then slit the two front and four rear tires of the Opel Blitz utility truck, while Bixente took the radio and strapped it on his back.

They broke the rear taillight of the BMW R75 motorcycle and were about to make their getaway when Bixente, who was about to take his seat in the sidecar next to Mikel, said, "Hold on. Those Nazis are getting too close to the Matador and company. Let me see if I can take a few of them out and distract them long enough for our friends to get away."

He took careful aim and started shooting at their enemy. At first the Germans could not figure out why some of their fellow soldiers were being shot down as they were taking very little fire from the top of the hill. Then one heard a shot being fired from the bottom of the hill next to their truck and realized what was happening. Soon they reversed their aim and started shooting downhill at the very same time that they heard the sound of a motorcycle roaring off.

A couple of hours later we finally reached the cabin where Bixente and Mikel were waiting for us. We quickly tended to Gerald and Julen's wounds, but Gerald had lost a lot of blood. Fortunately, Julen's wound was nothing that a few stitches could not remedy.

Manuel pulled out the MCR-1 radio and let the British know what had happened. He told them Gerald would need to be extracted along with me as he was in dire need of serious medical attention. Taking him to a hospital anywhere nearby would arouse too much attention, so it was not an alternative.

"Looks like you finally found a way to get out of this war and on top of it with a beautiful woman," smiled Manuel at Gerald.

"Well, she is a lot more pleasant to look at than you guys!" replied Gerald in good humor.

"I must tell you Countess, that my friend usually complains a lot more about everything. So the influence you are exerting over him is much appreciated. He is almost becoming pleasant, but just almost!" added Manuel, laughing.

Two days later, the Renault 6CV was finally fixed with the help of a local mechanic that was a friend of Gerald's, allowing Manuel and Bixente to drive us to the nearby village of Saint-Jean-de-Luz on the Bay of Biscay. There a small fishing boat took us out to a rendezvous point about four miles out to sea from the Spanish city of Bilbao, where a Royal Navy Motor Torpedo Boat was awaiting to transport us to Brighton.

Once on board, Gerald was finally able to get the necessary medical attention he sorely needed. By the time we reached Brighton, early the next morning, he was on his way to recuperating fully.

Lord Richard and Lady Leah Cook were there waiting to pick us up in their regal, bi-colored 1937 Rolls Royce Phantom III Touring Limousine. We all drove off to their magical estate, where we remained until the war ended, just over a year later."

"Ladies, if Manuel had been the one to pick me up at Banyuls-sur-Mer on that Motobecane motorcycle, who knows, he might be the man I would be married to today," said the Countess.

"He is awfully handsome," she added. Blushing as she did so.

"Well Countess, if you must know, Celia here, has long had her eyes cast on Manolo," I added jokingly.

"Trini, stop it! You are embarrassing me," replied Celia.

"Well my dear, I would not waste time in letting him know that you would be open to his overtures, as men like Manuel come around but once in a lifetime," the Countess advised Celia.

"And Carlos, slowly but surely that is what Celia did, and within a year and a half they were getting married. She will never replace Maria in his heart and she knows that, but she has made him happy and allowed him to move on and find peace in his life," added Trini.

14

"After World War II ended in June 1945," continued Trini, "Manuel told us how one morning he decided it was time to head home. He grabbed a backpack with the few clothes that he owned, said his goodbyes to Mikel, Bixente, and Julen, and then set out on foot towards Spain. He crossed over the border into San Sebastian and hitched rides to Burgos, then to Madrid, and finally arrived in Córdoba after almost a week of traveling, barely having anything to eat as he did not have much money to spare."

"Was he not afraid of getting caught by Franco's army and being shot or incarcerated?" asked Carlos.

"I guess after everything he had gone through in the last nine years he was not scared of anything, but we were," answered Trini. "There were still elements in Morente that maintained a healthy dose of outspoken resentment towards the Republicans. Chief amongst them was Antonio, my brother, who was the town's *Guardia Civil* representative, the military police that Franco used to control rural areas, and had never liked Manuel. I think it was more jealousy than hatred. My mother, Rosa, realized that this could become a dangerous situation, went to see Antonio the very same afternoon that Manuel showed up here at the estate. When she walked into the small building that housed the police station and a single jail cell, Father Juanjo was inside talking to my brother.

"Mother, what are you doing here, is something wrong?" asked Antonio.

"I am here to find out what you are planning to do about Manuel's return to Morente."

"Rosa," jumped in Father Juanjo, "I believe we have a moral obligation to alert the authorities in Córdoba. This could also bode well for your son and possibly get him a promotion."

"Antonio," said my mother, "has there not already been enough blood and tears shed all over this country for a godforsaken war? Have we not suffered enough even in this tiny village? Do you realize what this would do to my dear friend Araceli? After the pain she and Eugenio have endured for all these years, if you pick up that phone and tell anyone about Manuel's presence in this village you will stop being my son and I shall never speak to you for the rest of my life."

"Rosa, you are overreacting..." but before Father Juanjo could finish my mother glared at him and said, "Father, Manuel is a very close friend of Count Esteban. The same Count who is mostly responsible for the upkeep of the church, the house you live in, as well as the food you eat. You control the minds of the people of this village and Antonio controls their bodies with his authority, so if anything happens to Manuel, I will only blame you and my son. So, help me God, if a single word of Manuel's arrival leaks out, I will remind the Count every day of my life that it was your fault, so that he does not give you or the church a single *peseta*."

After a few moments of complete silence Father Juanjo looked at Antonio and said, "Your mother is right my son, it is time to forgive and let the wounds begin to heal."

"Thank you both, I knew you would understand," my mother said as she left.

The following Sunday at the church sermon, Father Juanjo talked of the need to mend, of moving forward without holding a grudge, of rebuilding and not blaming anymore. Nobody ever brought up the subject of Manuel and his role during the Civil War again."

"Trini, tell me more about the day Manuel arrived at the estate," pleaded Carlos.

"As the evening arrived, he at last broached the delicate subject of Maria. Don Esteban told him about what had happened in Morente since the time he had left."
"Nobody thought you were alive. I knew Maria was waiting for you and settled for me."
"You are wrong Esteban. You were always the one for her. She was in love with you, and that is why she forced me to help you escape to Seville," said Manuel.
"I do not know that I agree with you but thank you for saying that my friend. I doubt if either one of us deserved her," replied Don Esteban.
"Yes, on that I think we can both agree," smiled Manuel before continuing, "Well, Esteban, I should be going now. I cannot thank you enough for your hospitality."
"Nonsense Manolo, it is I who should thank you for your company. I have missed our conversations greatly. What are you planning on doing now?"
"Well, I fear my dream of becoming a bullfighter has passed me by, so to tell you the truth I am not quite sure yet."
"Would you do me a huge favor and come by tomorrow morning? Join me for breakfast and then let us go take a look at my herd of bulls and give me your opinion about them."
"I would be delighted."

The next morning Manuel showed up at the estate and joined Don Esteban for breakfast before getting on some horses and riding out towards where the herd was grazing.

After returning to the stables and dismounting, Don Esteban asked, "What do you think, Manolo?"

"Even my grandmother would not be scared of fighting those bulls," answered Manuel.

The various stable hands that were listening to the conversation were obviously mortified by the statement and were not prepared for the Count's response. He started laughing.

"Oh my God Manolo! I love your honesty my friend. Everyone here is too afraid to tell me the truth. Come, let's go talk inside."

They went into the library, where Don Esteban continued the conversation. "Why don't you come and work here and help me turn these cows into real fighting bulls?"

"You are not doing this just to try to help me, are you Esteban?" asked Manuel.

"Of course not Manolo. I am offering this to you for purely selfish reasons. No one around these parts knows more about bulls than you do. Besides I do not have anyone interesting to talk to around here! Also, I think Maria would like it if you helped me raise her daughter," Don Esteban added in a more serious tone.

"Okay, let me digest all this and let you know tomorrow," said Manuel.

The next day Manuel pedaled his bicycle into the estate to begin working for Don Esteban. From that moment onward they spent most of their time together.

"Esteban," Manuel said one day soon after he began working at the estate, "we have to start building a violent herd. I think we should go and visit what I believe to be the breeder of the finest fighting bulls in all of Spain."

186

"And who would that be?" inquired Don Esteban.
"Eduardo Miura, whose father and uncle own a ranch that he is taking over. It lies just outside of Seville," said Manuel.

Several days later on a crisp early morning that did not seem to want to awaken, Manuel and Don Esteban headed towards Seville in the Count's magnificent 1935 Hispano-Suiza J-12 Cabriolet adorned by Jacques Saoutchik's sensual coachwork. The mighty 690 cubic inch twelve-cylinder engine easily powered the car to speeds over 100 miles per hour, the flying stork mascot atop the polished stainless-steel radiator effortlessly gliding along, and soon they were motoring towards the small village of Lora del Rio, on whose outskirts lay Zahariche ranch, the home of Miura bulls.

Eduardo Miura greeted Manuel warmly. "It must have been over ten years ago but I still remember watching you fight a couple of *novilladas* and thinking to myself, this kid is special."

"Thank you, I am honored," responded Manuel. "Let me introduce my friend Esteban, the Count of Morente."

"Your Highness, I had the good fortune of meeting your father at the Maestranza bullring in Seville on a number of occasions. He was quite an aficionado and very knowledgeable. I was saddened to hear about his tragic death and that of your mother," the bull breeder told Don Esteban.

"Thank you."

"Well gentlemen, how can I be of service?" asked Eduardo.

Manuel explained to him that they wished to improve the quality of what was currently a mediocre herd and hoped that he may counsel them on how to go about doing it.

"First thing," began Eduardo, "is to find out which of the bulls are worth keeping, either for fighting next spring if they are now around three to four years old, or for breeding if they are older. The same applies to the cows that you are planning to keep for reproducing. The ones that do not fit the profile that you are looking for will need to be eliminated. Initially this is going to downsize the herd considerably and it will be some time before you are able to build it back up and make some money. Are you ready to make that sort of commitment?"

"Eduardo, in the long run, a reputable breeding program will be much more profitable, so we will just have to endure until we accomplish that. How large do you think the herd needs to be to be financially successful?" Don Esteban asked.

"If you can manage to sell about seventy-two to eighty-four bulls a year— enough for twelve to fourteen top notch bullfights— that would be excellent. You will need the herd to be around 700 head so as to be able to have enough quality bulls to choose from to sell for *corridas*, while at the same time leaving you enough to breed and continue strengthening the herd. For breeding you will need to have one bull for every twenty to twenty-five cows." Eduardo continued, "In the following weeks take the bulls and cows out to pasture one by one and hold a *tienta*, whereby each bull or cow is knocked down by a long, blunt wooden spear by a rider atop one of your Andalusian horses. The object of this is not to injure the animal, but instead to see how they react. Those that get up quickly and aggressively charge the horse that has assailed them, should be separated and kept. Those bulls or cows that seem scared or docile should be sold off. Remember that the only contact the herd should have with humans from this point on is when someone is bringing them food. And talking about that, because of the war and the food shortages there have been, most bulls have gotten too small and are not strong enough to endure an entire *corrida*. Make sure you get them to weigh at least a thousand pounds and that their diet is made up of mostly hay, for fattening them up, and oats, to give them energy. A couple of months before the bullfighting season starts, separate those bulls that you are going to sell for *corridas* in groups of eight, six for the fight, and two bulls as back up in case something goes wrong during the bullfight. The bullring managers want all the bulls in a *corrida* to have the same look and size, so make sure the separated groups are as homogeneous as possible. From now on, try not to buy bulls or cows from others to augment your stock, and instead develop your own breed of fighting bull, as in the long run this is what will make your bulls unique and get you the highest prices. In turn, when your herd gets to be of the quality that you want, my advice is that you only sell your bulls for fights and not to other farms for them to use for breeding."

They spent the rest of the morning and early afternoon on horseback wandering around the 1,500-acre ranch taking a look at the bulls and listening to Eduardo Miura talk about the characteristics that distinguish his bulls.

"The typical Miura is taller and longer than an average bull. They have large necks and small bellies, and their hides are fine and shiny, not rough or dull. The face of the bull also looks young and energetic. In the ring they are known to be very aggressive and have tremendous stamina."

As they were saying goodbye and thanking their host for the vast wealth of knowledge he had generously shared with them, Don Esteban told Eduardo, "I hope you come and visit us in Morente and allow us to repay some of your kind hospitality."

"Yes, I would enjoy that very much," replied Eduardo.

On the trip back to Morente, Manuel and Don Esteban could not stop talking about all they had observed that day. Both men started to spend the major part of their days together, and as they did, it was apparent to all of us that the bond between them was unique. Manuel stopped being another person that worked at the estate and instead became the confidant and most trusted adviser of the Count. The time that they did not spend out on the pastures observing the herd was taken up by lengthy oratory sessions in the library or being with Alexandra.

She was consumed with interest in the horses, and Manuel started to teach her to ride. He and Don Esteban would spend countless hours at the corral watching and coaching Alexandra on one of the ponies. No matter how much time she would spend riding, it was never enough, and she would constantly complain when either one suggested that it was time to end the session. The other pastime that mesmerized her was when every once in a while, Manuel would grab a cape and go out to the small bullring to show a prospective bullring manager the fortitude and resilience of bulls that were now being raised at the estate. Everyone would stop their chores and sit in the single row of seats that circumvented the plaza, as Manuel tantalized us with daring passes to our repeated shouts of *"Ole!"* He was so graceful and never showed any sign of fear. Alexandra would sit next to her father smiling and cheering like the rest of us, until Manuel felt that the poor bull was tired enough and sent it back to the fields to join the rest of the herd. Soon the bulls of the Count of Morente got a reputation as one of the up-and-coming breeds in Andalusia and some of the best-known matadors started to visit us to check out the bulls firsthand. Gitanillo de Triana, Luis Miguel Dominguin, and even the legendary Manolete, amongst many others, all came here."

"Manolete! Manolete came here?" Carlos exclaimed.

"Yes dear, he even gave us a short demonstration. It was like watching magic and elegance intertwined. He was quiet and reserved, except around Manuel and Don Esteban. Then he would become animated and talkative. It was so sad the day we heard of his death that awful day in August of 1947. It was as if everyone in Andalusia had lost a member of their family," replied Trini solemnly.

"Anyhow," Trini went on, "soon Alexandra was asking Manuel to teach her how to bullfight. At first Manuel was reticent to show her, but as you must already know, Alexandra is not easily deterred by anyone or anything! After continually being a nuisance about the subject, she finally was able to convince her father and Manuel to allow her to be taught. I think that initially both of them thought that like most children, she would get bored of the considerable training on a wooden bull on wheels, and all would be done and forgotten. The opposite was true! She thrived and would spend countless hours practicing every type of pass, until she wore out the poor ranch hands that had to push the wooden bull around! It was also obvious from the start that she was a natural. Her movements were unusually fluid and lacked the awkwardness common in a beginner.

"When she reached her twelfth birthday, Manuel allowed her to start practicing in front of calves, albeit with their horns heavily taped so that they could not pierce her skin. Still, a two-hundred-pound animal can inflict plenty of hurt if they barrel into you. Yet, every time Alexandra got plowed, and it happened on plenty of occasions, just when we thought she would finally give up on this silly endeavor of hers, she would brush the sand off herself, grab her cape and practice with even more intensity.

Manuel first taught her how to perform the different kind of passes with the heavy canvas cape.

"You must envision a bull's path before he starts his run. That is his rectangle, his area of influence. Your rectangle is the area where you stand. You must foresee these rectangles shifting constantly without ever overlapping. It is only when you the thrust the *estoque*, or sword of death, into the bull at the end of the *corrida*, that the two rectangles collide."

"A bullfight has three acts," he would tell her, "the first in which the bull is anxious, full of energy, where you must start to learn his movements. What side does he favor? How quickly does he turn his head after chasing the cape and does he flick his horns up? How fast does he turn around and charge again? Use the *veronica* pass— in which you carve a figure eight in the air with the cape as the bull glides past you— to find this out. It is the most difficult pass to make, but when it is executed well, it is also the most beautiful. First open the cape wide open as the bull drops his head and prepares to charge, lower the cape after the charge is averted while the animal passes as close to you as possible, and lift the cape again with a sweeping arc to send the bull away with the horns touching nothing but air. Towards the end of the first act you must bring the bull to the *picador*. To do this use the cape as if it where a fan. You distract the animal in such a way that it does not realize where it is going until all of a sudden it is in front of the horse."

"In the second act three different *banderilleros* each thrust two short spears in the bull's torso. Now the bull is angry and here the *serpentina* pass with its long sweeping cape movements keeps the bull from getting too close to you. As he starts to tire then you can use the more dramatic *gaonera* or *mariposa* passes, where you hold the cape behind your back as he goes by."

"In the third and final act you exchange the large cerise and golden-colored cape for the small bright scarlet one called the *muleta*. Now you use the *natural* pass, where your feet are planted, your left hand sweeping the *muleta* across your body and taking the bull with you, while holding the *estoque* in your right one. The most difficult part of the bullfight is the kill, the moment of truth. You must wait for the bull to tire enough so that he lowers his head, but not too long so that he is so exhausted that he no longer charges the *muleta*. Now you must fixate your eyes on a tiny region behind between the shoulder blades and lunge forward over the horns, for this is the only place where he will die quickly and honorably."

"By the time she was sixteen, Alexandra was killing young bulls that were not aggressive enough for bullfights, and instead would be sold to the local butcher shops. At nineteen, the bullring manager of the biggest plaza in Spain, Las Ventas in Madrid, after watching her perform at the estate, invited her to do her *alternativa*, whereby a novice is allowed to complete their first *corrida* against mature bulls in order to become a full-fledged matador. Everyone, not only at the estate, but also in all of Morente, could not have been more excited. The Count announced to the whole village that he would hire buses to drive everyone to Madrid and pay for the entrance to the plaza for those that wished to go see Alexandra at this momentous occasion."

"Manuel went off to Córdoba and Seville to talk to his friends in the business. They started to gather up a *cuadrilla*, or team for Alexandra, that consisted of two *picadors*, three banderilleros, who also acted as bullfighting assistants, and a *mozo de espada*, who took care of the swords and capes of the matador. He put one of the older and more experienced *banderilleros*, Cesar Calderón, in charge of the other five men. Manuel became the de facto manager of Alexandra together with the Count, who organized the transportation, meals, and hotels of the entire *cuadrilla* and took care of their wages and other expenses."

"I will never forget that glorious day in the spring of 1960. We could not contain our enthusiasm," continued Trini. "Alexandra looked so radiant in her shimmering suit with gold accents. She came out onto the plaza with the two other featured matadors on each side of her followed by the eighteen men that formed the three *cuadrillas*, with a large band playing *paso dobles*. I was seated between Celia and my mother. All she could say was, "My baby! My baby looks so young. Oh God, please protect her! Oh please Lord!"

We had wonderful seats just above the corridor, which separated us from the plaza. Just below us was Manolo with Alexandra and her team waiting for her turn to debut.

The other two matadors went first and although they fought well, they did not receive more than a shy ovation at the end of their work, as the crowds in Las Ventas are known for being quite demanding. When it was finally Alexandra's turn to fight the first of two bulls that afternoon, it was obvious from the moment she stepped into the arena that she was extremely nervous, as anyone would undoubtedly be if they were bullfighting in front of almost 25,000 passionate spectators for the first time! She appeared to be trying too hard. She seemed awkward and even frustrated. When the moment came to kill the bull, it took her three attempts to accomplish the feat, by which time there were murmurings of dissent descending from the crowd. When she ended and returned to the corridor, and as the next matador went back out for his second bull, she was practically in tears. Manuel put his arm around her without saying a single word and they watched the next two matadors perform. At last, almost forty minutes later, the time came for her to fight her second and last bull of the day.

Just before she reentered the plaza Manuel held her hands, looked into her eyes and said, "Just pretend you are back at the ring at the estate. You have practiced those passes for over ten years. Let them be! Do not think! Feel! Now go out there and show these peasants what it is to really bullfight!"

"Alexandra was suddenly transformed. You could sense the confidence building with every pass of the cape as she got daringly close to the huge beast."

"*Toro, Toro!*" she started yelling each time the bull went by to lure him back towards her. The crowd responded to the show of bravery with constant "*Oles!*" that got louder and louder. On the third and final act she killed the bull on her first attempt as everyone cheered from the stands and took out white handkerchiefs to implore the presiding dignitary to give her an ear of the bull as a sign of a great performance, which he did. Then she was hoisted upon the shoulder of one of the other matadors and paraded around the entire bullring followed by her entire *cuadrilla* while the crowd tossed carnations at her. We were all ecstatic and no one wanted to leave the plaza. That evening the Count took everyone out to dinner at Salvador, the restaurant where traditionally bullfighters and aficionados gather after a fight. As we entered the restaurant everyone inside got up and started clapping wildly. "Well done! Well done!"

The mood, as one can imagine, was very festive and was further perpetuated by the never-ending stream of bottles of fine Rioja. Towards the end of dinner Don Esteban stood up, goblet of wine in hand, and said to his daughter, "Alexandra, I think I speak on behalf of everyone at this table, when I say we could not be more proud of you!" Everyone clapped and yelled, "Here, Here!"

Then Manuel, who was sitting next to Don Esteban and across the table from Alexandra, got up, let the crowd settle down, and said these words that I will never forget: "Today the student has become the master. There is nothing else left for me to teach you my dear; I am now learning from you."

At that point she ran around the table and hugged her father and Manuel, tears streaming from her beautiful eyes. As Havana cigars and brandy from Jerez was being passed around, I overheard Don Esteban tell Manuel,

"Our little girl has become a woman. I believe we have not done our job too badly. Thank you, Manolo."

"It is I who should thank you Esteban, for letting me be a part of her life," replied Manuel.

"I could not have done it without you my friend," replied the Count.

The next day the principal newspaper of Madrid, the ABC, related how "the young and striking Countess of Morente showed great style, bravery and promise in her unveiling as a matador at Las Ventas yesterday afternoon."

Initially, after her successful start at Las Ventas, we all expected her to be highly sought after by the managers of the major bullrings around the country, but this was not to be so. It was quickly apparent that they were hesitant to take the chance on a female bullfighter. There had always been so much machismo associated with the sport; most managers were not sure how the crowds would respond to a woman matador. How would they react to seeing a young woman tossed by a bull? And how would the male matadors fighting alongside Alexandra feel? Would they think that the whole affair amounted to some kind of perverse freak show?

It was not till she befriended a rising young matador with a daring and unorthodox style and started headlining alongside him that she started to get exposure.

"Who was that?" Carlos asked.

"Manuel Benítez Pérez, although you are more likely to know him as 'El Cordobés', the one from Córdoba."

"He was sort of a rebel in and out of the bullring, and did not care what people thought about him nor whom he fought alongside with. We all knew he had a great fondness for Alexandra and many of us suspect he had a long-running affair with her. She has never admitted to it, but she has never denied it either. And how could she resist, because that is a man any woman would die to sleep with!"

Carlos could feel a burst of jealousy within him as Trini went on.

"The years that followed were filled with triumphs and the inevitable agony and worry that we all went through when she was occasionally tossed by a bull. Thank God that she has never been seriously gored!"

"And there you have it my dear Carlitos! That is the story of Don Manuel," finished Trini with a smile.

15

That afternoon Manuel and Celia returned from their voyage to Madrid. Carlos noticed that Celia was her same cheery self but that Don Manuel seemed distracted by distant thoughts and immediately headed to the library to have a long private meeting with the Count.

Later on that evening the mood at dinner seemed unusually somber, but towards the end the Count changed the solemn tone by announcing that the following day, Don Manuel, Carlos, and he would go hunting for wild boar, as a number had been recently spotted at the periphery of the estate.

The next morning at breakfast the Count told Alexandra to meet them in town for a drink at Pepe's bar around two o'clock in the afternoon, after the morning hunt. As the men took off on their excursion, the morning conversation started with the news that university students in Madrid had held demonstrations in the city the day before that had been forcefully ended by the heavily armed national police. They had been voicing their dissatisfaction with the continued crackdown on freedom of speech, women's rights, together with the government's control of the press.

"Until that monster dies nothing will change in this country," began Don Esteban. Carlos was taken by surprise by the comment. It was extremely rare to hear such a frank and critical statement about General Franco, specially coming from a member of a sect in society whose affiliations are usually very pro-fascist.

"What do you mean Don Esteban, are you not a supporter of Generalissimo Franco?" asked Carlos.

"My dear Carlos, I was. During the Civil War, I favored the Nationalists, as I felt the Republican government was leading the country into certain chaos. My view of General Franco slowly started to diminish as I heard rumors of more and more atrocities. Do not get me wrong; Manolo and his Republican friends also committed heinous acts. In wars nobody gets sainthood medals, but what led me to be particularly leery of Franco were the retributions towards his enemies that occurred for years after the Civil War had ended. The oppression of the Basques and the Catalans for the last thirty years by his regime has been particularly harsh and uncalled for. Also, with the passage of time, pledges he made at the end of the war turned out to be broken promises."

"Such as?" asked Carlos.

"In 1947 he proclaimed Spain to be a monarchy, but did not designate a monarch, as he never completely trusted that the exiled king's son, Don Juan de Borbon, would lead Spain in the right direction, for he perceived him to be too liberal. Instead he promoted himself to captain general, which is the king's rank, moved into the Royal Palace, and made people refer to him as Leader of Spain by the Grace of God. A title that historically has only been used by Kings. In effect he anointed himself King of Spain."

"Many would argue that to be born of royal blood does not necessarily make you fit to be a king, and there are plenty of examples in history books to make the point. Generalissimo Franco, they would say, with his autocratic power has been a more effective ruler than most any birthright king would have been during the past three decades. The trouble with having a supreme leader of any kind is that power is a seductive siren. It makes one feel immortal, and that one can never do or be wrong. Over time it distances you from the masses and then you become paranoid that someone will take that sacred power from you. This isolation moves you figuratively further from your subjects, so that in the end you do not know them at all. You can not relate to them as you do not have anything in common."

"In reality Carlos," began Don Manuel, "no one is free. Humans by their very nature of being social animals and belonging to a collective group, are bound by laws and rules that are established by others. To be truly free one would have to live without any contact with or influence from any other human. Yet while a democracy is an imperfect system to voice the opinions of the masses, it is the most fair. It reflects the most differences and is the most human. Let there be no doubt that it exacts a high price, the proof being the drugs, pornography and higher rates of crime that exist in our democratic neighbors, but is a direction that Spain must take."

"But how? How can things change when people live in fear of speaking out?" Carlos asked.

"In time, young man. Time is the great equalizer and patience her mistress. Cries for change like those we hear from the university students in Madrid will eventually be heard by the rest of the people in this country. Then they will rise up and join them," answered the Count. "Besides, not even General Franco can live forever," added Don Manuel, smiling.

"Well that day will not come soon enough," concluded Carlos.

The hunt did not bear any success but the three men continued to enjoy their chat until, after about four hours of walking, they ended up at the modest establishment owned by Pepe Pastor that served as the village social center and its only drinking establishment.

Pepe greeted them as they sat down at an empty table in the corner. On the opposite side of the room sat two men in their early twenties in torn jeans and ragged t-shirts that neither Don Esteban nor Don Manuel recognized. Pepe was bringing the three men some Manzanilla olives stuffed with anchovies to nibble on when Alexandra walked in. After greeting her father and Don Manuel she turned her attention onto Carlos.

"Well how was the hunting this morning," she asked jovially.

"Not very good, but the discussion during our walk was most enlightening," he answered.

"Yes, I imagine so," she laughed.

"What would you like to drink my dear?" asked the Count.

"I think I will have some Fino Sherry, thank you," she answered. "How about you Manolo and Carlos?"

"I will have a beer please," Carlos answered.

"A gin and tonic for me," replied Don Manuel.

Pepe set the drinks on the bar and Carlos began to stand up, but Alexandra smiled and said, "I will do that, you all look like you still need to rest from your morning walk."

As she walked to the bar one of the men from the other side of the room went up to the bar, stood next to her and said, "Hey pretty lady, how about a little dance?"

Before she could answer Pepe interjected by saying, "Leave the lady alone, she is not interested."

"Why don't you shut up old man and turn that old radio on so that I can dance with the lovely lady," said the young man.

"I am sorry, but I do not dance with strangers," Alexandra told the man.

"Well maybe I can change that?"

Don Manuel walked over to the bar. Carlos was about to follow him when the Count grabbed his arm and whispered to him. "Carlitos sit down and let the old man have a little fun." Carlos hesitantly sat down in his chair again.

"Young man, I do believe the lady has told you she is not interested in your company. Why don't you sit down and leave her alone?"

"Or what, you ancient corpse? What are you going to do about..." and before he finished his threat Don Manuel whipped out a left jab that sent the man reeling backwards.

"Okay you son of a bitch, now you are in real trouble!" The youth lunged towards Don Manuel, who easily sidestepped him, but not before delivering two quick blows to his kidneys. Carlos and Don Esteban were smiling as they watched the man awkwardly trying to bludgeon Don Manuel with his fists but failing miserably on each occasion. Don Manuel looked liked grace in a hurry. He continually inflicted pain on his inexperienced and brash foe, who started to bleed from his nose and mouth. One last uppercut by Don Manuel sent the man sprawling to the floor. As he was starting get back up his companion got up from his seat and took a switchblade from his pocket.

"Old man, I am going to cut you in pieces!"

"Sit down!" A thunderous voice filled with five hundred years of aristocratic blood barred down upon the man holding the knife. The man turned and looked towards Don Esteban, who was pointing his father's Rigby rifle at him. "It has been a long time since I killed a man, but I have not forgotten how to do it," threatened the Count as he slammed the Mauser action forward, chambering a 7mm bullet into the barrel. The man slowly went back to his seat and was accompanied there by his bloodied friend. Alexandra and Don Manuel were returning to join Carlos and Don Esteban at their table when Antonio, the local *Guardia Civil*, walked into the bar. He immediately acknowledged the Count and the rest of his party before turning his attention on the other table. When he saw the switchblade lying on the table, he took out his black baton from its sheath by the side of his left leg and pointed it towards the knife.

"What do we have here? You boys are obviously not from these parts. In my town we do not tolerate trouble," and with that he slammed the baton down on the table crushing the fingers of the right hand of the owner of the blade, the horrible sound of broken bones echoing in the room. The man screamed in pain but dared not move.

"I suggest you get out of here right now, and I hope never to see your ugly faces around these parts again, or my greeting next time will be a lot more painful. Do I make myself clear?" continued Antonio.

"Yes sir!" they replied as they scrambled out of Pepe's bar.

"Esteban, I had everything under control, there was no need to pull that rifle out, scare those poor boys and end our game," smiled Don Manuel.

"Well you know how I hate to let you have all the fun," chuckled Don Esteban in reply.

"By the way, thanks for coming to my rescue," Alexandra said as she looked at Carlos.

Carlos who was not sure if she was upset or just kidding around started to reply, "But, but I was…"

Alexandra interrupted him with a smile, saying "Never mind trying to come up an excuse. It is too late. Gentlemen should we make our way back to the house before we get scolded by Trini and Celia for being late for lunch."

"Ah yes, we certainly do not want that!" smiled the Count.

As they were leaving Pepe's bar, Don Manuel excused himself and went into the restroom. While Don Esteban and Alexandra were saying their good-byes to Pepe, Carlos overheard Don Manuel coughing loudly and opened the door to the lavatory to check on him. When he walked in he saw Don Manuel hunched over the sink coughing. There was blood in the basin.

"Are you okay Don Manuel?"

"I am fine. It is just a little blood from a blow I took," replied Don Manuel.

"I did not see you get hit by a single punch," Carlos replied back.

"I said I got hit!" Don Manuel answered annoyed.

It took all the courage Carlos had inside for him to say to Don Manuel, "I am not moving from here until you tell me what is going on."

Don Manuel turned suddenly around to continue to argue, but after seeing the look of determination on Carlos' face he simply said, "Not here, not now. I will talk to you later."

"Okay," replied Carlos as they headed out to rejoin Alexandra and Don Esteban.

After lunch, while coffee was being served, Alexandra asked her father and Don Manuel about her new quest to become a *rejoneadora*. Both men listened attentively to her explain the difficulty of finding plazas to fight for the upcoming season. *Rejoneo* was a natural option that combined her two greatest loves, she said, and it was a lot less dangerous than fighting bulls on the ground. Carlos smiled to himself, thinking it was almost a verbatim repetition of his conversation with her a couple of days previous.

"What do you think Manolo?" asked the Count.

"While it is certainly less dangerous, it is no walk in the park. On the other hand, the option is not bad considering the limited offers to fight on foot you are now receiving. You are a good rider Alexandra, but it will take a year of constant training to get you up to speed." Don Manuel replied.

"A year!" exclaimed Alexandra.

"Yes, at least that long," Don Manuel stated unequivocally.

Alexandra was about to continue her protest when her father cut her off by saying, "Why don't you think about it for a couple of days Alexandra, and see if you are willing to commit yourself to this new endeavor."

"Fine," she agreed hesitantly.

At that point Don Manuel suggested to Carlos and Don Esteban that they retire to the library for their customary drink and cigar.

After they had settled into the leather couch to begin their afternoon ritual, Don Manuel said, "Esteban, I am afraid I must tell our friend Carlos here what is going on with my health, as today he saw me coughing up blood and caught me in a lie about it."

"Manolo, as time goes on, your secret will inevitably be harder to hide. Besides, we are going to need Carlos to help Alexandra cope with the situation," said Don Esteban.

"What secret? What situation? What is going on?" asked Carlos.

"Carlos, everyone, including Celia, thinks that I just went to Madrid to visit my daughter Isabella, but that was not the principal reason for my trip. About a month ago I began to cough up a little blood a few hours after having a meal. At first I thought that it was probably an ulcer, but as the weeks have gone by the amount of blood has increased. Esteban and I decided that I should seek some specialized medical advice, and he suggested I call an old friend of mine from the war, Brigadier General Randall Lewis, the commander of the United States Air

Force base in Torrejon, just outside of Madrid, to see if I could be examined by the doctors there. I used the excuse with Celia that I was visiting Randall, and spent most of the day last Friday having a series of tests done. Right before we left Madrid to come back to Morente, Randall told me that his doctors had diagnosed me with intestinal cancer."

"What does that mean?" inquired Carlos.

"Well this word cancer I think is a term used by doctors when they do not really know what is going on. They feel the disease is too advanced and that surgery would probably be of limited benefit, especially at my age," answered Don Manuel.

"How much time?" asked Carlos, afraid to hear the answer.

"Six months, a year if I am lucky," replied Don Manuel matter-of-factly.

"Oh my God! I am so sorry!" Carlos looked solemnly at the wooden floor beneath him.

"No need to feel sad for me Carlitos. My life has been well lived, and if my time has come, so be it. We need to worry about Isabella, Celia and Alexandra, and figure out how best to help them cope with this."

"Jesus Christ!" said Carlos to himself, the man is dying and he does not even skip a beat and flinch. "I hope I have half as much courage when my time comes up."

As Carlos looked up again, he could see Don Esteban trying his hardest not to let the swelling of his eyes turn into tears.

"Don Manuel, just tell me how I can help. I will do anything," Carlos said sincerely.

"Well for one," began Don Manuel, "the more I think about it, the more I like this idea of Alexandra learning to do *rejoneo*. It will help to keep her distracted when we can no longer contain our little secret. Esteban and I have also noticed that she has come to trust you implicitly, and that you two have developed a close friendship. She will need you to be there for her to lean on. That, young man, is what I need you to do for me."

"Yes, yes of course Don Manuel," answered Carlos.

"Good, enough of this dour talk!" said Don Manuel emphatically ending the conversation.

16

By now Carlos had grown accustomed to seeing Don Manuel and Don Esteban enjoying their habitual morning coffee at the wrought-iron table with a top of concentrically arranged, tiny ceramic, jade-colored, luminescent square tiles. They would start each day by playing several rounds of dominoes before getting on horseback and taking a leisurely ride to check on the herd.

On this particular morning Carlos went up to his two patrons and after saying good morning asked them, "Don't you ever get tired of playing the same game every morning? After all, dominoes is just a game of luck."

Carlos knew by the disapproving look that the two men instantly gave him that he had uttered the wrong words.

"There is no such thing as luck. Luck is a human term for a fortuitous event that cannot be explained. Nevertheless the event occurred, it is real and there is a reason for it, we just do not know the what or the why," pontificated Don Esteban.

"In life, just as in dominoes, each decision that you take leads to a consequence. Deliberating properly on those decisions will commonly guide you towards more fructiferous results. This apparently simple game helps teach you that very complex and valuable lesson," added Don Manuel.

Nothing is as simple as it looks with these men thought Carlos as he walked away.

At lunch Alexandra announced that she had decided to wholeheartedly undertake the study of *rejoneo*.

"Wonderful my dear," acknowledged Don Manuel, "I will call our friend Don Álvaro Domecq, who has the finest stable of trained Andalusian *rejoneo* horses in the entire land, as we will need to supplant our own stable with at least a couple of more top-notch horses. Plus his son, Alvarito, is amongst the finest *rejoneadores* currently practicing the craft in Spain, and there is much we could learn from both of them. We will go to his estate just outside of Cadiz.

"I can see this is going to be a very expensive new hobby," joked Don Esteban.

"Father, I promise, I will make you proud, and become a great *rejoneadora*!" Alexandra said enthusiastically.

"Alexandra you have nothing left to prove to me. To most people we wish good fortune in life; with you I do not even have to do that, as you are already successful in the most important aspect of one's existence; you are successful as a human being," said the Count swollen with pride.

"Thank you, father, that means everything to me," replied Alexandra.

In the library following lunch, Carlos listened as Don Manuel began the discussion. "Esteban, I know you do not want to brooch this subject but we have to start looking for someone to take over my job here."

"Manolo, I am not sure that I am ready to do that just yet," replied Don Esteban earnestly.

"Unfortunately, Esteban there is no time to waste, as it will take a while to find the right person and for me to show them how we do things around here," countered Don Manuel.

"What about me?" interjected Carlos.

"What are you talking about my boy, you do not know anything about bulls except that when they are chasing you, they are much faster than you think!" replied the Count, who started laughing along with Don Manuel.

"Wait a minute, before you toss the idea out, listen to me for a moment." Carlos' tone made the men stop laughing and pay attention. "Alexandra is not stupid. The moment you hire someone, even if you say he is just here to help you Don Manuel, she is going to smell a rat. She knows that you would never trust anyone to manage the running of the bull program. She would know that something is amiss within five minutes of you or Don Esteban announcing it. I already know everyone at the estate and how things are done here. I know the financials of the program. All I have to learn is more about the bulls themselves. Surely Don Manuel, you could teach me that in the next year. Alexandra would not suspect anything was up, as all anyone of us would need to say if she asked is that I need more first hand-knowledge of the ranching operation to make it more profitable."

"He does have a point about our little girl Esteban. She will immediately know we are not being forthright. I think Carlos here needs to learn a lot but he seems capable of the feat. We would not have to spend as much money as if we were hiring someone new. Plus, you would still be around to help him if he gets into any trouble, and after being around me for almost twenty-five years you should have learned something about bulls by now," replied Don Manuel, smiling.

"I hope so!" said Don Esteban, laughing. "Well then Carlos, it is done. I will give you a raise for the additional responsibility you will be undertaking," Don Esteban added.

"No thank you, sir," said Carlos.

"Why not?" asked Don Esteban, surprised that he

would not want the extra pay.

"Alexandra will wonder about my increase, and in any case, I know that the *rejoneo* horses we will need to buy will not be cheap. I would rather that the money be used for that, which at this point and time is much more important."

"That is very generous of you Carlos. I shall not soon forget it," said Don Esteban. "If you do not mind now, I would like to have a private chat with my old friend here."

"Yes, of course sir," answered Carlos before leaving the room.

"What do you think, Manolo?" asked Don Esteban.

"I think he is capable of doing the job and unless I die in the next month or two, which I shall do the best to avoid, I have enough time left to teach him what he needs to know about rearing bulls. He is certainly smart enough."

"No Manolo, what do you think about Carlos and our Alexandra?" asked the Count.

"Oh, I see what you mean now. Well, I am sure you feel the same way I do, that there is not a man on this earth good enough for our princess. I must say though, that as time has passed by, Carlos is slowly winning me over—and I have been tough on him," answered Don Manuel.

"Yes, I agree with you. At first, I thought nothing could divert Alexandra's attention from her love of bullfighting, least of all a man. But I have caught her looking at Carlos in a way that shows she is captivated by him. At first it bothered me, but as I have gotten to know the young man, he has grown on me also. She is not getting any younger and neither of us will be around forever. She needs to start thinking of beginning a family," said Don Esteban.

"You know what?" asked Don Manuel.

"What?" replied his friend.

"We are sounding like two very old men!" With that, both of them started to laugh.

Two days later Don Esteban, Don Manuel, Alexandra, and Carlos were whisked off by the Hispano-Suiza towards Cádiz, 190 miles away. It was another beautiful spring day in southern Spain, and with the top down and the roaring engine, conversation within the automobile was difficult but nonetheless lively with Alexandra continually extolling the virtues of *rejoneo* and how exciting it was to meet the famed horse breeder and top level *rejoneador*. After almost three hours they reached the palatial estate of Don Álvaro Domecq. Bullfighters and the breeders involved in all of its facets constitute a very small but tightly knit group, and Don Álvaro warmly greeted Don Manuel and Don Esteban.

"It has been too long Manolo and Esteban! I cannot tell you how pleased I am to see both of you again, but the real pleasure lies in feasting my eyes upon your daughter. Countess you look more stunning with every year that passes."

"Don Álvaro, please, you are much too kind," answered Alexandra.

"Yes, much too kind," murmured Carlos to himself just as Don Esteban said, "This is Carlos Rodriguez Pérez, the manager of our estate."

"Welcome to our home, Carlos. Let's go and see my son Alvarito, who is practicing some moves with a few new horses on young bulls in our bullring."

"Is this not thrilling, Carlos?" asked Alexandra, squeezing his hand.

"Yes, quite," answered Carlos, thinking more about how her hand felt, momentarily touching his, than about watching a *rejoneo* exhibition.

They sat in the small ring, slightly larger than the one back in their home in Morente, and watched a young man atop a dazzling looking chestnut-colored stallion with a black mane. The rider was clad in a white shirt smothered by a short bolero jacket and pants coddled by black leather chaps. A broad straight-brimmed black felt hat was a fitting accent to the elegant attire. The horse was fidgety as he faced his foe. The equestrian tapped the large square-shaped stirrups against its belly and with that the horse raced toward the bull. At the last instant the horse swung its head to the right and then turned its body and head swiftly to the left, faking out its opponent completely. Alvarito then circled back around and this time the horse coerced the bull into chasing it not by sprinting away, but by keeping the distance between the two so tantalizingly close that the bull would keep charging. As the bull began to tire the stallion started to perform 360-degree turns, while at the same time avoiding the sharp horns of the beast. Everyone was shouting *"Ole!"* in unison throughout the demonstration that ended with Alvarito charging the bull with *banderillas* that were blunt at the end so as not to cause any sort of injury. As the bull was led away, the dashing rider dismounted and walked towards his father and the rest of the spectators.

Don Álvaro introduced him to everyone, but he was obviously smitten with Alexandra. "Countess, I am a big fan. To have the perseverance and dedication to pursue one's dreams against tremendous odds is something to be commended. To what do we owe the honor of your visit?"

"Well Alvarito, because of circumstances that I cannot control, I have decided to continue my career in the bullring as a *rejoneadora*. We came down to talk to you and your father about buying some horses, to get some training advise, and possibly watch you at a main event," answered Alexandra.

"We would be delighted to help in any manner we can. We have a number of fine Andalusians for sale that you can take out and ride for as long as you like. Each animal has its own character and nothing is more important in the art of *rejoneo* than having a perfect chemistry between the rider and the horse," said Don Álvaro.

"I am going to be performing in the next couple of months with the Peralta brothers, Ángel and Rafael, in Ronda, Marbella, Córdoba, Linares, Granada, and at the Maestranza in Seville," said Alvarito. "I would be delighted to have the company of such a beautiful dignitary at any, or better still, at all of those venues."

Carlos could feel his muscles tighten with every word Alvarito spoke.

"I do believe it is time for lunch and our wonderful chef, Charo, has been laboring at the stove for hours to prepare a feast for us," Don Álvaro announced.

Lunch did not disappoint. Everyone was served a glass of Domecq 'La Ina' Fino Sherry as they took their seats at the regal table. Next came platters of thinly sliced *Iberico* ham from the finest producer in the land, Sanchez Romero Carvajal, followed by baby squid and smelts *a la Andaluza*, lightly dusted with nothing but flour and fried in olive oil. The entrée was *flamenquines*, pork loin wrapped with Serrano ham, coated with breadcrumbs and egg, and then deep-fried. That was accompanied by a very rare Domecq 'Palo Cortado' Sherry. Don Álvaro related to his guests how the solera for this wine was established by his descendants in 1792, and that only one out of a thousand casks become this type of Sherry. Dark mahogany in color, it combined the delicacy of a *fino* with the richness of an *oloroso*. Macaroons were served to sweeten the meal.

Everyone retired to have coffee in the garden, surrounded by pink convolvulus, sea lavender and crown daises. Don Álvaro talked about the importance of selecting the right horse for each part of the bullfight.

"You must think of a *rejoneo* as consisting of four different parts. The first is when you enter the ring with the other *rejoneadores* before the fight begins. This is where you use a parade horse. It should be the most beautiful horse you own, but it also needs to be calm, as it will be marching next to other horses and surrounded by the entire *cuadrillas* and the marshals of the *corrida*. The music played by the arena band will be very loud and the crowds will be cheering for you to have success. The second part is when the bull first comes out into the arena. The bull is at full strength and very quick, so a very fast horse is essential. Here you have to spear him with the lances of punishment to weaken the animal and slow him down. For the third part you use the shortest spears, *banderillas*, or the shorter still *rosetas*. Your mount must be both fast and agile to fool the beast. The fourth and final part, the lance of death to kill the bull, requires the bravest and steadiest horse as the target area is very small."

"Noche is the perfectly suited for ending the fight. Luna is agile and quick, but probably not speedy enough to lead the fight. I would say that we need a show horse and a sprinter," concluded Don Manuel.

"Alexandra, let me escort you to the stables and show you some horses that fit those characteristics while everyone continues to relax here," volunteered Alvarito.

Carlos was loath to remain seated and not accompany Alexandra with her flirtatious host, but since no one else was getting up to join them, he decided it was not appropriate for him to do so.

After what seemed like an eternity, Alexandra and Alvarito returned to the garden. Alexandra was almost giddy.

"She made me give up two of our finest horses that I had no intention of selling," said Alvarito, smiling.

"Somehow I am not surprised son, as I would say that it would be very difficult for any man to deny her a wish," joined in Don Álvaro.

"You have to see these horses, they are beyond fabulous! You must come and see them!" she exclaimed beaming.

"Okay, okay, let's go and see them!" said Don Esteban.

As they walked to the stables, Alexandra asked Don Manuel, "Will you please try them out and make sure that I am making the right decision?"

"Yes, of course my dear," answered Don Manuel.

The two horses were still saddled up when they reach the main barn. One was the chestnut-colored stallion that Alvarito had been riding when they had first arrived. The other was another stallion, bigger and older, whose color was so white it bore a resemblance to porcelain, with the exception of a light grey mane.

Every one made their way towards the plaza to watch Don Manuel put the horses through their paces. Both stallions immediately took to his deft touch and it seemed he had ridden them for years.

"The old man knows how to ride," whistled Alvarito.

"He sure does," concurred his father.

After about thirty minutes Don Manuel finished the trial.

"Alexandra, I think you made two very wise choices. They are the perfect compliment to our horses," he proclaimed.

"Álvaro, why don't you and I go somewhere private and discuss the proper arrangements," Don Esteban suggested.

"Of course Esteban, let us go to my study," replied Don Álvaro.

"Father, I must insist that since I am relinquishing these two beauties, you must make it a condition of the deal that the Countess allow me to take her to dinner in Córdoba when we deliver the horses to Morente."

Before Don Álvaro could answer, Alexandra interjected, "It would be my pleasure Alvarito."

For the next fifteen minutes while Don Álvaro and Don Esteban were consummating the terms of the sale, Alexandra could not stop caressing the horses while saying, "I cannot believe these are going to be mine. I just cannot believe how lucky I am!"

"I dare say Countess, that it is they, that are fortunate to have you as their new owner," Alvarito said.

"You must not give me so many compliments, as I will start to deem them to be true," said Alexandra.

Carlos could sense his face turning red with anger. No woman had ever evoked such a reaction from him. He felt a rage he had not known existed within his body. He wanted to punch Alvarito and then kiss Alexandra as if it were going to be his last one.

Carlos was unusually quiet on the ride back to Morente. The journey seemed to take a lot longer than he remembered, for the other trio of passengers in the car though, it passed by in a hurry as Alexandra could not contain her enthusiasm.

218

"Father I can not thank you enough for the two amazing horses!"

"Nonsense my dear, besides, it is Manolo here, whom you have to thank for volunteering to spend a lot of time over the coming year to teach you how to ride them properly," replied Don Esteban.

"Not at all! I am actually looking forward to it, as nothing gives me more joy than riding a magnificent horse," chimed in Don Manuel.

It was almost eleven o'clock in the evening by the time they arrived back at the estate. Trini and Celia were there waiting with a light supper. Alexandra relayed the events of the day to her new audience while they ate.

"When are these amazing horses due to arrive?" asked Celia.

"Don Álvaro and his son Alvarito will deliver them personally the day after tomorrow," replied Alexandra.

"Oh that reminds me. Celia and Trini, can you make sure you prepare one of your outstanding meals so that we may repay our guests the wonderful hospitality they showed us today," asked the Count.

"Yes of course Your Highness," answered Celia and Trini in unison.

Soon thereafter everyone bid each other good night and prepared to retire for the evening.

"What is the matter with you?" asked Trini as she accompanied Carlos to their quarters.

"Nothing, why do you ask?" replied Carlos.

"Oh my dear Carlitos, jealousy wears an ugly scar. Anyone that would have looked at you during dinner and seen you sulking, could have figured out that something was amiss," answered Trini. "It was especially evident when the name Alvarito came up in the conversation.

Having watched him on television I can understand your envy."

"Very amusing, but I respectfully disagree with your theory. I am just tired from a long day. That is all," Carlos replied.

"Yes, that must be it. You look absolutely exhausted!" replied Trini smirking.

Two days later Don Álvaro and Alvarito arrived with the two horses, Nieve and Cola Cao. Every one in the house went out to the stables to watch the two magnificent animals as they were unloaded from the trailer. Alexandra could not contain her enthusiasm and it infected everyone with the exception of Carlos. Alvarito was constantly flirting with Alexandra and it was difficult for Carlos to not be bothered by it. Still he did his best to hide his sentiments. After lunch everyone retired to the garden, where the festive atmosphere continued. About an hour and a half later, Alexandra excused herself to get ready to go and have dinner at the finest new restaurant in Córdoba, and thereby fulfill her part of the horse purchase agreement by giving Alvarito her much sought-after company.

When Alexandra reappeared over an hour later, she looked so ravishing that for a brief moment none of the men said a word. Her silk chiffon black dress, with just the right amount of ruffles that came to rest above her knees, must have been from a Parisian designer of note, surmised Carlos, and was complemented by black patent leather stiletto heels.

"Darling you look like a gorgeous Andulusian evening," Don Esteban finally said, breaking the silence.

"Thank you, father," she replied.

"I am afraid I cannot express my admiration, as you have left me speechless, Countess," said Alvarito.

"Well thank you for that," answered Alexandra as she curtsied.

Dinner at El Churrasco restaurant was made all the more pleasant by sumptuous portions of Iberico pork sirloin barbecued over Spanish oak. The 1954 Lopez de Heredia 'Vina Tondonia' Rioja was the perfect frame for the meal. Alexandra found herself laughing at various times throughout the evening, as Alvarito's company was most entertaining.

Towards the conclusion of dinner though, Alvarito turned serious when he said, "Alexandra, would you do me the honor of allowing me to visit you more often."

"Alvarito it is I who am honored by your proposal, but my heart belongs to another," Alexandra answered.

"May I know who the fortunate man is?" Alvarito asked.

"I would rather keep it private for the time being if you do not mind, as I feel I should let my father and Don Manuel know before anyone else, and it is still too early to tell them," she replied.

"Yes, of course," he said in turn.

The next morning when Alexandra saw Carlos at the stables, she looked at him fainting disdain and said, "I should not even speak to you!"

"Why not?" replied Carlos, taken aback.

"Well for one, you were the only person that did not say anything about how I looked yesterday, and secondly, you did not wish me a nice time when I left last night."

"I just figured that you had plenty of men saying how attractive you looked and that you certainly did not need anyone else to say it," he answered.

"Lesson number one, Carlitos—women always need men to tell them how beautiful they look," Alexandra said coyly.

"I will try to remember that next time the occasion presents itself," Carlos answered back cockily.

"Yes, make sure you do that," replied Alexandra, flirtatiously.

17

The next months saw Carlos spending most of his time by Don Manuel's side. Don Manuel relayed the story of his visit with Don Esteban to the Miura ranch over two decades before, and that became the foundation of his newly formed knowledge about bull breeding.

"The most important decision you will make at this estate is which young bulls and cows to keep when they reach their second year. That is the future of the reputation of the bulls bred by the Count of Morente. You must never compromise that decision or you compromise everything we have worked so hard to accomplish. There will be years that for no logical reason do not produce many quality bulls. You must have faith in your conviction and not be swayed by anyone, even the Count."

"But the Count is…" Carlos was starting to object when Don Manuel cut him off.

"Yes Carlos, even Esteban. Remember always, that if you sell most of the bulls and cows to the local butchers, Esteban will earn a lot less money. That is right now, but if you are not selective enough, the herd becomes weak, and if that happens you will no longer be able to fetch a premium price for the bulls, which is where the most profit is made. Esteban is a strong-willed man, so it is not easy to disagree with him, but if you fail to do so when you know in your heart that you are acting in the best interest of the estate, then he will stop respecting you as the manager of his bull-breeding program. My father once told me that there are two ways to do things in life; the right way or not at all."

"Okay, I understand," acknowledged Carlos, half convincingly.

Soon it was the time of the year when the two-year-old bulls were separated from the rest of the herd and taken out, one by one, to an isolated part of the estate to be knocked down to the ground by horseman holding long wooden spears with rounded ends.

Don Manuel and Carlos spent weeks watching from a distance as each bull or cow reacted to the unceremonious act. Carlos would listen intently as Don Manuel gave his assessment of each animal.

"See how quickly that one got up and started charging the horse. That is one to keep. The one before got up and charged also, but too slowly, not fiercely enough. That one we will sell to a butcher."

Before long Don Manuel was letting Carlos make the first observations, and then adding comments or correcting him.

"Be tougher, more critical," Don Manuel would say to him over and over again.

The moments when Don Manuel was not teaching Carlos the finer points of breeding, he was coaching and critiquing Alexandra about her horsemanship.

"Don Manuel how is it that you are not even letting me practice with calves. All I do is ride horses everyday. How am I ever going to learn to be a *rejoneadora*?" Alexandra would say in frustration.

"My dear, to be a great *rejoneadora* you must first be one with your horse. Riding must become second nature to you. You must not think about your horse. Your sole focus has to be on the bull in front of you. The horse beneath you must feel safe. Your every touch giving it guidance. The tone of your voice a command, or reassurance. It must know what to do at all times. What movement to perform. What speed to approach the bull, to tempt it, to flee from it. It must never feel panic," Don Manuel calmly answered her.

A few months later she started to practice with calves and graduated to young bulls soon thereafter.

"She is amazing," Carlos observed one day watching her practice, while being seated next to Don Manuel in the estate's arena, "she learns so quickly. It seems like she has been doing it for years, she makes it look so easy."

"Yes, she is a natural. It is because she is so determined and fears nothing. The difficulty will be in not letting her rush to fight mature bulls too quickly," Don Manuel added.

"Good luck with that!" said Carlos.

"Yes, yes I know," concurred Don Manuel.

It was at lunch the following week that Alexandra brought up the subject of when her initial public *rejoneo* should be.

"Father, Don Manuel, I think I am ready. I have spent the last year training and the new bullfighting season will soon be upon us. I have been thinking about my first official *rejoneo*. My *alternativa* as a matador was in Madrid, and I think my inaugural *rejoneo* should also be at Las Ventas."

"Yes, that would be wonderful Alexandra," said her father.

"I think it has to be spectacular. Something daring to really attract attention, so that people do not say that I am just another washed up matador trying to continue my career," Alexandra continued.

"I want to fight a Miura."

"What!" exclaimed Don Manuel. "I would suggest bulls from the Count of La Maza. He is a breeder that is starting to get much attention from the cognoscenti."

"Don Manuel he may be an excellent breeder, but the general public has never heard of his bulls!" answered a discouraged Alexandra.

"Alexandra, you are not ready for a Miura," Don Manuel replied softly.

"But I am!" she exclaimed annoyed.

"Alexandra!" said Don Esteban raising his voice, "if Manolo says you are not ready, then you are not ready!"

After a minute of deathly silence Alexandra said, "May I be excused?"

"Yes of course," answered her father, before she stormed out of the patio.

Thirty minutes later Carlos found her walking alongside the road that led to and from the estate. From the red color of her pupils it was evident that she had been crying.

"I cannot believe it! I am ready! They do not understand. They have overprotected me my entire life and I am sick and tired of it!" she exclaimed not being able to contain herself.

"I do not disagree with them Alexandra," said Carlos quietly, somewhat afraid of the tempest that his comment would bring.

"What! Not you too!" she answered wickedly.

"Alexandra, hold on a second before you chop my head off," started Carlos calmly. "You are everything to those two old men. There is no way they would ever put you in harm's way if they felt it was too great a risk. I know you want to make a great impression, but even you must admit that fighting a Miura at your first official *rejoneo* is taking quite a chance."

"Alright, alright, if all three of you are against it then perhaps there is some sense to what you are all saying," she answered.

They continued walking while Alexandra began to calm down.

"Start out with the bulls of the Count of La Maza. Fight well and soon Don Manuel and Don Esteban will have no choice but to let you fight a Miura," Carlos assured Alexandra.

"Okay, I see your point. By the way Carlitos, I would never chop off that pretty little head of yours," she added playfully.

18

In the library one afternoon, after all the youthful bulls and cows had endured their test, while Don Esteban, Don Manuel and Carlos were having their Cognac and cigar, Don Manuel spoke up.

"Esteban, I have to tell you that my young apprentice here is getting the hang of how to do my job very quickly. I dare say his eye for spotting a brave bull is almost as good as mine."

"Thank you for the compliment Don Manuel, but I still have a lot to learn from you," Carlos interrupted.

"I also told him not too pay attention to you if you disagree with his conclusion on a particular bull or cow," Don Manuel added, smiling.

"Well that is nothing new around here. You haven't heeded my opinions for years!" said the Count laughing.

Don Manuel continued, "I think the three of us need to start going to bullfights together to introduce Carlos to the major bullring managers and matadors. I will tell them that it is getting time for me to retire and that Carlos will be taking over my duties at the estate. You know the bullfighting community does not take to strangers, so the earlier people get to know our lad here, the better. Plus the more bulls he sees fighting, the more experience and knowledge he will acquire, which will help him to direct our program."

"I agree Manolo, but we will not be able to keep our secret from our families much longer," said Don Esteban.

"I know Esteban. I have been dreading the day when I must tell our Alexandra what is happening, but I know I cannot postpone it much longer. My health is starting to deteriorate to the point where Celia has become very suspicious, and it is not fair to keep it from her either," Don Manuel answered sadly. "I shall tell Celia tonight and Alexandra tomorrow."

The next morning Carlos was in the kitchen with Trini when Celia entered to begin her chores. Her eyes were bloodshot and before she could finish saying, "Good morning," she broke down crying.

Trini rushed over to her and alarmed, asked her, "What is the matter dear?"

"He is very sick. He told me he is dying," Celia replied, barely able to answer.

"Who is sick?" asked Trini, afraid that she already knew the answer.

"Manolo, my dear Manolo," Celia replied.

Trini turned towards Carlos and said, "Carlos, would you mind giving me a little private time with my friend?"

"Yes, of course. Let me know if there is anything I can do," answered Carlos gently.

As Carlos walked away a feeling of helplessness swept over him. He felt empty and unsure of what to do. Don Manuel had become a father figure to him, and the confidence that normally prevailed in his manner was gone. He just started walking aimlessly about. He finally went over to the stables for no reason, except that he did not know where else to go. He grabbed a large wooden comb with wire ends and approached the stall that housed Noche. He normally did not go near the immense stallion, as he was usually quite jittery and nervous. Today however, the animal was unusually placid as he began to brush its long black mane. After a few minutes Carlos could feel the tears streaming down his cheeks and put his arms around Noche's neck. The stallion turned his head and then simply let in rest on Carlo's back, as if trying to console him.

Just then he heard his name being called out, "Carlos! Carlos! Carlos!"

It was Alexandra's voice. As he walked outside the barn, she spotted him and ran towards him, before throwing her arms around him. She was sobbing uncontrollably.

"Carlos, what are we going to do? How are we going to live without him? I am so scared. So sad."

"I don't know Alexandra, I am afraid I have no answer for you. What I do know is that we cannot waste a single moment that we have left with him. Pity is the last thing Don Manuel wants."

"I know that what you are saying is true, but it is still very bitter news and it will be a very difficult pill to swallow," she responded.

A mood of sorrow settled over the estate. It was as if one of the pillars was crumbling and everything was about to come crashing down. Don Manuel tried to keep Alexandra focused on her *rejoneo* career and went about his days as if nothing was wrong. Alexandra, who had previously been so fervent about her new undertaking, was much more subdued and went about it as an occupation rather than as a passion. Her debut in Madrid, though critically acclaimed, did not change her dour frame of mind. Carlos, Don Esteban and Don Manuel meanwhile, spent a good portion of the beginning of the bullfighting season at bullrings throughout Andalusia, introducing Carlos to the main characters at each of them. The excursions were accentuated with entertaining personal anecdotes by Don Manuel about the individuals they would meet. Not once did Don Manuel refer to his ailing condition or complain of the pain he was enduring,

231

and as time passed Carlos began to realize the enormous toll his death would take on all that knew him. He had grown to admire this man more than any he had ever met in his life, and knew he would dearly miss him when he was gone.

One particular morning, for the first time in over twenty-five years, Don Manuel did not come to work at the estate. Celia could hardly stop crying when she walked into the kitchen.

"He cannot get up, he has become so weak, and I know he is in great pain," Celia said to Trini, Alexandra and Carlos.

Carlos immediately went to the library, where he knew he would find Don Esteban.

"Your Highness, I think you had better come to the kitchen and speak to Celia," Carlos said.

"I will be there in a few minutes, I just have to finish up some things here," Don Esteban replied.

"Sir, I do not think this can wait," Carlos implored.

Seeing the look of anxiety on Carlos' face, the Count put down his pen and said, "Let us go then."

Celia, Trini, and Alexandra were in the kitchen, crying.

"What is the matter Celia?"

She told the Count of Don Manuel's condition that morning.

"I do not know what to do anymore Your Highness," she ended saying in desperation.

"Go home and take care of your husband," Don Esteban told her.

"But Your Highness, if neither of us can work who will pay for everything, how will we continue to live?"

The Count of Morente got on his knees and held her hands in his. "Celia, I need you to go home, I need you to take care of my friend. For as long as you live, Alexandra will make you sure your household never receives one *peseta* less than what both of you are being paid right now. Please go and give him as much comfort as you can. I will be there to see him shortly."

"Thank you so much Your Highness, but our house is very humble," was all Celia could think of saying.

"Celia if you think that where you live is going to prevent me from seeing Manolo, you are very mistaken about who I am, and what your husband means to me," Don Esteban replied.

With that he got up and excused himself. When he returned to the library he went over to his desk, opened a drawer on the right side, and took out a small black notebook and after briefly leafing through it, picked up the telephone and dialed a number.

"Brigadier General Lewis' office, how may I help you?"

"Yes, hello, I would like to speak to the Brigadier General please," replied Don Esteban.

"Whom might I say is calling?"

"This is the Count of Morente," responded Don Esteban.

"Just a moment sir," replied the monotone voice before Don Esteban was put on hold.

"Esteban, how are you?"

"Randall, I am fine but unfortunately our friend Manolo is not fairing quite so well."

Don Esteban then gave him a quick overview of his worsening condition over the last few weeks, ending by saying, "you know how stubborn Manolo can be and that he will never ask for help, and hence the reason for my call to you today."

"I do know how hard-nosed that old bird can be and I'm glad you called. Let me talk to my head doc here, Marc Rozenberg, and see what he recommends we do. Give me a few minutes and I will get right back to you Esteban."

"Okay," replied Don Esteban.

Ten minutes later the telephone rang.

"Hello, this is Esteban Vilches," answered the Count.

"Esteban, Randall here. I'm sending you who Dr. Rozenberg says is his best man, Dr. Douglas Merrill. He is packing some things as we speak and he will arrive in Morente tonight," said the Brigadier General.

"Thank you Randall," said Don Esteban.

"Don't mention it Esteban. Besides I owe the bastard! Keep me abreast of what happens, and if you need anything else just pick up the phone."

"I will do that," replied Don Esteban.

Don Esteban made his way to the barn where he asked one of the stable hands to saddle up Noche.

Don Esteban got on the stallion and whispered, "Okay, big guy, let's go see your master."

With that they galloped off towards the house of Don Manuel.

After asking several townsfolk, Don Esteban finally found the small but quaint house, neatly sandwiched between two similar looking ones, where Don Manuel and Celia lived. He tied up Noche to a wrought iron grill that protected one of the windows from any unwelcomed intruders. As he stood in front of the main door he came to the realization that he had never been to Manolo and Celia's house before and felt embarrassed by the fact. Celia opened the door and was clearly uncomfortable by the Count's presence at her home. She announced to her husband that he had a visitor as Don Esteban entered the bedroom.

"What are you doing here Esteban?" he asked.

"Well since you have never asked me to your house, I decided to invite myself," Don Esteban replied smiling, sitting on a small wooden chair next to the bed.

"Esteban, I am afraid I can no longer come to work for you. I would like to tell you that I will get better but we have always been honest with each other, and at this point in my life I will not start to do otherwise," Don Manuel said.

"Manolo, forget about work. Carlos is more than capable of doing the job. You have taught him well. You worry about yourself and let everyone take care of you."

"You know I have never been good at that," Don Manuel replied.

"Yes, I know," replied Don Esteban smiling, "but now you have to allow those that care for you to help in any way they can. They are also in pain, so even if there is little that they can do, it will make it easier for them to deal with this."

"Alright, alright," Don Manuel acceded.

"Good, I am glad we got that out of the way. By the way Randall is sending one of his best doctors to check on you. He is arriving tonight and tomorrow morning I will bring him by. Is there anything you need right now?"

"Esteban, you know that in all the years we have known each other I have rarely asked you for anything, but as I come to my end there is one very important thing you can do for me."

"Just name it Manolo, and it shall be done," replied Don Esteban.

"Isabella is young and I know she will be fine when I am gone, but please make sure that Celia is looked after," Don Manuel asked.

"Manolo you did not even have to ask for that. Celia is part of our family and she will never have to worry about anything," Don Esteban answered.

"Thank you," Don Manuel replied.

"Not at all," said the Count.

When Don Esteban returned back to the estate the first thing he did was find Alexandra and take her to the kitchen, where he knew Trini would be.

"Trini, as of tomorrow morning, you will go to Celia and Manolo's house and help Celia with the cooking, cleaning and any other chores she might need assistance with, until further notice. Whatever food, medicine or anything else needs to be purchased please pay with an advance I will have Alexandra give to you."

"But Your Highness, who will take care of things here if Celia and I are gone?"

"If you know of someone you can personally vouch for, then send them here to see Alexandra. If not, we will fend for ourselves. Believe me, while I know that you and Celia have no substitutes, and that we will not be eating anywhere near as well, we will make do for the time being."

"Yes Your Highness," replied Trini.

"Thank you," he answered.

Next he asked his daughter to find Carlos and meet him at the library.

"Both of you know by now the critical situation that Manolo is in. Carlos, after you complete your daily duties here you have my full permission to spend as much time as you can completing your education about bulls and the taking care of this estate with Manolo. Trust me, in two lifetimes you would never acquire even half of his knowledge, so take advantage of the precious moments you have left with him. Alexandra I do not think that there is anything I need to tell you about what to do in regards to Manolo."

With that, both of them left the room and started walking in silence and in no particular direction, almost as if lost.

19

The following day Don Esteban took Dr. Douglass Merrill to go see Don Manuel. After a thorough examination the doctor gave Celia several drugs and instructions on when to administer them. He told her that he would be back to check on Don Manuel the next day.

At lunch, Don Esteban and the doctor were joined by Alexandra and Carlos. Towards the end of the meal Don Esteban said, "Doctor Merrill, I know that you were under orders to come here, but I cannot thank you enough for attending to my old friend."

"Please Your Highness, there is no need to thank me, besides Brigadier General Lewis let it be known in no uncertain terms, that I am to make sure that Don Manuel is as well taken care of as possible, and to remain here for as long as it is necessary. I learned some time ago that it is best not to have a difference of opinion with the Brigadier General," said the doctor smiling.

"Yes, I imagine so!" laughed Don Esteban.

"May I ask you a personal question?" asked the doctor.

"Certainly, by all means doctor," replied Don Esteban.

"It is highly unusual to have us examine a civilian that is not American at the Air Force base in Torrejon, never mind be sent to take care of one hundreds of miles away. I am most curious to know Don Manuel's relationship to Brigadier General Lewis," inquired Dr. Merrill.

"Well good doctor, since the story is long and should be enhanced by Cream Sherry, why don't we all retire to the library?"

"Sounds like an excellent idea," agreed the doctor.

"It was in this same room one afternoon many years ago when Randall recounted the events that have brought us all here today," began Don Esteban. "He was in his early twenties, growing up in a middle-class neighborhood in Atlanta, Georgia when World War II began. Back then America stood by the sidelines, having sympathy for the British and French but hesitating to get involved in the immense conflict. It was the talk of the nation. What should be done? Which side should America join? Could America afford not to be involved in events that would decide the future of the world? The breaking point came on that horrific day of December 7, 1941 when the Japanese attacked Pearl Harbor, causing President Franklin Delano Roosevelt to declare war against Japan and its allies, Germany and Italy. Randall did not wait to get drafted and instead enrolled in the Air Force, having always been fascinated by flight. He was assigned to the Savannah Air Base near his home for flight training. By April of 1943 he was being shipped off to join the 61st Fighter Squadron, part of the 56th Fighter Group of the Eighth Air Force stationed at the Royal Air Force Station Horsham St. Faith near Norwich. I will never forget how he described his hands shaking as he took flight in his Republic P-47 Thunderbolt fighter on his first combat mission.

"I was as green as green could be! Excited and scared as hell," were his exact words. His mission was to escort a squadron of B-17 Flying Fortresses that were going to bomb the Bordeaux-Merignac Air Base that the Luftwaffe was using to launch long range fighters against Allied ships in the Atlantic. Everything was going according to plan, but just before they reached Bordeaux, a squadron of Messerschmitt Bf 109 fighter planes came out of nowhere and starting ripping the B-17s to shreds. Randall's squadron immediately started engaging the German fighters and soon the entire sky was being crisscrossed by dogfights. Randall remembered a Messerschmitt and his Thunderbolt coming right at each other, machine guns blaring, daring each other to dive off course and prevent a collision, knowing that whoever trailed off first would be at a disadvantage and be more exposed until the next run. The German finally caved in to the mad game of chicken, Randall was able to pick him off and the plane exploded in mid-air.

Before he was able to wipe the sweat from his forehead and celebrate his first kill, a bullet shattered the glass in his cockpit. Seconds later another penetrated the single-engine aircraft and black smoke engulfed the cockpit. He took the plane into a nosedive in an attempt to avoid his foe and at the same time play possum, pretending that he was crashing into the ocean below. The trick worked and the German pilot pulled up and went back to try to shoot down another B-17. Meanwhile Randall was pulling up on his stick with all his might to come out of his self-induced stall and prevent his plane from crashing into the water below. With just a couple of hundred feet to spare, the tough Thunderbolt finally swept upwards and he was able to regain control. But his troubles were just starting as his fuel tank was leaking badly and there was no way he could turn back and make it to England. He decided the safest route was to head south. He grabbed his radio and started screaming.

"Mayday! Mayday! Is anyone out there! Mayday! Mayday!"

Finally a voice came through.

"This is Gerald from French resistance."

"Thank God! This is Second Lieutenant Randall Lewis from the United States Air Force. My plane has taken a number of hits and is losing fuel quickly."

"What is your position?" Gerald asked.

"I am heading south of Bordeaux along the coast. My instruments are not working!" yelled back the frantic airman.

"Take it easy *mon ami*. I will guide you to safety but I need you to stay focused for this to work out," Gerald said calmly.

"Okay, I'm all ears Frenchy," replied Randall.

Gerald ignored the last comment and continued, "Use the coastline as your map. The next major town you will see on the coast is Biarritz about 100 miles south of your position."

"I figure I am flying at about half speed, so just over 200 miles an hour. I should be there in thirty minutes," replied Randall.

"I have to turn my radio off so that our German friends do not find me. I will come back on the air in twenty-five minutes," Gerald informed the airman.

"Don't forget about me Frenchy," Randall half pleaded.

"Do not worry *mon ami*, I am not going anywhere until you are safe," Gerald reassured him.

"Thanks, I owe you a beer when this is over!" said Randall.

"Roger that. Over and out," replied Gerald.

As soon as he got off the radio Gerald looked up at Manolo and the three other men in the group.

"Well, he does not know how lucky he is that I just turned on the radio to check in with London! Matador, you and Julen take the motorcycle and make your way to the road south of Ascain. Go about five miles on it and you will come to the only meadow around these parts that is flat and long enough for our new friend to land his plane. Grab him and get out of there fast, as no doubt our German friends will not take long to spot a low-flying American plane leaving a trail of smoke behind. Julen, you will provide cover for the Matador if anything goes wrong, and come back on foot through the mountains."

"Gerald, how will he be able to spot us? That meadow is not that easy to find from the air," asked Julen concerned.

Before Gerald was able to answer Manolo jumped in with an answer, "The smoke from a fire. I know it is risky, but Julen is right. It will be tough for him to pinpoint our position without his instruments."

"Okay Matador, but be careful," warned Gerald.

"Before we go, I will grab an empty bottle and put some gasoline in it so that we can start a small fire quickly," Manolo said.

By the time Gerald turned the radio back on, Manolo and Julen were long gone.

"Can you see a large town yet?" asked Gerald over the microphone. "Good to hear your voice again Frenchy! No, no town yet. Oh wait! There it is. I see it now," replied Randall.

"Good, now keep going down the coast for another twelve miles and you will shortly come to a large bay with a small fishing village in the middle. Once there, turn southeast and head ten miles inland or about 3 minutes flying time. The skies are clear here, and you should see a column of smoke coming up from a small fire next to a large field. That will be your landing spot. Two of my men will be there to welcome you to the Basque country," Gerald instructed.

"Okay, I see a large bay, and yes, there is the small village. I'm heading southeast and timing it," answered Randall.

The three minutes seem to last an eternity as everyone around the radio started to get anxious. Finally Randall came back on the airwaves.

"No sign of a fire anywhere."

"Keep looking *mon ami*. My men are there," Gerald answered as convincingly and relaxed as he could.

"Nothing yet Frenchy, and I'm about to start flying on vapor. Plus I do not see many places to land this plane in these mountains! I hate to say this but I'm starting to get really nervous!" said the panicked airman.

Gerald was about to say something to calm Randall down, when the American came back on the radio.

"Hold on Frenchy! I think I see something. Yep! It's smoke all right! Okay, time to drop my wheels and land this baby. Shit! My landing gear won't open! That damn Kraut flyer must have damaged it! I'll have to eject and parachute down, but I'm too low so I have circle back around and gain some altitude.

"Do not turn south! Turn north!" yelled Gerald into the microphone, but it was too late. By turning south and circling back that way, Randall flew directly over Ascain where a very surprised pair of German soldiers, smoking some cigarettes while taking a break from their mundane duties, spotted the American plane and started running to alert their superiors. Meanwhile Randall came back on the radio.

"I can't get her to go above 2,000 feet so I'm going to have to take my chances with the parachute and hope I'm high enough. See you soon boys! Over and out."

Back on the ground Manolo was wondering why the hell the American was not landing the plane, until with his binoculars, he could see several large bullet holes in the undercarriage of the P-47 Thunderbolt and realized what was wrong.

"Damn it!" he swore when the American turned south to circle back.

"Julen we are not going to have much time before the Germans show up, so keep your eyes peeled to see where this cowboy lands so that we can get out of here as soon as possible."

"Yes Matador," Julen replied, while his eyes continued to look upward.

They saw the P-47 Thunderbolt first, streaking across the sky pursued by a large swath of smoke until it exploded into a fireball about a quarter of a mile from where they were standing. Soon an oversized umbrella with a man dangling from it appeared.

"Oh God! He is coming down too fast. This is going to be ugly," said Manolo.

Without prompting, both men started running towards the lone flyer. As Manolo had feared, he had landed too hard and when they reached the young Second Lieutenant halfway up the side of a mountain, it was obvious that he had fractured his right leg. Randall was writhing in pain. His fibula had broken in two, and part of the bone was grotesquely sticking out through the skin.

"Good afternoon. I see you have not done much parachuting," said Manolo smiling.

"You can say that again buddy!" replied Randall good-naturedly, in spite of his condition.

Manolo then went over to a tree nearby and broke off a branch.

"This should do the trick. Julen give me your belt," he asked him as he took off his own old brown leather one. "This is going to hurt a little but we have to get you fixed up enough until a doctor can take a look at you," said Manolo.

He reset the bone back into its original place, took the branch and tied it tightly with the two belts around the top and bottom of Randall's leg to immobilize it. Randall wanted to scream bloody murder but just ground his teeth.

"Next time I want a pretty nurse to do that, and just a tad more gently," he said in good humor.

Manolo was about to reply to Randall's comment, when they heard the sound of a fast approaching motorcycle. Manolo held his hand up, signaling for the other two men to be silent, as the BMW R75 with a sidecar, went screeching by them on the road thirty yards below.

"Okay let's get out of here before we have any other company or those two Germans come back. They tell me the guest accommodations at the local Gestapo headquarters are not too comfortable," Manolo added sarcastically. Randall had of course heard the horror stories of Gestapo torture sessions, but until that very moment they seemed quite distant. Now the possibility was imminently close and he was terrified by the prospect.

They had just propped up Randall, who had one arm around the shoulder of each man, when the unmistakable rumbling of a halftrack caused them to lie back down quickly.

"If they spot us with that, we are dead meat," said Julen.

"Pass me your backpack," Manolo quietly ordered Julen.

He then took out the bottle of gasoline that was still ¾ full, and pulled out the cork stopper that prevented it from leaking. Next he grabbed a handkerchief from his pocket, dipped it into the gasoline soaking it completely and leaving half inside the bottle and using the other half as a wick by re-inserting the cork tightly in the middle of the white cloth.

The German armored Panzer halftrack rounded the bend below and came into the view of the three men.

Standing in the back of the odd-looking vehicle were ten soldiers, two of whom were manning the menacing 7.92mm guns on board, with another two soldiers in the protected cabin up front. Suddenly it came to a standstill, as it must have gotten word by radio from the motorcycle up front, that the plane had crashed and to be on the lookout for the surviving pilot.

Manolo did not wait long to light the makeshift fuse and darted down the steep slope towards the road below like a mountain goat, holding the bottle of gasoline in one hand and his Astra M400 pistol in the other.

"What the hell does he think he's doing? He is going to get himself killed," asked an incredulous Randall.

"I don't know, but just be glad he is on your side and not fighting against you *mon ami*," whispered Julen.

"I hear that!" replied Randall quietly.

As one of the soldiers was about to alert his comrades of their incoming enemy some forty feet directly above them, Manolo shot him in the face and launched the crudely concocted Molotov cocktail into the halftrack. As soon as the bottle hit the deck, it broke and the ensuing explosion killed the rest of the soldiers in the back. The two other soldiers in the front cabin, engulfed by the fumes, tried to flee from their vehicle but Manolo had already landed on the roof and promptly shot them in the back before they were able to realize what was happening. He quickly climbed back up to join Randall and Julen, his face covered in soot from the explosion.

"Come on, let's go!" he commanded.

Randall was in tremendous pain but dared not complain in light of their predicament. Soon they reached the road and started heading for the Motobecane hidden behind some trees around a bend about 75 yards away. They were 40 yards from the corner when the BMW appeared out of nowhere and the driver came to a screeching halt. The German in the sidecar already had his ERMA Werke MP 40 Submachine gun out and was starting to fire at them. Both Julen and Manolo instinctively threw Randall to the ground behind them, before pulling out the pistols from their holsters to defend themselves. Julen went down from a bullet to the chest but not before he took down the driver of the motorcycle. Manolo shot the other German squarely between the eyes and immediately turned towards his fallen friend.

"Julen, everything is going to be okay. Just hold on, my friend," said Manolo as calmly as he possibly could, while he tore off the bloodied shirt that concealed the bullet hole.

"Matador, it is okay, I am not going to make it. Being around you these last few years has given me the courage to face death. I cannot feel anything except for peace. I see white..." and then Julen was gone.

"No!" screamed an enraged Manolo.

By then Randall had crawled over to where Julen was lying and propped himself up on one knee.

He had never seen a man die and he started sobbing.

"He died because of me!" was all he could say.

"No, he died for his country. The same country you are fighting to free. To get rid of the tyranny that is here!" replied Manolo before adding, "But we have to go now before more Germans show up. Because if you were to die now, then Julen's death would have been in vain, and that would be unpardonable."

"Are we just going to leave him here, in the middle of the road?" asked Randall through his tears.

"There is nothing we can do right now, except to get out of here. Julen would understand that."

As Manolo helped Randall walk towards their motorcycle, he stopped as he passed by the two dead

Germans, took out his knife and slashed the tires of the BMW.

"It should take those Nazis some time to move that halftrack out of the way, and by then we will be long gone. He grabbed their weapons and ammo, and then continued to aid Randall until they reached the Motobecane. It took them over an hour to return to the cabin, as they took seldom-used back routes, some more akin to dirt paths than paved roads. When they finally did reach the cabin, the look on Manuel's face said it all and nobody spoke. Bixente and Mikel helped clean the airman's wound while Gerald got on the radio to inform the British that they had rescued their lost American pilot. Manolo meanwhile went outside to be alone. After about an hour, Gerald joined him by his side, but did not say anything and just stared at the sky above.

"I keep thinking that there is something I should have done differently. That bullet could have easily been mine," Manolo said solemnly.

"But somebody decided it was not to be your last day. From what our cowboy inside told us, I would have done the same thing as you. It is the senseless consequence of this horrible business we are in *mon ami*. It is as simple and tragic as that."

"Yes, I guess so, but it still does not make it easier."

"As soon as it gets dark, Bixente and I are going to drive our new houseguest down to Saint-Jean-de-Luze to get him to a doctor," said Gerald. "Besides, if we do not get rid of him quickly and he keeps calling me 'Frenchy', I will do the Germans a favor and shoot him myself!"

A couple of hours later, Mikel and Bixente were helping Randall get into the back of the Renault, but before he got in he turned towards Manolo and said,

"Thank you for everything you have done for me. I shall never forget this day."

"Do that on Julen's count my friend, not mine," answered Manolo. Randall nodded in agreement.

That evening the doctor that would fix Randall's leg would tell him that if Manolo had not set it as well as he did, he would have walked with a limp for the rest of his life.

In the twenty-seven years since they met, Manolo has never asked Randall for anything until last year, when at my behest, he called him to see if he could be physically examined by one of his doctors. You are here today because I, and not Manolo, called Randall to tell him of his friend's worsening condition. And that my dear doctor is why Brigadier General Randall Lewis, Commander of the United States Air Force Base in Torrejon, sent you to a little village in the middle of nowhere in southern Spain to take care of an old man."

"Well that makes things pretty clear, I must say," replied the doctor.

"Carlos and Alexandra, will you please excuse the good doctor and me so that we can have a chat in private," asked Don Esteban.

After the two of them had left, Don Esteban said, "Doctor, I need you to be completely forthright with me and tell me just how poorly my friend is doing."

"Your Highness, to be totally honest, I am surprised he is still alive. I cannot believe that he has been able to endure the pain he must be going through without complaining. He is in critical condition, and the best I can do is just to make him as comfortable as possible for the short amount of time he has left," answered the doctor.

"Thank you, and now doctor, would you mind if I had a moment to myself," asked Don Esteban.

"Yes, certainly."

The 18th Count of Morente sat alone on the old leather couch, snifter of Cognac in hand, and stared out the window as life passed him by.

20

Carlos got up early the next day and drove his SEAT 1500 to Morente to visit Don Manuel. As he knocked on the wooden door he felt uneasy, as he did no know what to say to Don Manuel.

Trini opened the door and greeted him with her characteristic smile. "Come in, no one is going to bite you," she said as she sensed his discomfort.

He went in and followed her through the pleasantly appointed house to the main bedroom.

"Manolo, look who the cat dragged in this morning to see you," said Trini as she left to help Celia in the kitchen.

"Everyone is showing up around here these days. Jesus, I have not died yet! But come on in."

"How are you feeling Don Manuel?"

"Well Carlitos, I have had better days, but the drugs this Doctor Merrill is giving are almost making me forget about any pain I might have," answered Don Manuel smiling.

"I am very glad to hear that," said Carlos. "I wanted to ask you if there were particular things at the estate that you think I should be focusing on, and any advice you might be able to give me?"

"My dear Carlos, you are more than capable of running the estate on your own from this moment forward. You have good instincts, let them be your guide. Trust them. What you will need to do is keep an eye on Alexandra. Her father will not be strong enough for the two of them when I pass. You have to be the shoulder she can lean on," replied Don Manuel.

"Yes, you can be sure of it Don Manuel," said Carlos.

"Good. If there is one bit of wisdom I have learned that I can leave you with, it would be to live as it were your last day, for life is much shorter than we ever imagine it to be; love, those you cherish; honor, those you love; dream, for that keeps you alive; fight, to make your dreams come true, and let others attend to mediocrity."

On his way back to the estate Carlos could not stop thinking about what Don Manuel had told him.

In spite of the brave façade that Don Manuel was putting on for all to see, it was painfully obvious that he was rapidly deteriorating.

The estate seemed to be in a constant state of disarray as everyone was either coming from or going to Don Manuel's house. The atmosphere was solemn and an awkward air prevailed.

Then, four days later, the inevitable moment occurred. Trini told Carlos as he knocked on the door of Celia and Don Manuel's house on his daily morning visit that he had peacefully passed away in his sleep.

It is a curious thing when someone dies, thought Carlos. No matter how prepared you think you will be, you are never really ready for the actual moment. There is a hollow feeling inside that can never be filled. He stopped by the side of the road as he headed back to the estate, consumed by the overwhelming loss, and burst into tears. When he did arrive at that the estate he went straight to the library where he knew he would find Don Esteban.

"Don Esteban, Don Manuel is no longer with us," was all he said.

"Thank you Carlos, does Alexandra know yet?" he asked.

"No sir," replied Carlos.

"Okay, let me go and tell her myself," Don Esteban said. "Oh, and Carlos, please call Alberto Solis, the general manager of the Parador Hotel in Córdoba, and have him set aside twenty rooms for this coming Saturday and Sunday under my name. Over the next two days we will let him know the names of our guests staying there. I will take care of all the charges."

"Of course sir," replied Carlos.

Ten minutes later Carlos saw Don Esteban returning to the library where he went to his desk, got out his notebook and for the next few hours started making telephone calls.

Carlos then headed to the stables, the most likely place that Alexandra would be at. He found her brushing Noche, softly singing to him, tears in her eyes. When she saw Carlos she walked up to him and put her arms around his neck without saying anything. Carlos just held her while gently caressing her long dark hair.

On Saturday afternoon a black 1964 Lincoln Continental with its trademark suicide doors arrived at the estate, escorted by four policemen on their Sanglas 400 motorcycles. The two front seat occupants, both United States Air Force officers, simultaneously opened the rear doors of the gargantuan automobile and stood at attention. Brigadier General Randall Lewis and his wife stepped out of the car and were warmly greeted by Don Esteban.

"I am sorry about the circumstances that have brought you here today, but welcome back, Randall. Debbie, a pleasure to see you as always."

"I only regret not being able to come sooner and say goodbye properly to my friend," replied the American General.

"Trini here, will escort you to your room. Please do not hesitate to ask for anything that might make your stay more comfortable," said Don Esteban.

"Esteban, I trust the only thing we will miss is Manuel," replied Brigadier General Randall Lewis and Don Esteban nodded in agreement.

Later that afternoon, Alexandra returned from Seville with the Minister of Foreign Affairs of Cyprus, Aristos Kemitzis, and his wife, Litsa. Gerald Hirigoyen and the Countess Christiane Wenckheim arrived from Biarritz in their striking, candy-apple red 1957 Facel Vega FV2B convertible. The Brigadier General and the Foreign Minister both embraced the Basque man while Trini hugged the Countess and welcomed her back. The three men then headed off to the library where they joined Don Esteban and Carlos. Trini led Christiane to her room in the villa. After helping the Countess put her things away Trini asked her if she was going to join the men in the library.

"Oh no my dear! They need their time alone. Besides, soon they will end up drunk and reek from the smell of those ghastly cigars. I would rather help you in the kitchen. By the way, how is dear Celia?" the Countess asked genuinely concerned.

"I think she is still stunned and it has not fully sunk in. Then again, I am not sure anyone else feels differently," Trini replied, the sadness apparent in her voice.

"Yes my dear, I am afraid you are right," said the Countess.

The next morning everyone made their way to the church in Morente, which was soon overcrowded. There were so many uniformed RAF pilots, that it seemed half the British air force was in attendance. El Cordobes,

Diego Puerta and Curro Romero, amongst other noted bullfighters, were chatting with Don Eduardo Miura and Don Álvaro Domecq, along with the large contingency of others in the business. All the village folk were there. Laurent Manrique and his wife Michelle were talking to Gerald, Christiane, Mikel and Bixente.

Father Juanjo began the service with his customary oratory prowess. Even he was in awe of the sizable gathering. Finally it was time for Don Esteban to give the eulogy for his friend. He looked particularly old and frail on this day. Whatever slight chatter might have been going on came to a standstill as the booming voice of the Count of Morente echoed throughout the small church.

"Lord!" he bellowed, "I am angry at you today." He then paused for a moment before continuing. "I know it is blasphemy to speak in such tone in your house, but if this is a place where truths be told, then you will surely forgive my words. Who will lift my dreams into reality if he is not here? Who will bring me back down to earth when I start thinking too highly of myself? Who, Lord? Today I would fight you to get him back. I would fight you with every ounce of my flesh, with every drop of my blood, and you would certainly have to take my last breath away to defeat me. I know right now you feel safer having my friend by your side, but for all the years I knew him, I was the one that was richer than thou. Every time anger overcomes me at the thought of his loss, I feel his hand on my shoulder pushing me away from my rage, as if saying that everything is going to be all right. I keep thinking how poor the people must be who never had him walk in their lives. How blessed we are to have been enriched by his presence in ours. I know that there will be days when I am walking and all of a sudden, I will stop as a thought of him takes me to another place, a different time. A smile will undoubtedly appear. A ray of light.

Later on, many of us will get together. We will have too much to drink, and men who have rarely shed a tear will drown in them tonight. We will rejoice from the memories of how he touched our lives, and pain at the thought that no new ones will be created. Honor, nobility, dignity, bravery…words that are not fashionable and now rarely spoken, will be repeated over and over again. But then fashion comes and goes with the whims of the seasons, while the few men like Manolo leave their imprint on us forever. The greatest sin we can commit is to forget Manolo, and I stand here in front of you and our Lord, and swear that the day I forget will be the day I die. Thank you, Manolo. Thank you for being in my life."

Every soul was in tears as the Count of Morente finished his speech. The casket was loaded onto the hearse outside by a group of RAF officers and taken to the small cemetery at the estate of the Count of Morente. Once there, Don Esteban, Carlos, Aristos Kemitzis, and Gerald Hirigoyen went over to the hearse to act as pallbearers. Randall Lewis began to walk towards them to help when his wife Debbie grabbed his hand.

"Honey, don't you think you are too old, with your bad back and all, to carry such a heavy thing?"

"No, not today dear," replied the Brigadier General.

Laurent Manrique was about to join them but Jacques intercepted him and handed him his cane.

"He was like a son to me. Do me the honor of letting me carry him."

"Certainly uncle," replied Laurent as he stepped aside.

As the six men slowly carried Don Manuel's casket to its final resting place, it would mark the first time in almost 500 years that someone that was not a direct descendent of Manuel Vilches Díaz, the 1st Count of Morente, was burried there.

Later on that evening, most of those who had attended the funeral went over to Pepe's bar to celebrate Manuel's life.

When Don Esteban arrived, he went over to the counter and told Pepe, "Put everything on my tab."

The old bartender looked at him and with tears in his eyes replied, "I am sorry to disagree with you Your Highness, but Manolo was also my friend. Although I do not have much and my bar is humble, it is my house, and today no one shall pay here."

"Thank you, Pepe," said the Count as he reached over and shook his hand.

As the evening progressed Carlos ended up seated at a table with Gerald, his wife, Randall, and Don Esteban.

The Brigadier General was recounting the story of his first encounter with Don Manuel in his folksy southern drawl. "I have never been so scared as I was that day, but watching the Matador in action gave me a sense of courage I never thought I had. He made everyone around him feel safe. Give me ten soldiers like him and I can conquer anything."

"I cannot believe he is gone. Out of all of us I was convinced he would be the last to go. He wore a cloak of invincibility. I never, never thought he would die," Gerald uttered as he broke down crying.

By this time the Basque man was quite drunk and his wife told him, "Darling, I think it is time we headed back to our room."

As Gerald tried to get up, he stumbled. Carlos immediately got up to help the Countess carry him out of the bar, but the look in her eyes stopped him in his tracks.

"Young man, I have carried this man for the last thirty years and for as long as I am alive, I shall be the one that continues to carry him. Thank you."

The mood at the estate in the days following the funeral of Don Manuel was quite gloomy. Everyone seemed to want to talk about Don Manuel but was afraid to do so. No one knew how to start to heal.

Celia showed up for work a week after the funeral and when Don Esteban saw her, the first thing he told her was, "Celia, what are you doing here? You do not need to be here. Take off as much time as you need."

"I know, Your Highness, and I very much appreciate that, but all I end up doing is sitting alone at home thinking of Manolo. Crying and feeling miserable. Coming to work will be a good distraction for me. Besides, Manolo would not approve of me being paid and not working."

"I understand Celia, but if you feel you are not ready to return, then please know you do not have to," Don Esteban told her.

"Thank you, Your Highness," she replied.

As Celia was leaving for the day, she sought out Carlos. When she finally found him, she handed him a bag.

"Carlitos, Manolo always had much fondness for you, even if your memories from your first meetings make that difficult to believe," she said, smiling. "This was his favorite piece of clothing and I think he would have wanted you to have it."

"I do not know what to say Celia, except thank you very much," Carlos responded.

After Celia departed, Carlos took the worn bag to his room and opened it. Inside was the old leather vest that Manolo customarily went hunting in and wore during his war days. There was a small wicker chair in the room, and Carlos went over to hang up the vest on it. As he spread it open, a small zipper inside the bottom left side caught his eye. Curious, he opened the small pocket expecting to find it empty. Instead, he was surprised to find a small envelope folded in half. It had obviously been in the pocket for a long time as it was frayed and stained. It was not addressed to any one. For a second he thought about not opening it, feeling he was invading someone's privacy, but his curiosity got the better of him. There was only one page inside and he carefully unfolded it. He immediately saw that it was a poem. The word Maria was neatly scribbled on the first line. Carlos was stunned as he began to comprehend its significance.

Maria

As the morning sun awakens,
it casts its first shadow on a solitary figure yonder.
The warrior stands lost in the moment,
until the man within reveals his anguish.

Now he just stands stoically,
a shield decorates his left arm, while his right hand
bears his sword.
His veins are breached, scars wander all over his
torso,
blood his only clothing.

The leather sandals strapped to well-worn soles do
not move,
he has fought with all his might.
The Christian and Moor that runs thru his being,
preventing him from surrender.

When his body leaves this earth,
the richness that he sought,
would be your love to surround his soul.
It is I.

Carlos read it over and over again. "What am I suppose to do with this?" he kept asking himself. Soon he realized he could not show it to anyone, so he carefully put it back into the envelope and returned it to the pocket it had been hidden in for some thirty years.

21

Both Carlos and Don Esteban were surprised when over lunch just a week and a half after Don Manuel had been buried, Alexandra informed them that she had just gotten a phone call to do a *rejoneo* that coming Sunday.

"Alvarito Domecq took a nasty tumble while practicing yesterday and Jorge del Puente, the bullring manager of the Linares plaza where he was scheduled to perform, called me and wanted to know if I would take his place alongside the Peralta brothers."

"My dear, do you think enough time has passed for you to be emotionally prepared to do a *rejoneo*?" Don Esteban asked concerned.

"Father, ever since Don Manuel died, I have spent most of my time practicing in our arena. Being with the horses that he loved so much has helped me begin to heal during this difficult time. I know that wherever Don Manuel is, he will be watching me this Sunday and I would like to make him proud," Alexandra countered.

"Alright then, I guess you should go ahead and do it," said the Count.

After they had finished lunch Carlos accompanied Alexandra to the stables. She had been distant ever since the funeral. He wondered if she felt vulnerable or simply needed the time and space to mourn. Still, he sorely missed her company and used the opportunity to engage her.

"I will call Cesar Calderón this afternoon and have him get your *cuadrilla* ready. Meanwhile I will make the hotel reservations and arrange for the transportation."

"Thank you Carlos. I appreciate that," Alexandra replied.

"Oh, I forgot to ask you earlier, whose bulls will you be fighting?" Carlos inquired.

"Those of Don Eduardo Miura," she answered.

"Miuras?" Carlos said caught off guard.

"Yes why, do you think I do not have the ability to fight a Miura?" she answered sharply.

He knew it was a loaded question. The idea of entering into an argument with Alexandra, especially one in which he knew he was not going to win, did not appeal to him at all.

"I have no doubt at all in your capabilities Alexandra, I was just a little surprised that is all."

"Good, then I am going to go and do some riding while you make those telephone calls," Alexandra said as she started walking away.

Carlos did not like that fact that she would be facing two Miuras on Sunday. It was too soon. At least she would be fighting atop a horse and not on the ground, he told himself to feel better.

On Sunday morning, they started making the 80-mile journey to Linares. The plaza there was like many in Andalusia, but had become world famous because on August the twenty eighth of 1947, fate had dealt Spain a terrible hand as it was here that the country's idol, Manolete, was mortally gored by Islero, a Miura.

Jorge del Puente, a graying and amiable Andalusian gentleman of some sixty years, greeted them as they arrived. He kept thanking Alexandra for agreeing to join the spectacle on such short notice. The horses were taken to the stables and cared for. It was not long before the Peralta brothers arrived and settled in.

At six o'clock the gates to the plaza were opened to the public, and the capacity crowd started to fill every seat in the stands. The pageantries began soon thereafter and the crowd's excitement grew in anticipation of a splendid recital. It had been decided beforehand that the Peralta brothers would go out first and second, signifying that Alexandra would fight the third and the last bull, the sixth.

Finally the first bull came roaring into the arena. Carlos was in the alley that separated the fans in the stands from the bulls in the arena. Even from behind the protective wooden barrier seeing a Miura so close up made him uneasy.

Ángel and Rafael Peralta were excellent horsemen but they lacked the flair of the very finest *rejoneadores*. The crowd applauded their efforts but one could sense that they were reserving their praise. As Alexandra came out on Cola Cao she cut a dramatic figure on the spirited animal. She encouraged the young stallion to tempt his fate as he came perilously close to the bull's horns. Soon the crowd was on its feet, but Carlos did not like the fact that she was taking so many chances. She rode Luna to put the *banderillas* on the bull, but instead of leaning over to do it, she twisted her body so that her back was to the bull as she placed them perfectly. The crowd cheered wildly. For her final act she exchanged the mare for Noche. Even on this stage, replete with amazing horses, Noche stood out. The stallion reacted to Alexandra's every gentle touch. Noche became an extension of his rider. She took the lance of death from her *mozo de espada*, Luis Castelero, and had Noche run in tight circles around the bull until at last she made him almost come to a standstill alongside the Miura, while she thrust the lance into the bull's upper torso. Then Noche leapt out of harm's way, turning severely. As he did, he came up limping. The bull died instantaneously and although the crowd was passionately applauding, Alexandra paid no heed to them, quickly dismounting to check Noche's left rear ankle. The presiding dignitary awarded her two ears but all she could think about was the injury to her horse. While Ángel Peralta came out to fight his second bull, Cesar Calderón, Luis Castelero, and Carlos listened while Alexandra talked about what strategy she would use for her second bull.

"I cannot ride Noche again today. I can use Cola Cao for the entrance of the bull and to put the *banderillas* because of his speed, leaving Luna for the kill as she is less jittery."

Cesar Calderón shook his head. "I do not know if I like that Alexandra. To run a horse for two straight acts without a rest is asking a lot of him, and these bulls are fast. We could be begging for trouble."

Carlos looked towards him as he was speaking and for a moment his long, lean figure, sent a chill down his spine, as he looked like a perfect effigy of Manolete himself.

"But Cesar, Cola Cao is just not calm enough for the lance of death and Luna is not quick enough to begin the fight," countered Alexandra.

Luis Castelero finally spoke and came up with a compromise they all agreed could work. "Alexandra, like you suggested, ride Cola Cao for the entrance and the *banderillas*, but make sure you do not push him hard at the start of the fight, don't get too close to the Miura, so as to reserve his energy for the second act. Leaving Luna fresh for the final act."

The crowd greeted Alexandra warmly as she came out for the last bull of the day. Cafetero wore black and white spots, and as beautiful as the Miura was, Carlos did not like the look of this bull from the moment he laid eyes on it. He was eighty pounds bigger than any of the previous bulls, which made him stronger and faster. He also had a dangerous tendency of flicking his horns up suddenly and unpredictably. The bull's speed caused Alexandra to have to make numerous attempts to place the *banderillas*, and when she went to replace Cola Cao with Luna to bring the fight to an end, she was visibly frustrated.

While she switched horses, Carlos went up to Cesar and Luis and told them, "I want both of you to move around the ring and be as close to that bull as possible in case something happens. I am not sure that bull is weak or tired enough yet."

Cesar was about to be patronizing but decided against it once he looked into the young man's eyes.

"God how I want this fight to be over," thought Carlos.

While Luna was older and more serene than Cola Cao, she was no Noche. That, plus the added fact that Cafetero was still moving much too quickly, making it difficult for Alexandra to get close enough to the Miura to kill it, started making the crowd rumble in disapproval.

"Forget the crowd, calm down Alexandra, do not hurry, this bull is still too strong," muttered Carlos anxiously.

After circling the bull on several occasions Alexandra went in to thrust the lance of death but as she leaned over, the Miura thrust his horns upward and caught the hind leg of Luna, which made Alexandra lose her balance. She was thrown off the horse.

"No!" screamed Carlos as he jumped over the fence and into the arena while the 9,000 people inside the plaza held their breath as the Miura turned around to attack the fallen rider.

Cafetero barreled into the defenseless Alexandra, one of his horns penetrating her stomach, before casting her aside like a rag doll. Cesar reached the bull first and was able to distract him away with his cape just before Carlos got to Alexandra.

"Alexandra!" he called out as he turned her over. Blood was gushing down her leg. "Oh my God! Alexandra stay with me. I love ..."

"I know," she said as she opened her eyes and caressed the tears streaming down his cheek.

"Carlos, we have to take her now," said Luis Castelero as he gently moved him aside so that the rest of the assistants and other bullfighters could pick her up and quickly take her to the local infirmary.

After a few minutes the bull was led back to its pen. The people stayed in the stands, not knowing what to do except replay the horrifying scene in their minds. Finally, they slowly departed.

Up in the stands, an old man with a black beret sat next to his grandson. They waited for the majority of the plaza to empty before starting to exit. As they were leaving, the young man turned around and saw Carlos still on his knees, holding his face with both hands, in the middle of the arena.

"Grandpa, I am not sure I can see another fight."

"Yes, I understand," said the old man, gently patting him on the shoulder as they left.

The End

About the Author

Born in the United States and raised in Spain and England, Emmanuel is a graduate of the University of California at Davis. In addition to his Economics and Spanish Literature degrees, he studied Viticulture and Oenology. In 1989 Emmanuel became the twelfth American to pass the Master Sommelier exam in London, England and one of the few to pass on his first attempt. Emmanuel is the proprietor of Miura Vineyards and co-owner of L+i wines in California, the Managing Director of Clos Pissarra in Priorat, Spain, co-owner of the Miura Beer Works and the Café Islero Coffee Company.

The Miura Affair is Emmanuel Kemiji's first published book where he combines his love of literature, Spanish history and culture, and all things wine- and food-related. He is currently working on a second book which takes us through the history of rice...

For more information on Emmanuel, please go to his website: miuravineyards.com or visit him on Facebook: @emmanuelkemiji

www.ingramcontent.com/pod-product-compliance
Lightning Source LLC
Chambersburg PA
CBHW070325260626
47160CB00003B/952